Only a Fling

Kasper Ridge, Book 1

Delancey Stewart

For my Dad

Chapter One

Succeeding at Failure (Harder than it Looks)

WILL

"D o me a favor and put your phone away," Dad said the second I strode into his office.

I shoved my phone, which had been in my hand, into the pocket of my pants, simultaneously pushing down the irritation that rose inside me at the command.

Dad never changed—and it wasn't that he was angry or domineering, he wasn't. He just expected people to behave a certain way, and he'd had enough experience with me to get out ahead of any disappointments I might offer him.

"I need all your attention on this rebuild on the Esplanade, Will."

For a second, hope awoke inside me, crawling from the bed where it had decided to take an indefinite slumber a long time ago.

"Yeah? I can do that." I stood taller. I'd been waiting for the opportunity to take the reins, for the moment when I'd proven myself sufficiently to my father to oversee one of the massive luxury construction projects his firm was known for. The Esplanade project was going to be huge, and I'd been second on so many projects now, it felt like maybe it was finally my turn to lead.

"Good, Markie will need your help."

"Markie?" I felt my shoulders slide back down. Of course. Markie.

I was not a Markie fan. Markie was a tough woman, good at what she did, but with a couple bags of Fritos perched high on her massive shoulders. It was pretty clear she'd had to work hard to get ahead in the male-dominated world of construction, and at this point, she assumed every guy she worked with expected her to be incompetent. She made up for it by turning herself into the kind of foreman people were afraid to piss off. Me included.

And she had a dog everyone hated but no one had the guts to tell her was a disaster. He was a pitbull/daschund mix named Buzz, every bit as ornery and bullying as Markie.

"Yep. She's running the show. Best we've got, son. And this project is critical."

I tried to absorb that blow without letting it show on my face. And I sucked in a deep breath, girding myself for what I knew was coming out of me next. Because really, what the hell did I have to lose? "Dad? When will you trust me enough to run a project?"

Shit, I was thirty-one. The United States Navy had trusted me enough to put me in charge of a seventy-million dollar jet. But my dad wouldn't trust me to run a construction project with plenty of help. Maybe my Navy career hadn't been as glorious as his, but I'd done it, dammit. I'd flown, I'd fought, and then I'd decided it was time to move on.

Only I hadn't moved far. Dad had offered me a job at his firm, and I'd accepted. Because I'd actually hoped it might be a big enough place to grow, to finally show him I was a capable adult.

To maybe even make him proud. Of course, as soon as I'd gotten here, I'd screwed up. And it was clear Dad was never going to let me forget it.

"Not this one, son. This one is critical, and Markie's got it handled. Just be there to run defense for her, carry some of the weight when she needs you, and help manage the schedule." Dad's attention was already back on the screen in front of him. That was my cue to go.

Frustration bubbled inside me. "Dad."

He looked up again, his eyes widening slightly, like he was surprised to see me still standing there. "Will?"

"Do you think you'll ever trust me again?"

His lips tightened and I saw a muscle jump in his cheek. His steely eyes held mine for a beat, and then they softened. "Yeah," he said. "I hope so."

Hope.

He hoped he could trust me.

Someday.

I left his office and returned to my own, using every bit of restraint I had to keep from slamming the door. As I swiveled to gaze out the plate glass window, I let my mind wander back over every stupid thing I'd ever done, every act that had solidified my father's belief that I'd never be as good as him, never be ready to take on the weight of his trust.

It was a long and exhausting stroll down memory lane. But beyond all the silly shit I'd done in the Navy, the one thing I knew Dad couldn't forgive was directly related to my work here. I'd trusted someone to do what they said they would. I hadn't been a good enough leader to demand it—or to doublecheck it. And a man had almost died as a result. Since then, I'd been the most competent manager Dad had, the most engaged, the most organized. But it still wasn't good enough. It would never be good enough.

My phone buzzed in my pocket where I'd shoved it earlier, and though my dark mood suggested I ignore it, the name on the screen piqued my curiosity. I hadn't talked to Ghost in a while, but word was going around that he'd taken on some crazy project up in the mountains in Colorado. A hotel or something.

I didn't know if running a hotel was what the guy needed, but I knew he needed something. After everything that had happened...

"Ghost," I said, hitting the speaker button and sliding my phone onto my desk.

"Fake Tom," he said, his voice warm and cheerful. It felt good to have someone address me by my callsign again. Even if I'd hated the name at first. A wash of nostalgia flooded me on hearing it on his lips. I missed it. And him. I missed all my squadron buddies. "How's it going, man?" he asked.

"Living the dream."

"I bet," he said. "Still working with your old man building those luxury condos on the beach?"

"Pretty much sums it up," I said.

He paused. "Don't sound too excited."

I wasn't going to get into it. Especially not if Ghost had just called to shoot the shit. All of us seemed to have agreed to look out for Ghost a little bit, and the last thing he needed was to hear about my petty gripes with my dad. He had bigger things to worry about.

"I heard you bought some hotel or something in the mountains," I said.

He let out a laugh. "Not exactly. My great-uncle left me the place. Me and my sister."

Ghost's sister Aubrey was a spitfire. She'd come to visit us a few times in Lemoore, and the girl was tougher than some of the drill sergeants I'd met.

"So you're living the resort life now? Rubbing elbows with the apres ski set, I guess?"

"That's the plan, but we're not there yet. Which is part of why I'm calling you."

"Aw, Ghost, you didn't just call to say hello because you missed me?"

"You know I do," he laughed. "And that is actually exactly why I'm calling you."

"I'm touched."

"In fact, I miss you so much I have an idea for you."

"Hold me. I'm frightened."

"Probably should be. Want to come up here and run the renovation on this place? I've got proposals from some top-notch crews, but I need a project manager who knows construction and can keep the whole thing on schedule. Run the show. Herd the cats." Ghost's tone was light but I sensed an undertone that hinted he might be in trouble.

I dropped into my chair, my mind whirling. "I do have a way with puss—ahem, with cats," I joked, mostly to buy a little time to think. I knew next to nothing about the project Ghost was proposing. But I had heard him say I'd be in charge. "Tell me more."

He paused, and I sensed the bad news was coming next.

"Well, I couldn't pay you much," he said, and my hopes fell. I needed an actual job. I didn't have a ton of expenses, but I did have some bills. "But I could give you free housing and a percentage."

"A percentage of...?"

"Of the Kasper Ridge Resort property."

"You're talking ownership?" Maybe Ghost was a little desperate if he was willing to pay me in equity. Still, I found myself considering it.

"I mean, I should let you know the place is in the red right now."

Of course it was. "So let me get this straight." I looked out the window at the deep indigo expanse of the Pacific stretching to the horizon and tried to imagine exchanging it for rugged mountains, pine trees. "You're offering me a low-paying job, a share of a failing business, and a shitty room in a run-down resort?"

Ghost chuckled. "I figured it was a long shot."

"I'll do it." The words were out before my brain caught up. But that was pretty much how every bad idea I'd ever acted on had come to life. Why quit now? One more way to disappoint Dad.

"Seriously?" Ghost sounded surprised, like he'd figured this was a long shot at best.

"Yeah, I'll do it. I'm sick of playing second fiddle to burly chicks in combat boots with bad breath and no sense of humor."

"That's weirdly specific."

"Send me the details."

"You got it," Ghost said. "And Fake Tom? Thanks, man."

I hung up, my insides churning with something that was either excitement or dread. I had no clue what I'd just agreed to, besides having to tolerate people calling me Fake Tom again, but even that held a certain appeal.

Maybe this was the chance I'd been waiting for. I wasn't going to let it pass me by. And when it was over? Maybe Dad would finally see me as something other than a disappointment.

Chapter 2
Don't Mess with a Woman in a Hard Hat

LUCY

The grinding sound of machinery grated through the cool mountain air, sending a shiver up my spine. There were piles of dirt all around, my crew moved here and there, and Mateo was making quick work of the dig with the backhoe, meaning soon we'd be on to the more exciting parts of the build.

I lived for this chaos. There was something satisfying about the noise and the mess around me. We were driving the earth to meet our will—or the will of the ridiculously wealthy family paying us to build them a mountain home, but whatever—creating organized destruction, all in the name of accomplishment.

Just as I allowed myself a smile, the grating, sifting noise of the backhoe digging changed, replaced by a stomach-lurching, bone-shaking thump I knew too well. I heard it twice more, but kept my head down, leaning over the plans I had spread on my worktable.

The backhoe shut off and I turned to see Mateo striding toward me across the site, a grim look on his face.

"Boss. Hit rock."

I swallowed the aggravation I felt. "Bound to happen up here. We do this just about every time, right?" I shot him a confident smile.

"Thought we were gonna get lucky this time. I was more than halfway done." Mateo took off his hard hat, the crinkles around his light green eyes appearing as he returned my smile with a more doubtful one of his own. He had to peer down at me because he was at least six feet tall and I wasn't anywhere close. Somehow, though, Mateo never made me feel small. I'd known him forever, and I trusted him like a brother.

"I don't put much stock in luck. Things that come too easy aren't usually worth having, in my experience."

My friend squinted at me, the low western sun highlighting the smears of gritty dirt on his tanned face. "Now you sound like the old man."

He was right, and my heart warmed as I thought about it. "I guess he was bound to wear off on me some time." I gazed around at the weary men surrounding me, waiting for next steps. This was only part of the crew I'd have up here once the excavation work was done. We just needed to get the site plumbed and poured before the fun part would begin, but digging in the mountains was never without adventure, and encountering rock down beneath the soil was to be expected.

"Let's call it for today. We'll get to ripping that rock early tomorrow and hopefully can get these lines plumbed starting in the afternoon. Depending on how much rock is down there."

Mateo wiped a hand across the back of his neck and pulled the hard hat from his head. "You sure, boss? Another hour of daylight here."

"It's Friday night. Go have fun, guys. But not too much. I need you tomorrow at six."

"Right," Mateo said, shaking his head. I knew his night wasn't likely to be too exciting. He was a single dad, raising a little girl on his own. "We might have time to watch *Frozen* again."

"I love that movie," I told him, earning a grin before Mateo turned and headed to his truck.

The crew slowly made their way to the vehicles parked here and there around the site. When everyone was gone, I double-checked to make sure all our equipment was secure, and then hopped into my truck. I had plans of my own tonight.

* * *

"Girl, how do you look like that when you spend all day covered in dirt and sawdust?" Bennie pulled me into a hug as I approached the little round high-top table where my girlfriends already sat with pints before them.

"Like what?" I asked innocently, batting my eyelashes.

"Shut up, you know exactly what she means," CeeCee scolded, pulling me in for a hug next.

"I like getting dressed up," I told them, smoothing the skirt of my red dress and adjusting a curl over my shoulder. "It's like exploring the two sides of my identity. Hard-assed construction boss and actual girly girl."

"Well, you do both pretty well. How's Papa?" Bennie pushed a glass and the pitcher my way, and I poured a beer after settling onto a stool.

"He's doing fine. He's busy playing poker tonight with the other old timers. I just hope he takes it easy on them this time. I don't know what I'll do if I have to listen to him complain for another month that none of his friends will speak to him."

"He's a card shark, huh?" Bennie laughed.

"He's just tricky, I guess." Papa was smart. Shrewd, maybe, was a better word. But my grandfather was also the kindest person I'd ever known, and even though I liked to complain about him to those who knew his quirks almost as well as I did, I wouldn't trade a single thing about him. Not the way he complained about my terrible cooking, or the way he stuck his nose deep into every project my construction business took on. He was a know it all maybe, but he'd earned the right—and he'd taught me literally everything I knew.

I sat back in my chair and let the tension run from my fingertips and toes, soaking in the laughter and warmth of my friends, and the people around us in the Toothy Moose, one of two local bars in Kasper Ridge. It was this place or Bud's, and you didn't go to Bud's unless you were under twenty-one and desperate to test out your fake ID, or hoping to run into someone you hadn't known since birth, since it was halfway down the mountain. The Moose was home base for most of the locals up here, and hanging out in the cozy mountain bar felt a lot like relaxing at home.

"You guys seen what's going on up at the old hotel?" CeeCee asked, her big brown eyes shining with some kind of unspilled gossip.

I sat up straighter. I knew something, but I wondered what

these ladies knew. I'd been talking with Papa about it just this morning, and about the proposal I had put in at the request of the mysterious new owners.

"Did it finally collapse?" Bennie asked. It was a fair question. Kasper Ridge Resort had once been a pretty fancy ski resort, the kind of place just big enough to attract celebrities, but small enough to give them the freedom to enjoy themselves without crowds of tourists. But that was decades ago, and the guy who owned the place hadn't done a lot to keep it up in his later years. The roof that protected the receiving drive out front had collapsed a few years back, and my crew had gone in to pull the debris out of the driveway. Just in case anyone ever needed to get to the front doors again. The place was a hazard, really.

"I might have heard some things," I said. "What do you know?" Besides the request for proposals the owners had put out to construction firms as far afield as Denver, my knowledge was limited to permits filed and equipment requisitioned, and some of my guys had told me they'd helped out constructing some kind of temporary lodging structures behind the place at the start of the summer.

"That old guy that owned the place died and left it to some family of his, I guess," CeeCee said.

I frowned. The RFP had come from an LLC, so I didn't have a lot of insight into who was actually funding the job. "What kind of family?" Up here, property left to family sometimes didn't turn out well. Folks who hadn't spent years living in the mountains didn't really understand what it was to exist up here. They didn't get the culture, the harsh conditions that cropped up regularly in terms of weather, or the unspoken rules about privacy and community that mountain people just seemed to know. The last thing we needed was some slick banker type thinking he could turn the place into the next Aspen or Beaver Creek. Even though having a tourist destination up here would help keep some money coming into the local businesses, we didn't need that kind of reputation.

"A brother and sister," CeeCee said. "They're Kaspers. Mabel at the market said they came in to buy some things and told her about what they're up to." CeeCee was glowing. She was a good person—one of the best, and I'd known her since preschool, but CeeCee loved to gossip.

"Anyway," she went on, leaning forward as she got into her story. "Get this. I guess there's some kind of map or something. The old man was crazy, right? And he put together like, a treasure hunt or something, for his niece and nephew to figure out. That's why they're here."

"They came up here to nowhere ridge to go on a treasure hunt?" Bennie looked skeptical. "What's the treasure? A bunch of rocks?"

"The old guy—Marvin, I think?—he was rich, right? He ran the place when it was a fancy resort in the eighties. Famous people popping in all the time? My dad says he went there once when he was a kid and there were pictures everywhere of the guy with celebrities."

"He and Papa were friends a long time ago," I told them, remembering what Papa had told me this morning. "But they hadn't talked in years. And Marvin either ended up poor or senile, because the place is in serious need of work," I said. "But it does sound like the new owners are looking to renovate."

Both my friends were watching me now.

"You already knew," CeeCee accused, clearly disappointed that she hadn't gotten to share the juicy gossip first.

"I only know they're looking for help getting the place running again. It's a huge job."

"You putting in for it?" Bennie asked.

"I already did," I told her. "It would make the year for me, and probably next year too. Plus I could hire back all the guys I had to let go when things slowed down. And it'd be great for Kasper Ridge. All those local guys working so close to home? And think about the business the tourists would bring when the place is done." Excitement forced my words out faster than usual, and my whole body bounced in my chair. It would be a great opportunity to be involved in something that would really help our community, and would pretty much seal my own future (and Papa's).

"Your eyes are all sparkly," Bennie said. "Also, ew. Tourists."

"Tourists mean money for the town. And this job would seriously make my company," I said, allowing myself to dream a little in a way I'd told myself not to. "And if I win it, no one will ever question my abilities again. Woman or not."

"That dress says woman," CeeCee said, pointing to the flouncy red dress I'd pulled on after my shower.

"And so do those shoes," Bennie agreed. "I swear, you're the only person who wears heels up here, Luce."

"I like to dress up. And getting dressed up after work shouldn't make anyone think I'm less serious about the job while I'm there. I'm out to prove I can do both. Women can be kickass foremen."

"Forewomen," CeeCee corrected. Her forehead wrinkled. "Forepeople?"

"I'll drink to that," I said, lifting my glass. I wasn't going to think about all the jobs I'd been turned down for because of my gender. I was going to get this one.

"To the new Kasper Ridge Resort," Bennie said, joining the toast. "You better get that job so you can give us an inside peek."

We touched our glasses and drank, and then CeeCee dropped her last piece of gossip with a gleeful smile. "Guess what else I heard? The guy running the place now? The nephew? He was a Navy fighter pilot, and he's bringing up a bunch of his buddies to help. Soon Kasper Ridge will be swarming with hot men."

I shrugged. Hot men, in my experience, were not all they were cut out to be. Good for a weekend or a summer, maybe. But hot men from out of town didn't stay long in Kasper Ridge.

Chapter 3
The Stale Smell of Disappointment

WILL

Not surprisingly, Dad wasn't thrilled at my news.

"You've got work to do here, Will. You can't just leave."

"That's why I'm giving notice. I've only ever worked for you and Uncle Sam, but I'm pretty sure that's how people do it in real jobs." I did realize that quitting meant there might never be another opportunity to show my father how capable I was and regain his trust. But maybe leaving was the only way to finally move on, to prove that I could actually trust myself.

Dad sighed and rubbed a hand over his jaw, his steely eyes

cutting right through me in the way they'd done since I was a kid. It made me wonder what exactly he saw there. Whatever it was, I was pretty sure it wasn't what he wanted.

I stood in his study at my parents' house, a kind of wood-paneling-meets-the-beach space my mom had put together for him. I'd always wanted something similar one day. A big house like this, a wife like my mom, who made sure I was always happy, comfortable. Someone to raise kids with.

I'd always wanted to be exactly like my dad.

Only, maybe it was time to step out of his shadow.

"Colorado, huh?" Dad asked, sinking into one of the leather side chairs next to his desk.

I took that as a cue to join him. We had dinner here once a week, on Sundays. Mom was still clanging around in the kitchen, and so I'd followed Dad to his office with a tumbler in my hand, steeling myself to tell him my plan.

"Yeah," I confirmed. "I doubt you remember the guy, Ghost? Archie Kasper."

"Like Casper the Friendly Ghost, right?"

"Yep." Callsigns were one language Dad and I both spoke fluently. Of course his was Terminator, and mine ended up being Fake Tom. That's what you got in the Navy for coming in with great ideas for the callsign you really wanted—they gave you something as far from it as a bunch of drunk, adrenaline-dependent twenty-something-year-olds can conceive. I'd wanted Maverick. It worked for Tom Cruise in *Top Gun*, and he and I shared a last name. Kind of.

"Yeah, I remember the guy. There was all that stuff in the news a couple years ago about him. And Sugar gave me some of the inside scoop when he decided to get out. Sounds like he got lucky."

"I don't know if I'd put it that way. He's been pretty messed up about the whole thing for a long time." I stared into my tumbler, thinking about the days right after Ghost's mishap, when it had looked like he might even be courtmartialed. Sugar had been our CO at the time it happened. Naturally, he and Dad were old squadron buddies and Dad always knew more than I did about everything.

"So you think he's the right guy to throw in with now?" Dad was regarding me with that narrowed gaze again. "He steady?"

"Yeah. Maybe."

"Better be sure, Will. Markie's not gonna take this lightly, you walking away from the Esplanade job."

I doubted Markie would care in the least. And her dog had peed on my boot just that morning. I looked forward to telling them both. "I'll let her down gently."

Dad put down his drink and steepled his hands before him, his elbows resting on the leather arms of the chair, and his still-impressive biceps popping beneath the sleeves of the thin cashmere sweater he wore. The guy was impeccable. Always. It was frustrating. "All right then. Just hope you know what you're getting into."

As soon as the words were out of the old man's mouth, a weight slid off my shoulders, and I could practically hear it landing softly on the plush carpet in his office. I was free.

"Thanks for understanding, Dad."

He chuckled. "Not sure I understand," he said. "But I guess I get needing some space, needing to do your own thing for a while. You've been a good son, Will, staying close, keeping an eye on me."

If only that had been my reason. It sounded a lot more noble than being chickenshit and never wanting to take a leap and have to deal with Dad seeing me fail. But maybe I'd been failing up close for too many years now. "I think it's been the other way around."

Dad rose and dropped a big hand on my shoulder. "It's a big

opportunity," he said. I'd told him about Ghost's plans, about his intention to put me in charge. "I think you're up to it."

This was high praise coming from the one man whose words really mattered to me, and I was happy to take it. "Thanks."

"Let's go help your mom finish up and break the news to her. She'll be sad to have you so far away."

I would miss my mom. She was the one person who always believed in me, no matter what. "It's a quick flight."

"Takes longer when you're not the one flying," Dad said, giving me a wry half-smile.

"True."

* * *

Two weeks later, I was in the car, Southern California in my mirrors and what I hoped was a future filled with opportunity ahead of me in Colorado. As I traded traffic for desert and finally, desert for trees, something inside me loosened, and by the time I was twisting and turning up the two-lane road, following signs to the town of Kasper Ridge, I was certain I'd made the right choice.

Of course pulling into the round driveway at the front of the Kasper Ridge Resort had me thinking something else entirely. The place was a disaster.

"Fake Tom!" Ghost was stepping out the front door as I slammed the driver side door shut and took in my first lungful of thin, crisp mountain air.

"Ghost. Good to see you, man."

I stepped close and hugged my friend, clapping him on the back as I released him, and feeling the grin stretching my cheeks wide. It was good to see him again. A little like coming home.

"Mandatory bro-hug," a female voice called out, and a curvy, compact woman with a mass of dark hair waving down her shoulders stepped out the revolving doors to stand at Ghost's side. "It's a wonder you boys ever got anything done in the Navy, what with all the hugging."

"Shut it," Ghost said.

A laugh escaped me as I took in the woman at Ghost's side.

"You remember my irritating sister, Aubrey?" Ghost pointed at her and she turned to him and stuck out her tongue before extending a hand to me.

"Fake Tom, right?" she asked.

"Will works fine, too. Nice to see you again, Aubrey." I had met her a couple times, but I didn't remember the pretty glow on her cheeks or the light of happiness in her eyes. The mountains clearly agreed with her.

"Let's get the obligatory crap out of the way," she said. "Cuz I know I'll get asked. What's the story with your callsign?"

A little of the weight I'd managed to throw off as I'd driven up landed back on my chest. "Long story."

"Nice try," Ghost said, stepping to my side. He threw an arm around my shoulders, and his voice was full of glee as he explained. "This guy, Will Cruz, showed up thinking that with all his thick hair, blue eyes, cool-guy attitude, and similar last name, he might just let us all know that he was going to be called 'Maverick.'"

"Like the movie," Aubrey said, and I could see the flicker of amusement in her eyes.

"Right," I confirmed, having little choice in the matter. I'd gotten used to the story by now and braced myself for her laughter.

"But that's just not how things work," Ghost explained, taking his time with it. "I knew other guys who came in with good ideas. Things like 'Killzone' and 'Death Star.'"

Aubrey laughed. "Seriously? Death Star?"

Ghost dropped his arm and looked more serious for a

second. "When you plan your whole life to fly and you finally get there, you've probably been thinking about it for a while. You get ideas."

"Right," she said, waving her hand for him to continue.

"Anyway, those guys who come in with the good ideas—and women," he corrected himself suddenly. "There were female pilots too"—Aubrey nodded ferociously at this amendment— "well, they were the ones who got things like 'Cupcake' and 'Pretty Pony.'"

"That's cruel," she said.

"That's how it works," he said. "So this guy?" He jabbed me in the chest. "Maverick here? The guy was a legacy too—and his dad had a kickass callsign—Maverick thought he was writing his own ticket. So we gave him what he wanted. Kind of."

Aubrey shot me a look that told me she imagined some of the humiliation that had initially come with the assignment of this callsign, and I found myself liking her.

"I got used to it," I assured her. In fact, at this point, my call-sign was part of my identity, maybe more than my given name. It tied me to guys like Ghost, to the bonding moments we'd all shared, and to a time in my life where I sometimes felt like I was accomplishing things, doing well.

"Let's give you the tour," Ghost said, grabbing my duffle from the back of my SUV. "You can leave this here for now." He indicated the car.

They turned and we went inside the resort through the grand revolving door, and I could see immediately the potential of the place. It featured incredible high ceilings dripping with dusty chandeliers, and a reception desk that must have cost a fortune when it was originally installed and would look amazing once we got it cleaned up. There were two staircases winding up behind the desk, meeting on a landing and then continuing up to some unseen floor above, and doorways leading in several directions from the main lobby.

"Elevator, library, bar, restaurant, entertainment wing," Ghost said, pointing from one place to the next. "Don't take the elevator yet."

"Noted."

"Come meet Wiley," Aubrey said, practically skipping toward the huge doorway Ghost had said was the bar.

Unlike everything else I'd seen so far, which was dusty and decrepit, the bar was pristine. The brass rail in front of the huge wooden structure was polished to a high shine, and the glass shelves behind the bar were fully stocked with more gleaming bottles than I had seen in one place before. The walls were lined with photos, many of them in black and white, and all of them featuring a white-haired man with a wide smile.

"I see you've got your priorities in order," I said, taking in the impressive space.

"'Course I do. Bartender was the first hire I made," Ghost said. "Fake Tom, meet Coyote."

A tall man with a messy shock of dark hair and friendly brown eyes grinned at me from the far side of the bar, and strode over to shake my hand before turning to plant a kiss on Aubrey's cheek. They stood smiling, nearly glued together.

"My boyfriend, Wiley Blanchard," Aubrey said.

"Were you Navy?" I asked him, thinking he'd gotten a pretty cool callsign. I didn't know the guy, but that didn't mean much.

"Nah, Ghost is just generous with the nicknames. He must be happy about you being here, cuz when he's pissed he calls me 'Picket.'"

I felt my eyebrows creep closer. "Picket?"

"His last name means 'white fence' in French," Aubrey explained.

"Clever," I said, smiling at Ghost.

"Just keeping in shape," he said. "Anyway, Wiley and I went to school together back in the day, when Dad was at Pax River."

The Naval base in Southern Maryland. I knew of it, but I'd never been stationed there. Like me, Archie and Aubrey Kasper grew up in the Navy.

"Well, good to meet you," I said.

"I'll give you the rest of the tour and then we can come back here so you can try the Kasper's premium whiskey," Ghost told me.

"Sounds good."

The place was huge, with two wings of guest rooms and a third wing with spaces for events, a movie theater, a sports shop, and more. My room was in what Ghost had called the 'staff wing,' and he explained that one day these rooms would house guests too, but that for now it just made sense for us to live in the hotel. The plan was to rebuild the guest wing this summer, hopefully in time for the winter season, and to tackle some of the common areas. Next year, the rest of the resort would get shored up and shined.

I settled my duffel on the couch in the living room of my suite. It was a little run down, but it would work.

"So what do you think?" Ghost asked me later when we were settled at the enormous bar, a glass of Wiley's famous Half Cat whiskey in front of us. "You ready to whip this place into shape?"

I felt a slow smile creep over my face. It felt good to be trusted, to be given the confidence of someone's belief in me. "Yeah," I said. "I think I am."

"Good, because tomorrow we've gotta pick a construction company. I've got a couple front runners, but there's a local one I think might be the right choice."

"Great," I said, eager to get started.

"But for tonight," Ghost said, raising his glass, "I'm just happy to see you again, man. Thanks for coming."

We touched glasses, and for the rest of the night, we relived some of our better memories and carefully avoided those dark cobwebbed corners of our shared experiences. Ghost seemed happy, and I hoped to help keep it that way.

Chapter 4

The Man with Ocean Eyes (Is Clearly a Pain in the Ass)

LUCY

I spent the rest of my weekend standing on the edge of a job site watching as Mateo ripped away at the enormous slab of rock we'd hit. We couldn't continue the build until it was cleared, and we couldn't revise plans at this point. Rock was normal. This was a little much, however.

"This is putting us behind schedule," I complained when Mateo stopped the machinery and stepped down to take a break and update me on the progress.

"Worried about your perfect record?"

I glared at him. Mateo had been on my crew since I stepped into this role five years ago to help Papa. "You bet I am."

I'd never let a job get behind schedule. And when nature interfered—as it always did at this altitude—I caught us back up. It's what I was known for. That, and being the only female foreman in at least a two-hundred mile radius.

"You want me to get up there for a bit?" I asked Mateo, nodding at the huge hydraulic breaker we'd brought in to handle the rock.

A wry grin spread across his handsome face. "Nah," he said. "I wouldn't want you to break a nail."

I shot a quick jab at his arm, but my anger was feigned. Mateo was the only person who I would allow to talk to me that way—I trusted him more than I trusted anyone. He knew exactly what I was capable of. So he was allowed to make jokes.

He climbed back up into the cab and soon the rock pummeling started up again, the sound jarring the birds from the nearby trees and filling the quiet mountain air. I'd put my ear muffs back on to block out the noise, but when I felt my phone vibrating in the pocket of my jeans, I pulled the ear protection off and stepped into the relative quiet of the little trailer we'd hauled up for this job. My office.

"Hello?" I hoped they could hear me. It sounded like Mateo was making headway out there.

"Guessing I've got the right number. I can hear the construction." The voice that came through my phone was stern and commanding, and for a moment, I felt a little bit like I might be in trouble.

"Who's this, please?"

"My name's Will Cruz. I'm managing the restoration at the Kasper Ridge Resort and wondered if you'd have some time this week to stop by and talk about your proposal. If you're still interested in the job. This is Lucy Dale, right?"

"Yes, this is Lucy. And I'm very interested in the job. When is good?" I pushed down the little chirp of excitement inside me that threatened to push my voice an octave higher.

"Monday would be best," the man said.

"How's first thing? I've got a build going, but can probably afford to start a little later Monday." I couldn't. But I'd figure it out. The last thing I wanted was to look like I didn't have things under control in front of this guy, who was evidently the last obstacle between me and the job that would make my career—and allow me to ensure Papa was always comfortable and that Kasper Ridge Construction remained viable.

"Nine o'clock?"

"How about more like seven? Gotta start early when the weather's good up here." A little flicker of doubt lit within me. It sounded like this guy was going to be in charge, and he definitely wasn't a local. I wondered how painful it might be, leading him through a huge project like the resort's reconstruction. As long as he was willing to take my lead, it'd be worth it for the pay and security.

"You know where the place is? Top of Kasper Highway?"

"Everyone around here knows where it is," I told him, trying not to sound annoyed or smug but feeling a little of both.

"See you then, Lucy."

I turned back to the job at hand. If I managed to bring in the resort reconstruction, my guys wouldn't have to worry about having work for at least a couple years. There was plenty to do there, and the plans I submitted involved multiple phases of construction and renovation. I wanted to do that for my crew. For myself too.

* * *

Monday morning had me parking in front of the once-grand hotel and striding confidently toward the revolving doors, my heels clicking on the potholed concrete sidewalk out front. Everything here needed work, and my brain was already flying through the sequence of repairs we'd begin, the cadence of effort that would be required to bring this place back to life.

A little chill shot through me, and it had nothing to do with the fading coolness of the late spring morning, or the piles of snow scattered around from what was hopefully the last snow of the year. I wanted this job.

A man sat on a straight-backed chair at one side of the darkened lobby, and he jumped to his feet as I strode into the space.

"Hello," he said, a half-smile pulling one side of his full lips up. He had thick dark blond hair mussed to perfection, sparkling blue eyes and a build that suggested hours in the gym. He also dressed in a way that told me he was more city than country, all shined-up loafers and linen, though I was one mountain girl who could appreciate dressing up.

"Hello," I said. "I'm Lucy Dale. I'm looking for Will Cruz."

"Oh," he was clearly surprised, but recovered himself quickly. "You're Lucy." He repeated this as if needing to clear it up for himself.

"I am," I confirmed. "Are you Will?"

"Last I checked, yes." He stuck out a hand to shake, still giving me a questioning look. He had to have known I was a woman based on my name, and we'd spoken on the phone. I hoped his reaction wasn't about to lead to an abject rejection based on gender.

"Something wrong?"

"Not at all," he scratched his square chin between his thumb and two fingers for a second, shaking his head slightly. "I guess I just wasn't expecting a construction foreman in a dress."

"Yeah. I get that a lot," I said, keeping my voice flat. The way I dressed for a business meeting was appropriate, plain and simple. Black sheath dress, patent wedge pumps (stilettos would get you a broken ankle up here, especially on a site), and a hot pink blazer. "Don't worry, I don't wear a dress on the job site. But I do like to dress for interviews, and I assume that is what we're doing here today."

"It is." He dropped his hand and straightened. "Come on with me and we can talk a bit." He turned and led me through an enormous doorway at one side of the lobby, and for a moment I had the sensation I expected Dorothy might have had upon opening the door on the Technicolor world outside her little farmhouse after she'd been dropped into Oz. The bar we entered was beautiful, and it was clear work had been done in here already to fix it up. The bar itself shone in mahogany, wrapping imposingly down one entire side of the room. The rest of the space was open—clearly furniture still needed to be brought in, but there was one small round table in the far corner with a few chairs. The windows let in the early morning light, and the brass rail along the edge of the bar gleamed and sparkled.

"Wiley's not usually in here this early," Will told me. "But I can grab you a soda? Some water? Orange juice?"

"I'm fine, thanks." I was doing a good job keeping cool, but my stomach wasn't going to tolerate anything at this point. I was nervous. This job was important.

"Okay then." Will pulled up a chair across the table from me and we dug in. "Lucy, you come highly recommended up here, and the proposal you submitted makes a lot of sense. Can you walk me through the phases you've proposed here?"

My proposal was on the table before me, and it was a comfort in some small way. I'd put a lot of work into that, visiting the hotel several times and walking the grounds in an effort to understand what would be required. I hadn't been inside, but there'd been photos in the request for proposals, and Papa had known a bit more than I'd expected him to about the way the place used to be.

"Sure. But can I ask you something too?"

"Shoot." His full lips tipped up in a half smile, like this was an amusing turn of events, and I tried not to be annoyed.

"Where did you come from?"

"Los Angeles."

Right. That was about all I needed to know. This guy might be in charge, but he was going to need his hand held all the way through this project. Of course I couldn't tell him that yet. I still wanted the job.

"I was in the Navy," he said after a brief pause. "And I've been running jobs for Cruz Construction in Orange County since I got out."

So at least he had some construction experience.

"High rises? Condos?" I asked. I'd been to LA. I didn't think they dealt with many of the same issues we had to consider at ten thousand feet.

"Pretty much. Shopping centers, the occasional clifftop home."

I couldn't hold back the sigh. The renovation of the Kasper Ridge Resort was a double-edged sword for folks up here. The town could use the influx of money and tourism, no doubt. But could we tolerate shiny city people wandering around like they owned the place?

"Got it," I said. "So let's talk about the resort."

For the next hour, I walked the man through my proposal, doing my best to ignore the fact that there was something distractingly compelling about his confidence and low-key arrogance. I also had to ignore the fact that he smelled fucking amazing—some combination of cedar and tropical island that pulled at things inside me I was trying to put a lid on. I'd let myself get carried away by out-of-town hotshots before. And I'd learned that city boys didn't stay up here long.

If anything, this guy could be a fun fling, but it would be for someone else. Maybe CeeCee or Bennie. Working for the guy—teaching him what construction looked like at this altitude and in this rugged environment—would surely squelch any attraction I had for him pretty quickly.

"Fake Tom, have you seen the—"another man stepped into the bar, pulling himself to a stop when he saw me sitting at the table with Will. "Oh, hey. Sorry, didn't mean to interrupt."

The guy looked vaguely familiar, but I didn't think we'd met before. Unlike Will Cruz, he didn't look entirely out of place here.

"Ghost. This is Lucy Dale. She runs Kasper Ridge Construction. Just going over plans for the reno."

I stood, extending a hand to the man Will had called Ghost. "Hello."

"Hi Lucy. Thanks for coming in," he said, shaking my hand. He was businesslike, serious—but not arrogant. I liked him. "I'm Archie Kasper."

Kasper. That explained a lot. This was the guy who owned the place. "You're Marvin's nephew," I said. "My grandfather was a friend of his. A while back."

Archie's eyes lit a bit at this. "Oh yeah? I'd love to meet your grandfather some time. Uncle Marvin is turning out to have been a bit more mysterious than I think we realized as kids."

He didn't say anything more about it, but I sensed something buried there, beneath the simple statement. I wondered if he was talking about the treasure hunt CeeCee had told us about. It all sounded a bit crazy to me.

"Can I ask why Will calls you Ghost?"

Archie shot a look at Will, and then met my eye again. "Sorry, yeah. We flew together in the Navy. We'd agreed, I thought"—at this he glared at Will again—"to use names and not callsigns with vendors, but I guess old habits die hard."

I turned to Will, who stood across from me looking both one hundred percent comfortable and completely out of place at once. He was too polished, too perfect for the mountains. But the compelling thing was that he seemed to settle right into the fact. Comfortable in his own skin, I supposed. Or too arrogant to ever consider that he might not belong.

"What's your callsign then?" I asked.

"Nah, it's—"

"That's Fake Tom," Ghost supplied.

"I see." I did not see, but was beginning to feel pressure to get back to my own job site. I glanced down at the plans spread across the table. I didn't have time to dig into the meaning behind Will's strange nickname. I needed this meeting to end. With me getting the job, of course. "So..."

"Right," Ghost said. "I'll let you get back to it." He turned and left us alone in the bar, and we retook our seats.

"I think your plans make a lot of sense," Will said. "The timeline is pretty tight..."

"We work hard when the weather's good," I told him. "And I've never missed a deadline. I can give you several local references if you like."

"Sure," he said. "You can email those to me."

Will, clearly, was in no hurry this morning.

"All right, well. If you don't have any other questions for me," I said, hoping to wrap things up.

"I'll be in touch if I think of any," he said, and his tone made me worry that I was being turned down.

"When do you think you'll have a decision?" I pressed. "My summer is scheduled, but I can move things around if needed."

"I'll be in touch," he said again, and I didn't like the dismissive tone that came with the words.

We were walking back to the lobby now, side by side, but I stopped and turned to face him. "Listen," I said. "I know you're new up here. So I'll just warn you. I don't know who else you're talking to, but if they're all locals, I've worked with every single one of them. In some cases, I've cleaned up after them. John Racket will tell you what you want to hear, start late, go over budget, and drag the thing out at least six months past the deadline he sets. Alex Kramer will tell you he's the foreman, but you'll never see him again until the job's over. He doesn't like to leave Denver. If you want someone who knows what it is to build up here, I'm your man."

"You're my man," Will repeated, turning it into a question and a joke at once.

I didn't crack a smile. I'd had enough experience to know he was questioning whether a woman could even be a contender, but I'd also had plenty of experience making sure I was taken seriously.

"Don't let the dress confuse you," I told him. "I'm the best."

I didn't wait for him to respond. Instead, I stuck my hand out, shook his, and saw myself back to my truck. "I'll wait to hear," I called out the window before heading back to work.

I wanted this job. I also suspected that working with Fake Tom-slash-Will would be aggravating. Good looks, bulging muscles, and whatever sexy scent he wore couldn't make up for his arrogance or what he didn't know about mountain construction.

But I wanted the job anyway.

Chapter 5

The Foreman is a Fox

WILL

I watched Lucy Dale climb into the cab of her big white truck as my head tried to wrap itself around the conversation we'd just had. This woman was a walking set of contradictions, and I was slowly coming to terms with the surprise I'd felt as she'd revealed each one. The first one, of course, had been her actual physical presence. I'd called Lucy Dale of Kasper Ridge Construction expecting someone like Markie back at my dad's company. Maybe a little rougher around the edges, since this wasn't Southern California. Maybe someone rugged and tough. A touch of flannel here and there, maybe a pair of boots. Maybe a pit bull.

It wasn't my style to judge a book by its cover, but Lucy Dale had a hot, tight little cover I just hadn't been prepared for. I hoped I hadn't let it show.

Who expected a construction foreman to turn up in high heels that made her curvy legs look three thousand miles long, and a dress? Her dark hair had been pulled back into a high ponytail, and it had taken every ounce of self-control to keep my mind from wandering into fantasies where I pulled that rubber band out and watched as the waves fell down her back and shoulders. Or wrapped that ponytail around my fist and backed her into a wall..

Couple the sheer attractiveness of the woman with the ferocious take-no-prisoners attitude beneath it, and... well, shit.

"How'd the interview with the forewoman end up going?" Ghost asked, striding back into the bar where I'd returned to do my best to make some notes on Lucy's proposal. He was smirking, which told me he knew exactly how it had gone.

"About like that. Too hot for the job, probably."

Ghost slid into the chair across from me, his dark eyes on my face. "She was hot. And I'm definitely not trying to hire a fuck buddy for you to play with all summer, man." One hand came up to rub at his chin, which sported the scruff most guys let grow once they'd left the restrictions of active duty behind. "But she's also the best up here, according to everyone I've talked to."

"According to her too," I pointed out.

Ghost smiled at that. "So she's a little cocky. You'll get along great."

"If by a little, you mean she pretty much told me I'd be a moron not to hire her and tried to make it clear she thought I had no idea what I'd be doing up here." A hot little zing ran through me, remembering the way she'd cut down her competitors in that matter-of-fact way. It took some balls, and it also led me to believe she probably had the ability and track record to back it up.

"You talking to a few more today?"

I nodded, my mind already settling pretty firmly on Lucy Dale as the only real contender, despite my dislike of her condescending attitude. "I'll see who else there is. Having her around could be distracting. Plus, she thinks she knows more than me."

"She probably does. I'm guessing she was learning about high altitude construction when you were still building Lego jets and planning to be called Maverick."

"Can we let that go?"

"Probably not."

"Shit."

"Get over yourself and hire her if she's the best," Ghost said. "And keep your dick in your pants if you do."

I crossed my arms and frowned at him, pretending to be offended by his suggestion. I wouldn't be tempted to mess around with her because I'd be too busy being annoyed by her thinking she knew more than I did about construction. I'd come up here to run the show, and I wasn't about to hire a contractor to do it for me or tell me I had no idea what I was doing. "I have more control than that."

"Of course you do." He started to rise when I remembered something else I wanted to ask him.

"Hey Ghost," I said, and he sat back down. "Is there a ladder around here?"

"Yeah..."

"One of the lights in my room isn't working, and when I got up on the bed to see if I could change it, I could see something shoved into the fixture."

Ghost sat up straighter, his eyes brightening. "Something? Like what?"

"I don't know, man. But whatever it is, it doesn't belong up there and you're lucky it hasn't caught the whole place on fire. Some kind of paper or something."

"Let's go," he said, pushing to his feet so fast he nearly toppled the chair over. Maybe Ghost wasn't doing as well as I'd thought. He was pretty excited about a piece of paper.

I followed him to a utility closet on the third floor where my room was, and then let him into the room with the ladder, pointing at the fixture I'd tried to reach the night before.

Ghost set up the ladder and was on top of it faster than I would have thought was possible. "Ha," he said, reaching over the globe of the fixture and tugging on the paper I'd spotted in there. "Yes!"

He was really excited about old garbage. "Got it?"

"Dude, do you know what this is?" He was still on top of the ladder, smoothing the bit of paper he'd extracted on the top rung. It was yellowed and wrinkled.

"Garbage?"

He shot me a grin, and something in my stomach felt uneasy at his expression. "What's going on, Ghost?"

He climbed down and crossed the room, holding the scrap out to me. "This," he said, "is part of a map."

I took the old piece of paper and examined it. It was faded and soft, and there was a dotted line crossing it from one side to the other, along with a few other marks scrawled on it. "Where is this map going to take you?"

"To a treasure, hopefully."

I barked out a laugh before realizing that Ghost was dead serious. "No shit."

He nodded. "Come with me."

In Ghost's room, he showed me three other pieces of the same map, laid out on the dining room table of the suite. He fit the piece we'd just found next to another, in the bottom left corner. "Shit," he breathed. "This is the path to Lola's Gate."

"Lola's Gate?"

He looked up at me for a long minute, and then let out a breath. "You better sit down."

Ghost told me a story then, about his great uncle Marvin getting a little crazy toward the end of his life, about the resort being deeply in the red, and about the old man hiding some kind of fortune. There was this map, and a poem the guy had left.

"And this," Ghost said, pulling a big brass key from a side table next to the couch, "is the key to Lola's Gate." The key had a cross imprinted on it that matched the one printed in the corner of the map. And the dotted line on the piece I'd just found did seem to lead to the cross on the map when we lined up the ripped edge.

"Why do you think this key goes to Lola's Gate?"

He showed me a photo of the poem on his phone.

> *A ticking clock*
> *A lonely dock*
> *My riches wait*
> *Find Lola's Gate.*
> *Blood of my blood,*
> *Heart of my heart,*
> *Take this key.*
> *When you're ready to start.*

"No idea," Ghost said. "But it's the best clue we've got right now."

I wasn't sure if this treasure hunt was a worthwhile distraction, considering the tight timeline and the lack of funds we were operating on to bring this resort back to life. But Ghost seemed pretty excited about it, so I decided to play along for now. "Okay. So where is Lola's Gate? Did you already try the key?"

Ghost looked at me as if he was disappointed. "We don't know where or what it is. But Marvin's wife was my Aunt Lola. That's all we've got. So no, we haven't tried the key. I'll go fill in Aubrey and Coyote."

"Okay." It seemed that treasure hunting was going to be one of my responsibilities this summer in addition to pulling off a potentially impossible high-speed, high-altitude reno.

"And you need to go hire Lucy Dale."

"Right," I said, less sure about that than I was about this insane treasure hunt Ghost seemed about to lead me into.

I'd hire her, but I was going to talk to the other contenders first. And if she ended up working here, I'd make it perfectly clear who was going to be the boss. I'd had enough of playing second string.

Chapter 6
Pot Pies and Gossip

LUCY

"Tell me everything." Papa was sitting on the porch at the end of the day, his customary glass of whiskey wrapped in his hand as he watched me descend from the high cab of my truck in the driveway.

"I'm barely out of the car, Pops, wanna give me a second?"

"No need. I know you go three hundred miles a minute and your brain is already inside the house having a glass of wine. I was just trying to catch you out here before it's too late."

He wasn't wrong. "Well," I said, slamming the truck door and carrying my messenger bag to set down on the top step of our porch. "I'll tell you a few things. I'm not sure we have time for everything if you want dinner at a reasonable hour tonight."

"We'll eat cereal. If you try to cook, you'll burn the house down or give me food poisoning again. Tell me everything about the today."

I sighed, letting out the tension from another long day on the job and letting that crack about my cooking go. It hadn't been food poisoning.

"We finally got through the stone we hit and managed to finish excavating the foundation for the custom home. Plumbers started work on the lines today, so we're on track."

"You know that isn't what I want to know." Papa frowned at me.

"The resort is a mess." I tried to tamp down the excitement that leaped to life within me when I thought about the opportunity to make the place new again.

"A big mess," Papa agreed. "But it was kind of a mess when it was open. Marvin wasn't a guy for details getting in the way of a good time."

I let that sink in a little. Papa hadn't told me much about Marvin Kasper, or whatever he knew about him. "How well did you know the guy?"

Papa, who had raised me from the time I was about five when my parents had died, gave me a look I hadn't seen before. "I knew him pretty well at one point. He didn't grow up around here, so not like I knew some of the other old timers, mind you."

"The place is called Kasper Ridge. Marvin Kasper wasn't from here?" I'd always assumed he was.

"The family used to live up here. A generation or so before my time. Marvin owned a bunch of the land, and that's why he ended up here. Built that resort."

"Huh. When did he build it?"

"Oh, back in the fifties. But the place was already there. Just not as big."

"I didn't know that." I thought about the grand circular drive, falling apart now, about the sweeping staircases behind the front desk. It must have been magnificent at one time. "They've got the bar looking pretty nice," I told Papa.

"Did you go over there to talk or to drink?" he asked, grinning at me.

"It was seven in the morning. We were talking."

"Did you give him your 'I am woman, hear me roar' act?" Papa's watery eyes never left my face and I squirmed as he peered right past the armor that protected me from less observant people.

"Maybe a little. I have to. People expect a man, so I have to show them why I'm better."

Papa nodded, but I got the sense he was absorbing my words, not agreeing with them. "Did you get the job?"

"Don't know yet," I said, wishing I felt more certain about the chances. Wishing I'd been better able to read Will Cruz and his intentions. "The guy hiring was some slick city boy. Former fighter pilot."

"Yeah?" That clearly piqued Papa's interest. "What'd he fly?" Papa had flown helicopters in Vietnam and was always eager to talk shop with another pilot.

"We didn't really get into that. But Bennie and CeeCee told me that Marvin's nephew, Archie, was a jet pilot and that he told his sister Aubrey that a bunch of the guys he flew with would probably be willing to come help."

"Don't listen to the gossip mill, Lucy. You know better than that." Papa repeated what he'd told me a thousand times. Key advice if you were going to survive in a town as tiny as Kasper Ridge with your sanity and any lick of privacy.

"Well, it seems accurate so far. I guess Archie and Will flew together at some point." I did my best not to picture the arrogant man I'd met this morning in a uniform, but failed. He might be a jerk, but he was undeniably hot.

Papa nodded his head, clearly thinking. "What about that other feller?"

"Who?"

"Bartender, I think. Came in a month or two ago?"

"I didn't meet anyone else."

"From Maryland, sounds like."

"Papa, if you already know, why are you asking me?"

Papa smiled innocently over the rim of his tumbler. "Just making conversation."

"Well, I'm going in to grab a shower. Dinner in forty-five, okay?"

"Kind of a long time for cereal," he teased.

"We're not having cereal."

"I like cereal."

"I'm going to put those frozen pot pies in the oven. I think I can handle it."

"Don't burn the place down."

I sighed loudly.

"You're the best, love." Papa chuckled.

"So are you."

I went into the little two-bedroom house and straight through the cozy living room to my room in the back. Papa had insisted I should have the master suite, with the bathroom included, since I was the one working at this point. I think some of his willingness to swap rooms when I returned home was that this room reminded him of my grandmother too much. It reminded me of her too.

Mimi had passed ten years earlier, and Papa had seemed to become an old man almost overnight. I'd gotten a call my last year in college during finals week that he'd been injured on a job site, and had skipped my last test to rush up to see him. He'd been okay, but shaken. And that was when I'd made the decision to return home for good, to take over the business eventually. It had been an idea I'd been toying with for a while anyway. This just gave me a reason to make the decision. Now, at almost thirty, it still felt like the right thing to do.

Even if being single in Kasper Ridge wasn't always easy. I didn't have a dream of a house with a picket fence and a couple of kids, not like Bennie and CeeCee did. But every now and then, it did get a little lonely up here surrounded by the people I'd known my entire life.

And when new folks came to town, they didn't tend to stay. Not everyone was cut out for life in a place like this.

I stepped into the hot shower, working to keep my mind from Will Cruz and the job I desperately wanted. The job was the thing I should have been considering as the hot water sluiced over my tired muscles and through my dirty hair. Instead, my mind was lingering on the way Will's muscles had challenged the fabric of that soft looking long-sleeved T-shirt he'd worn, about the confident smile he'd shot me as soon as we'd met.

The guy was in over his head up here. That much was clear.

But he was also stupidly attractive, and if I was offered the job, remembering that he was a client would be critically important. Almost as important as reminding myself that he wasn't a permanent fixture in Kasper Ridge. Like all outsiders, he was only temporary, and if he was good for any kind of romantic involvement, it would be only a fling.

A fling I had no intentions of having.

Chapter 7
Making the Most of our Messes

WILL

Lucy was right.

I talked to the other two companies who'd put in compelling offers for the work on the resort, and while both guys seemed friendly and professional, it was the references I checked in with who really sealed the deal. I might not have bothered calling references, except Lucy's parting shots about her competition had stuck in my mind. And I wanted this done right—I'd left Southern California to prove myself, and that meant no shortcuts.

If I was ever going to be able to show my father what I was

capable of, to earn his respect, I had to make sure this job ran perfectly.

A week after I'd first spoken with her, Lucy Dale was striding confidently back through the lobby doors in the late afternoon, wearing another dress—this one blue—and sandals that made it weirdly difficult not to stare at her painted toenails.

But her toenails were not my concern, I reminded myself. We had a lot to accomplish, and we were going to be working together. Today's meeting would set the tone. Lucy needed to know for sure that I was in charge, in case there was any question.

"Hello," she said, her confidence projecting through the relative gloom of the lobby.

"Good morning," I said, reaching out to shake her extended hand.

She was formal and businesslike, and her skin was soft and warm—and a second later she was pulling her hand away with an irritated expression. Had I held that shake too long?

Dammit. I knew this would be awkward. I did fine around pretty women—but there was something different about Lucy that had me reverting back to the discomfort I'd felt around my first crushes in middle school. What the hell was wrong with me?

"Ready to get started?" she asked me.

"Yep, let's go." We were doing a comprehensive walk-through, checking her timeline against Ghost's ambitious opening plans to prioritize the most critical parts of the operation.

Lucy carried a tablet and every time we moved, she jotted more notes into it, nodding her head and muttering to herself.

"It's going t be a full court press to get this place ready for guests by November," I told her as we climbed the stairs to the third level to look at the first wing of guest rooms.

"My crew can get the critical work done," she said. "You won't have to worry about safety and stability. And this," she said, waving an arm to indicate the peeling wallpaper in the hallway and the ripped up carpet piled to one side. "This stuff won't be an issue once we've got the demo done and we can see what's really under all this."

I tried not to let the obvious mountain of work ahead impede my confidence. "It's a mess, but I'm sure you're right."

She shrugged, stopping in the middle of the hallway, her shining hair and tanned long legs a stark contrast to the decrepit old space. "It's cosmetic." She stepped over to the wall, taking hold of a piece of peeling paper and pulling it free. "And no matter how attractive or unattractive things are on the surface, it's the stability of the structure underneath that we need to be concerned with." She shot me a fierce look, her eyes narrowed and her lips pursed, and I had the bizarre sensation that she wasn't talking about the resort, but that she meant me somehow.

"Right. Well, stability is my middle name." My mouth was going before my brain had even gotten into the game, and I wanted to sink into the hole in the floor at the end of the hallway and disappear.

"So you go by 'Will Fake Tom Stability Cruz' then. Is that right?" One dark eyebrow was arched over her blue eyes and her mouth hitched up. The sudden shift to sarcastic humor took me off guard a little.

"You can just call me Will though," I said.

"It's definitely less of a mouthful."

"It is." We continued our tour of the property, Lucy making constant notes on her tablet as we did and me working to keep my mouth in check, and my body too. Lucy was smart, and I'd just figured out that bantering with her could be fun. I bet lots of things we could do together might be fun, but we were not going to do any of them. I had the clear sense she was merely tolerating me anyway.

As we finished up, I took her to Ghost's suite, which he and Aubrey used as a kind of headquarters office, since the offices off the lobby were in as poor of shape as the rest of the place.

When Archie pulled the door open, he waved us in, looking a little worried. My heartrate ticked up immediately. I didn't like Ghost being worried about anything, it was part of why I was here.

"Everything okay, Archie?"

"Yeah," he said. "Just a lot to do here, right? Have a seat. Nice to see you again Ms. Dale."

"It's just Lucy, please," she said, taking a seat and crossing her ankles as she smoothed the skirt of her dress.

I pulled my eyes from her legs and back to where Ghost was sitting across from me. "Plan's looking good and Lucy's ready to get her crew starting on demo tomorrow."

Lucy said, "We'll get everything cleaned up so we can account for anything that might be a surprise along the way—"

Ghost raised a finger. "Surprise? You mean like discovering things you didn't expect."

"Right, like water damage or mold, old electrical, that kind of thing."

I was fairly certain Ghost hadn't been talking about those kinds of surprises. He was fixated on this ridiculous treasure hunt. So much so that he'd had me write some silly shit about it into our vendor contracts and then had his lawyer proof it. I thought he was off his rocker, but it was clear that Ghost and Aubrey thought this treasure was real and they were determined to find it. I thought we'd be better off standing up a profitable business instead.

"And did Will talk to you about the contract clause I added? About finding other kinds of things?"

Lucy's eyes crinkled a bit at the corners, as if she found Ghost's treasure hunt amusing. She'd been a little surprised when I'd pointed out the clause, but she'd reacted professionally, as I was sensing she always did. "He did. And I'll brief my crew. Anything we find in the course of demo or construction comes straight to you."

Ghost looked relieved. "And if it proves to be valuable—"

"We get a share." Lucy waved this away. "I don't think you need to worry," she said. "We're here to do a job, and we're careful and professional. My guys would turn in anything they found anyway. That's just the kind of people I hire."

"Well, that's good to hear," Ghost said.

"But you really think there's something hidden here, don't you?" she asked, watching him carefully.

Ghost looked between us and let out a sigh. "I don't really know," he admitted. "There's something, definitely. I don't know if it's here or somewhere around here, up in these mountains. Uncle Marvin was... well, he was secretive sometimes, even when he was alive. So I'm definitely curious. And it wouldn't be the worst thing to find out that he hid a fortune around. It would definitely help with the bottom line."

"Well, whatever we find will come straight to you," Lucy said seriously. "No worries there."

"Thanks," Ghost said.

"Final contracts are signed," I told Ghost. "We're ready to roll."

Lucy nodded. "We'll be here early tomorrow morning."

"We'll be ready," Ghost said, and I could see the eager excitement on his face. I just hoped we weren't all biting off more than we could chew.

It felt like we were wrapping up, and just as I was about to stand to escort Lucy out, the doors to the suite burst open again, and Aubrey and Wiley came in, their hands full of heaping plates.

"Oh!" Aubrey said, spotting Lucy and stopping short so that Wiley almost crashed into her from behind. "Oh hi! You must be Lucy Dale, yeah? Will wasn't kidding about how pretty you are."

I felt the heat rush to my face. Dammit. I was never telling Aubrey anything again. Her mouth was always a mile ahead of her brain.

Lucy turned to look at me, that eyebrow high again as her lips hitched into the half smile I liked more than I should. Thankfully, she didn't say anything about that. "I'm Lucy," she confirmed. "You must be Aubrey Kasper."

"And this is Wiley," Aubrey said, turning to indicate her tall boyfriend at her back. "We've got meat. You staying for dinner?"

"Oh, no," Lucy said, rising and picking up her tablet.

"Stay," Ghost suggested. "Unless you have other plans. You can get to know the team, and—"

"Let's not push her," I said, coming to my feet. I wanted to keep Lucy at a professional distance. A safe distance. "She already said—"

"If you insist," Lucy said, shooting me a huge smile. "Let me just make a quick call." She slid her phone from her bag and strode to the corner of the room.

"Awesome," Aubrey said, practically bouncing out to the grill on the enormous patio.

"I guess she's staying for dinner," I said, working hard to summon disappointment over this turn of events. It was pointless though, something in me was rallying at the idea of sitting close to her, maybe making her laugh.

Ghost chuckled and took a step closer. "Maybe you'll be able to get your shit together if you spend a little time with her.

This whole puppy dog eyes thing you've got going on right now is going to be a problem."

"What? I don't—" *Shit. Shit, shit, shit.*

"All set," Lucy said, stepping close again.

The damned heat flooded my body again as the scent of her hit me, and I wished I'd worked harder to send her home. Either way, I needed to get myself in check. If Ghost had noticed some reaction to her, I wasn't doing as good a job as I'd thought of hiding my interest. And this was a situation where any interest at all could jeopardize everything. "I'll be right back." I basically ran, heading out the front door of the suite and down the hall to my own room, where I planned to do as Ghost suggested and get my shit together.

Once there, I braced myself in front of the bathroom mirror and stared at the guy I found there. I looked put together enough. Intelligent, capable. So why was I turning into a bumbling douchebag every time I had to talk to Lucy? I needed to get over this issue right away, or I'd flub this job and prove my father right.

Not for the first time I wished Lucy was more like Markie back at home, that all that capability didn't come in such a gorgeous little package that smelled like frosting and oozed competence. It was a lot to ignore.

I splashed some water on my face, gave myself a stern talking to, and went back to the big suite at the end of the hall, where I found Lucy sitting on the couch next to Aubrey, Wiley explaining how he'd come to be here with them.

"And it just seemed like the right thing to do. I was at the end of the road back in Maryland, and ready for something new." He winked at Aubrey.

"So are you still planning to go home at the end of the summer?" Lucy asked, and I noticed Aubrey stiffen a little. I knew Ghost hoped Wiley would stay, but we had a couple leads on local bartenders if he decided not to.

Wiley wrapped a big hand around the back of his neck. "I've got good reasons to stay," he said. "Ghost says I could run the bar and the alcohol program for the whole resort. But there is the distillery to think about back in Singletree."

"He'll stay," Ghost said confidently, and I sensed he didn't want to go too far down that road. That was something Wiley and Aubrey needed to work out.

"And what about you?" Lucy asked, turning to face me with a glass of whiskey in her delicate hand. "You came in from Southern California to help your friend. What will be next for you?"

I was mid-pour on my own whiskey, so I finished and went to sit in the vacant spot at the end of the couch. "I'm not sure," I said truthfully. "I guess I'm here as long as Ghost needs me."

"According to the plans you drew up, that'll be at least a year," Ghost said.

"You planning to keep working through winter?" Lucy asked, and from the tone of the question I could tell there was only one right answer.

"Interiors only, yeah."

She nodded, looking dubious. I hated that she doubted me. She and Dad would get along great.

"And then back down to the city," she suggested.

A feeling of despair washed through me unexpectedly when I thought about my condo, about Dad, about the life I'd had until just a week ago. "Not necessarily."

Lucy raised that eyebrow again and took a sip of her drink, and I was glad when Ghost and Aubrey began talking about other aspects of the resort, taking the focus off me.

Chapter 8
Some Hot Guy from LA Makes Me Nervous

LUCY

G etting the Kasper Ridge job was everything I wanted, and as I finished up dinner and said goodbye to the small group at the resort, I hoped I was up to it.

"You'll do great," Papa said when I expressed my concerns to him later that night. "You keep your crew close and tight, don't take shortcuts."

"Never do," I said, settling down on the couch beside him. "You taught me that."

"Good girl," my grandfather said, giving me a warm smile that made me feel like I'd won the lottery. He was the only parent I'd really ever known, even though he wasn't technically my parent at all. But he'd taught me everything I knew about the world, and he was my champion. Always. Which was why I never wanted to let him down. "Tell me more about the resort," Papa said, giving me his full attention even though there was a poker tournament on television.

I tucked my legs up beneath me and told him everything I'd learned so far, telling him about the people, the peeling wallpaper and missing floorboards, the front drive that needed a new overhang. And then I told him about the odd clause Ghost had written into our contract.

"What is he expecting you to uncover?" Papa asked, sounding interested.

"Sounds like he really believes there's some kind of treasure there. Something his great uncle left." I loved the idea, I just hoped it wasn't going to distract from the real work we needed to do.

Papa chuckled, and for a second I wondered if he'd known about this. "Did I ever tell you how Marvin and I met?"

"I don't think so."

He grinned and crossed his hands over his stomach, settling in for a tale. "He musta been about ten, I'd say, and I was a wee little thing. Maybe four or five.

"His father had built the original Kasper Ridge Resort, only back then it was just a little building on the side of a hill, a couple ski runs, a few guest rooms and a restaurant. His folks didn't live here though. The place was run by a manager—my dad."

"I didn't know that," I said, surprise making me sit a little straighter.

"Yep. Marvin used to come stay for a couple weeks in the summer, and Dad became part babysitter, part resort manager."

"Seems like a lot to ask of an employee," I pointed out.

Papa lifted a thin shoulder. "Things were different back then, I guess. I didn't think much of it, just knew that this wise older feller would come up to play with me every year. And he was wise, Luce. He was a city kid, you know. Growing up out there in Los Angeles."

A noise escaped me, thinking of some other slick city fellow from LA. "Oh yeah?"

"But he was smart. And full of ideas. We weren't allowed to go off the resort property," Papa continued. "Which gave us a pretty big run, really, if you included the ski mountain. But Marvin always had adventures for us. We'd be pirates or cowboys, exploring and discovering things. He had a mind for stories, and I was always thrilled to go along for the ride. It was like every summer was a trip to a whole different world."

"Sounds like an interesting guy," I said. "So you stayed in touch, all those years? And eventually he came here to stay?"

"By the time he came to stay, the world had changed," Papa said, shaking his head. "But yes. He brought his wife, and the two of them turned that hotel into something spectacular. I didn't see him much then—he was busy entertaining celebrities and living the high life, I guess. He came to see me once or twice a while before he died though."

"So recently?" I began wondering if maybe I'd met Marvin Kasper at some point.

"You were never around—working," Papa said, answering my unspoken question.

"Do you think he might have left some kind of treasure for his nephew and niece to find?"

Papa's eyes crinkled at the corners as he grinned, his chest shaking a little with a silent laugh. "Oh, I bet he did," he said. "I bet he did."

"What do you think it would be?" I asked, a little surprised that the treasure hunt might actually be real, that Papa believed it could be worthwhile.

"Knowing Marvin, it could have been anything at all. He made treasure maps for me all those years ago. Would send me hunting all over these hills for little treasures he'd nicked from guests at the hotel."

I giggled, pressing a hand to my mouth. "Really?" I imagined two little boys roaming the hills in search of stolen lighters and cufflinks.

He laughed at the memory, then shifted gear. "When are you getting things rolling on the renovation?" Papa asked, pulling my mind back to the present.

"First thing tomorrow," I told him. "Mateo's gonna finish up over at the home site, and I've already pulled back in six of the guys I had to let go last year. They jumped at the chance to get on a local job, something that will keep them busy for at least a year." A little flicker of pride warmed me at the thought of providing that kind of security for them.

"I bet."

"I'll have a small crew for the initial phase, but then Mateo will bring the rest over when they finish up the custom build."

"You've got a plan," Papa said.

"Always."

"And the city slicker you told me about?"

My mind slipped back to the suite where I'd had dinner sitting across the table from Will, his blue eyes catching the lights and his cocksure grin doing strange things to my stomach. He was too damned handsome for his own good. Or maybe just too handsome for my good. I was going to need to be careful—I'd caught him watching me a few times during the evening, and his attention lit a strange little glow in me. I liked his eyes on me. I wanted him to notice me.

But on a rational level, I didn't want any of it. It would only complicate things, and potentially get in the way of the job.

"I'll manage him."

"Isn't he the one in charge?" Papa asked, purposely riling me in the way he'd done since I was tiny, checking my own arrogance.

"That's what he thinks, yeah. But he'll figure it out pretty quick."

"Don't get too cocky, Luce."

I smiled sweetly at my grandfather. "Not cocky. Just confident."

Papa made a doubtful sputtering noise and turned the volume back up on the poker tournament he was watching. "Gotta focus now, Luce," he said out of the side of his mouth. "That bastard Louie thinks he can beat me Thursday night. I'm gonna take him for everything he's got."

"Papa, go easy on your friends. If you take all their money, they won't want to play with you anymore."

"Nah. That's why they play with me. They gotta keep trying to win it all back."

"Then let them," I suggested.

Papa turned to me, his eyes wide. "That would be dishonest."

I blew out a sigh. "You're impossible."

"When you're my age, you can be whatever you want."

I dropped a kiss on Papa's cheek and headed back to my bedroom. It was going to be an exciting week. I was looking forward to getting back to the resort, getting started on the job that would make my career.

And if I was honest, I was excited to see Will again. But as a little flame of desire burned inside me at the thought of his broad firm shoulders and that dimple next to his smile, I realized that maybe honesty wasn't the best policy where Will was concerned.

Chapter 9

You're Doing Great. Do Better.

WILL

The renovation started smoothly. Lucy ran a tight ship and I did my best to stay in the background, steering from behind. I'd been micromanaged plenty of times, and while I checked in on things a little more than she probably realized—a benefit of actually living on the job site—I was confident she was doing a good job. And that meant I was doing a good job.

I was just beginning to relax a little bit when Ghost pulled me aside one night in the suite where we'd had dinner and laughed with Aubrey and Wiley before they'd headed off to their yurt out back.

"I need to tell you some things," Ghost said, pouring himself a healthy glass of whiskey and not meeting my eye.

"This can't be good." I followed suit. If he needed whiskey to tell me whatever it was, I probably needed whiskey to hear it.

As I poured, my mind took some very dark side streets, and I imagined this was where Ghost told me it had all been a mistake. Or that in even this short time he'd realized I wasn't up to the challenge. Or worse, that maybe he'd talked to Dad, heard about the one time I let down my guard and put too much faith in the crew—the mistake that had me cost me Dad's trust. And my confidence, if I was being honest.

"Dude." Ghost's voice held an edge of annoyance, and I looked up abruptly at my name, realizing a beat too late that I'd been zoned out.

"Sorry. Just imagining heading back to LA, asking Dad for my job back." I hated the idea and my gut churned. I poured whiskey into it to see if it would help.

Ghost dropped the heavy glass tumbler on the long dining table. "Shit. You're leaving?"

"What? No. I figured you were about to tell me I should."

He shook his head. "Didn't expect that," he said, a bark of mirthless laughter escaping him. "No, not at all. I need you more than ever. And I'm gonna ask something of you that is going to piss you off."

"I'm not giving you a foot massage." It wasn't the time for jokes—I knew that. But my mouth had a mind of its own sometimes, and I figured Ghost could use a little levity. I was worried he might be about to break down. Or cry.

"Funny. No."

He moved to look out the window toward the back of the property. An array of heavy machinery was scattered across the wide open space, the gentle slope of what would be the ski mountain rising up behind it in the falling darkness.

"This has to happen faster," he said.

A spike of uncertainty raced through me. "Faster?"

"Yeah. Like twice as fast. I need to book guests in to ski this winter."

"Are we looking at the same resort here? That's impossible. Look at the place."

"We don't have to be one-hundred percent operational. But we need a few rooms, outdoor spaces done, an operational restaurant, and at least one chair lift."

I shook my head. "What's the sudden rush?"

"I've been digging through the books, looking at my own accounts. We don't have enough runway to drag this out until next year. We need to get income this winter or the whole thing will fail."

"What about bringing in investment?"

Ghost frowned at me. "I've thought about it. It's a last resort. Between you, me, and my sister, it's already a complicated equity arrangement. I don't want some big firm that's going to send in management and tell us what to do just because they own a stake."

"Maybe we need it."

Ghost stared out the window again. "Can we find some way to make it happen faster? Get the outdoor spaces finished ASAP? There's gotta be a way."

I was torn. On one hand, Ghost was being completely unreasonable. Rushing led to oversights, and I wanted this job to be the one that went off perfectly. We didn't have enough people or time—or money—to do what he was asking. On the other hand, it sounded like if we didn't make it happen on this advanced schedule, it might never happen at all. And then we'd all lose. And I'd be heading back to LA exactly where I started. Except with another failure next to my name.

"I'll make it happen." My mouth again. Getting ahead of my

brain. Only this time, I knew it was saying the only thing I could say.

"How?" Ghost asked.

"Not sure yet. But don't worry. I'll figure it out." I finished my whiskey and went back to my room to dig through every idea I could come up with and see if any of them might work.

So much for things going well.

Chapter 10
Unreasonable Construction Banter

LUCY

For the first two weeks of work, I did a good job dodging the Will Cruz-shaped bullet around the job site.

Friday morning of the second week, I pulled the truck up behind one of the dumpsters and hopped out, reaching back into the truck for my tablet and hardhat.

"Morning."

A deep voice out of nowhere had me jumping and I let out a squeal as I whipped around to find Will standing just behind me. He had to have been waiting behind the dumpster.

"Shit, didn't mean to scare you."

I recovered quickly. Shrieking like a little girl wasn't the way I wanted to assert my authority here. "You didn't scare me."

"You always screech like that when you get out of your truck?"

I turned to face him, taking in the smirk on his face and the way his muscles bulged as he crossed his arms over his chest, awaiting my reply.

Ass.

"How's it going?" he asked.

So we were going to make small talk now? I'd arrived here in a fine mood, ready to reengage with the project that would make my career, solidify my reputation, and give my crew and myself the security we all needed. But now I found myself irritated, jumpy, and strangely aroused. Not for the first time, I wished Will wasn't so goddamn handsome.

All this, and it was only five after seven. I had not had enough coffee to handle Will. "Yep, going good," I said, following him to the table where the plans were laid out. We gazed down at them together as I waited for whatever he wanted to check in about.

The sound of the loaders broke through the tension and snapped me back to the job at hand.

"I brought the skid steer and track loader to clear the debris around the side and back to get us a clearer path to the patios," I told him, pointedly looking at the plans and avoiding his ocean-eyed gaze.

"That's good," he said. "I'm gonna want you guys to bump up construction on the outdoor amenities on the other side too. The hot tubs have to be operational this winter, which means the east side needs to get attacked asap."

Annoyance sizzled through my insides, and I squinted up at him. I hated that this guy was taller than me. I didn't have much of a chance of intimidating him at five foot three, and right then

I needed to communicate in a look how completely outrageous the words he just uttered were.

Where the hell had this come from? Had the guy just woken up today and decided to change everything? I knew his inexperience would become an issue. I reigned in my simmering anger and adopted the tone one would use with an errant toddler.

"Will, we already went over all the plans. This thing is going to happen in phases, remember? The eastern assets are part of phase three, which means, no hot tubs until the first floor grounds are cleared and laid, and the interior electrical and water have been revamped."

"Yep." He grinned. "And all that needs to happen a little quicker so we can get the amenities in before the winter. We're doing a soft open for guests this December. Archie's pushing things a bit."

"Will," I said as calmly as I could manage. "It is July. We have plenty of challenges with this whole yurt thing you've got set up at the back of the resort over there"—I gestured toward the woods where Ghost and Aubrey had erected six huge yurts and an outdoor kitchen, and had been talking about booking guests in for the end of the summer—"but getting the place winter-ready by this December with the assets we have now is completely impossible."

He nodded. "That's what I told Ghost. But it doesn't matter. We're gonna have to figure it out."

I stood to my fullest height and looked straight into those ridiculously intense blue eyes, trying to tamp down my irritation at his apparent belief that plans were merely a suggestion.

"I'm telling you that the plans we agreed on are the ones we'll need to follow if you want this done on time and on budget. I know what I'm doing. I've done it hundreds of times before."

His face hardened slightly at the implication that maybe he hadn't done this before.

"Maybe I can bring in a second crew to focus on the additional work."

"Absolutely not. I've already got you to contend with. I don't need another jerk up here who thinks he knows what he's doing."

Will sucked in a breath, and any congeniality left his face. "I actually do know what I'm doing."

"I'm not totally convinced you do. That's why you hired me to manage this job and keep things on track. If you knew what you were doing, you'd know that this idea is insane and potentially dangerous." I was angry, but I tried to keep a reasonable tone, even in the face of this unreasonable demand.

"I'm actually the one managing this job, and I'm aware that this is not what we initially planned. But I am asking for your input here. We don't have a choice. Archie makes the decisions," Will said. I realized he didn't look thrilled about the change of plans either.

"It's never a good idea to push a project like this. We don't want shortcuts."

Will looked distressed, a frown pulling his lips down and the bright blue eyes dimming as he stared down at the plans. "I know," he agreed.

I needed to find a way to figure things out. I couldn't lose this job, and I didn't want it to spiral out of my control either. "I'll take a look at the plans and the timing," I said, still irritated, but soothed by the fact Will was actually asking for help instead of demanding I perform magic. "And I'll have some suggestions for you and Archie tomorrow."

"Thanks. I'm working on it too. Just wanted to let you know that things are shifting. We'll figure it out." He gave me one stiff nod and turned to watch the guys loading the remains of the old patio, expertly scooping and dumping it into the waste containers.

"I'm going to get started," I said. With that, I put my hardhat on my head and walked away from him as a huge SUV pulled up behind my truck.

I headed past the first dumpster and turned to watch as the car stopped and both front doors opened. Will's posture changed as a man emerged from the driver's seat, his arms opening and a loud whoop leaving him. Will practically skipped over to give the man a bro-hug.

"Brainiac! You made it, Sir!"

Brainiac? Sir?

The guy Will called Brainiac was every bit as well built as my irritatingly handsome nemesis, only this man had salt and pepper hair and his face was just a little more touched with age. He had a seasoned, debonair look to him.

Was this place some kind of hot guy magnet? I thought back to what CeeCee had said about Ghost bringing up a bunch of former military guys to help out. That would explain the nickname too. Brainiac. Another callsign.

Just as I was about to turn away and head around the side of the building, Will called out to another person.

"Monroe! So good to see you." A woman appeared from around the back of the SUV, and Will swept her into an embrace as I took in the long wavy blond hair, the tall curvy figure, and the confident posture. Who was this? And why did my stomach twist as I watched her talking to Will, a couple inches closer than was strictly necessary?

I tore my gaze away and turned on my heel, heading back to do what I had been hired to do. It was none of my business who my employer had visiting him here.

Still, there was something about the way he'd embraced

"Monroe," and my mind kept spinning around the annoying attraction I felt for Will. But none of it mattered.

I needed to focus and get myself straight. And figure out how to do the impossible on a limited budget and a ridiculous timeline.

Chapter 11
Getting the Band Back Together

WILL

Seeing Brainiac and Monroe pop out of that SUV almost rescued me from the shitty mood that arguing with Lucy had launched me into. Almost, but not quite.

I watched Lucy's flannel and denim-clad figure disappear behind the enormous dumpster and a wash of feelings poured through me that I couldn't even begin to sort through. The woman was a conundrum. Part of me wanted to wrap her in my arms and protect her—she was so small and adorable. But another part of me wanted to fight with her and pin her to a wall and make her listen to me, and maybe kiss her just a little bit and potentially rip all our clothes off and convince her that sex would solve whatever issues we had.

She was frustrating, and not just because I knew she was acting as the voice of reason on the renovation. I'd never been completely in charge before, as my dad had pointed out so many goddamn times. And so maybe I'd never really realized that being in charge meant you were the one caught in the middle between the client's unreasonable demands and the foreman's clear view of what needed to happen when and how fast would be safe and smart to proceed.

Lucy was right. And Ghost demanding suddenly that the whole east patio be functional for winter was way outside the scope of what we'd planned to accomplish this season. I knew that.

But I also knew I had to succeed at this. Because if I failed at managing this job, if Ghost had to send me packing, what exactly would I be going back to? The only way I wanted to return to Dad's business was as a success. As a leader he couldn't shove to the side any longer. As his equal.

Pushing Lucy at the very start of this project might not have been the right move. But she exuded capability and confidence. I had a feeling she'd make things happen, if only to spite me. And since I couldn't pin her to the wall and rip her clothes off, I'd have to accept her spite instead.

Although there was always the possibility of a nice hate fuck...

"Head in the clouds again," Monroe teased, punching me in the arm.

"Nothing's changed, I guess," Brainiac threw in. "Where's Ghost?"

"Upstairs," I said. "So he was serious. We're actually getting the band back together."

"Oh god, no singing, Fake Tom," Monroe moaned. "You're strictly backup."

"Nice," I told her. "I seem to remember that you don't exactly have sultry tones either. Remember that night at the O-Club in Osan?"

"No way she could possibly remember that after all the shots she put away," Brainiac said.

"I remember parts of it," Monroe said, her chin tipping up. She might look like a pinup girl, but Monroe was as tough as any of the male pilots we'd flown with. And I'd always suspected that, like me, she probably felt like she had something to prove. "And I know I sing better than Fake Tom."

"Maybe," I conceded. "But you'd never catch me on top of the bar belting out a Mariah Carey tune."

"Fuck," Brainiac cringed. "I can still hear the high notes Monroe unleashed that night. Takes me to a very dark place."

"Speaking of very dark places," I told them. "Let me show you guys around Ghost's luxury resort. Want me to grab your bags, Sir?"

Brainiac stepped in close, his breath in my face and his eyes nearly slitted as he growled, "quit it with the 'Sir' stuff."

"Yes, Si... Ah, okay," I said. Brainiac had always outranked me. I was a junior officer when I'd joined the squadron and he was a lieutenant commander. It was going to be a hard habit to break.

"You can carry my bag, Tom," Monroe purred, thrusting a sea bag into my arms from the back of the SUV.

"You know they make suitcases with wheels now, and you're out of the military," I said, hefting the enormous thing onto my shoulder. "Time for an upgrade?"

"This works fine," she said, sniffing and lifting a shoulder. Monroe had never been what you expected her to be. She was tough, practical, honest, and the single biggest player I'd known when we were active duty. If fighter pilots had a bad reputation where one-night stands were concerned, Monroe certainly lived up to it, though she was careful never to sleep with anyone in our squadron.

I led my old friends inside the dark lobby, Brainiac letting out a low whistle as he looked around the space. I'd been here long enough now that I didn't see the broken chandeliers and peeling wallpaper anymore, but had begun to see possibilities instead. But for these two, that wasn't the case. They saw what was here now, and it wasn't much.

"This is a shit show," Brainiac mused. "Ghost has really lost his damn mind, huh?"

"I don't know," Monroe said. "The space is great. That reception desk is incredible. I think there's a lot of potential here."

"Potential for a lawsuit when someone falls down those stairs," Brainiac said, pointing out the missing bannister as we climbed the sweeping staircase behind the reception desk.

"That's what the construction crew is working on," I told them. "That's why I'm here, actually. Managing the project."

They both gave me a look that made me think they doubted my abilities, but I tried to shrug it off.

I dropped Monroe's bag at the top of the stairs. "We'll put it in your room when we figure out where Ghost wants you." Brainiac deposited his leather duffle next to the worn sea bag, and we headed for Ghost's suite.

The door opened just after I knocked on it, and Aubrey bounced on the balls of her feet when she saw who I'd brought.

"Oh, this is really happening!" she sang. "Archie! Look who's here! We've got our events manager and the engineer who's gonna get that old lift running again!"

"No shit," Ghost said, appearing from around the corner. "You guys made good time." He gave each of them a warm hug, then stepped back and looked at Brainiac. "I thought you weren't sure you could get away, Sir?"

"Don't call me sir," he said. "And I'm taking a sabbatical." Brainiac was an engineering professor out at Archmont University in Northern California. He was a classic engineer, except all the social awkwardness and lack of conversational skills had been poured into a pretty intimidating package, especially now with the silver-black hair and the I've-seen-some-things look in his eyes.

"Well, it's good to see you both," Ghost told them. "We've cleaned up a couple more rooms. We'll get you settled and I'll show you around and we can talk through plans."

"I'm gonna head back out to work," I told them. "Dinner tonight?"

"Definitely," Ghost said. "But we're heading into town. Be ready to leave at six."

I gave him a quick exaggerated salute, and Monroe and Brainiac both rolled their eyes. It was nice being around my squadron mates again. Felt a little bit like coming home.

* * *

I went out the back doors of the east wing and looked around. The ground out here was covered in pine needles and leaves, debris blown up in piles against the walls of the hotel, but this was where the east patio that would hold the hot tubs and tiered seating was intended to go. The part we'd planned for spring, but which Ghost had just pressed fast forward on.

The plans called for an extension of the hotel structure itself out to one side, and the clearing of a lot of trees and land to create the patio.

Lucy was right and I knew it. This part of the project required a whole different set of machinery and manpower than what she'd planned for phase one on the west side. Phase one was supposed to be clearing debris and cleaning up, renovating structure only where it was unsafe and then interior renovation through the winter months to get the lobby and one wing of guest rooms up to snuff to open for next summer.

I considered how it might be possible, caught between what I had already approved, and what I needed to do to make sure Ghost's dream didn't die on the vine. Because if his dream died, mine did too and Dad would only ever see me as a failure. As I stared up into the towering trees facing the mountain, I took a deep breath. The sound of machinery filled the air now, Lucy getting her crew to work—and I knew what I needed to do.

Chapter 12
I Have No Moments

LUCY

I had almost gotten past the anger that had roared through me at Will announcing so blithely that we were going to accelerate the entire plan—a plan that he approved, and that I'd put meticulous care into making sure we'd be able to execute. And once I got past my anger, which was something I'd always struggled with, I was usually able to think clearly and begin to execute.

But then he appeared again.

"Hey," Will said, striding around the back of the enormous

wall of windows that faced the mountain at the back of the resort. "Got a minute?" he asked.

I kept my jaw from popping open through sheer force of will and a little bit of residual anger. Yeah, he looked like a freaking model, but he was an irritating and entitled asshole. I needed to remember that. A demanding one who clearly had no idea how to manage a job like the one I was forced to work with him.

"I have very few, now that you've stolen six months from the schedule, actually." My tone was icy and hard, and I was proud of myself. I'd already had a few ideas about how to actually accomplish the ridiculous feat of simultaneously renovating the west wing and building the east patio, but I wasn't ready to tell him that just yet.

"About that," he said, coming to stand next to me. The crew was busy clearing years of debris from the sides of the building and the land that stretched down on the western side toward the old outbuilding and ski lift that sat beyond.

I let out a sigh and faced him, crossing my arms over my chest like a shield. "Unless you've got some kind of time machine—"

"Maybe you could just listen for a minute," he suggested. His tone was friendly, but the words were pointed and he had interrupted me.

I hated being interrupted.

"Maybe you could wait until I'm done speaking before you start," I said. "That's how polite conversation works. We take turns."

His steely eyes narrowed for a fraction of a second and his lips pressed into a line before a smile crept across those glorious features and my traitorous body lit up like a damned Christmas tree. But only on the inside. I'd never let this guy see the effect his stupid good looks had on me. I was stronger than that.

I was stronger than him.

"Apologies, Firecracker," he said, emphasizing each syllable in a very annoying way. "Continue."

"It's Lucy." I blew out a frustrated sigh, partially because some silly part of me had lit up when he'd nonchalantly given me a nickname. I hated how I reacted to this man. It would be best if I could just get on with the job at hand. There was no reason we had to interact in person. He could like, email me or something. "I was just saying again that this demand to accelerate the development of the east patio is going to require an additional set of resources I hadn't planned on for this phase, and that—"

"That's what I wanted to talk about," he said.

The top of my head was close to blowing off. "You just interrupted me again. And we already talked about it. Like an hour ago!"

His chin dipped down, and for a second I had the feeling of being looked at as a child, or as the tiny woman I actually was, not as a figure of authority. "Sorry about that," he said, his voice smooth and silky. "I just wanted to reassure you about it, though. I think I've got a solution."

"Great. I can't wait to hear it."

"I'll foreman that project. I just need resources. Men and machines."

"So we'll be what, partners?"

"No. I'll still be in charge. But that doesn't mean I can't get my hands dirty. I've handled an excavator before, you know."

"Shoveling all that sand down in Southern California," I said, nodding.

His face hardened slightly, but there was something else in his eyes, something dark and smoky that had muscles tightening deep within me in response. "I have the distinct impression that you don't respect me, Firecracker." He stepped a tiny bit closer, not inappropriately so, but enough that I thought I could feel the heat radiating off his T-shirt covered chest.

I tilted my chin up to him, not giving an inch. "Respect is something that has to be earned, Fake Tom," I whispered, emphasizing the name I knew he had a love-hate relationship with.

"I bet I could earn your respect," he murmured, his eyes dropping to my lips, then lower.

My body heated at his attention, and I had the urge to remove the flannel shirt I'd pulled over my tank top. "Really?" I challenged. I knew I should have walked away, should have ended whatever this was. But I couldn't.

Will nodded, but just when I thought he might lean in and whisper something in my ear, or even kiss me, he stepped back.

Will looked around, took a deep breath, and turned to me again. "Do you think we could work with John Racket to get another crew and some more equipment up here?"

I swallowed hard, doing my best to get my mind back to the work. Back to being mad at this arrogant jerk. But it was still lingering on the way I'd reacted when I thought he might touch me. I'd actually wanted him to touch me. "I don't work with that asshole. I go in after him to fix what he screws up."

Now I was just fighting Will on principle. His idea actually wasn't bad. But Racket would be unlikely to give up a crew or any equipment. We'd never been especially friendly, and I knew from gossip around town that he was pissed off about losing this job.

"Look, Lucy. We just need some warm bodies and some equipment. I can follow the plans you put together for the east side and get it done while you handle renovation on the west. If we work together, we can do this. It's just about resources."

"So you're going to accelerate the payment schedule too then, speaking of resources?"

Will nodded. "Yeah. Of course."

"I'll have the new budget for you tomorrow." I wondered where the financing would come from if things were tight enough that Ghost thought the whole operation would go under if we didn't get guests in right away. But that was above my pay grade. As long as my men got paid, I didn't care.

"Sounds good. Thank you." He smiled.

"Let me make some calls." I'd actually made a call right after I'd calmed down from our last chat to see about the equipment we'd need from a place in Colorado Springs that I'd rented from before. The guy owed me a favor for giving him a deep discount on a custom cabin, and he'd been eager to pay me back. But Will didn't need to know how I worked my magic, only that I could do it without breaking a sweat or a nail. "I'll make it happen."

I looked up when he didn't say anything else to find him looking at me, a glint of something burning in those deep blue eyes. What was it? Attraction? Admiration? Lust? I was usually so good at reading men, but this guy... he was so polished on the outside, there was no figuring out what was really going on inside.

It would be far better if I didn't have a frustrating desire to find out. He was like a mystery to be solved—just like this whole damned place. But I decided right then that no matter what happened, I was not going to play detective. Not now, not ever. Not with this shiny hot city boy.

"We done here?" I asked him, pulling my gaze from his.

"For now," he said, winking and sending my temperature spiking again.

* * *

That night I met CeeCee and Bennie at the Surly Fox for dinner, needing a night out to help clear some of the irritation and annoying desire that I felt related to Will and the resort.

"So there'll be skiing this winter?" CeeCee asked. "That's amazing!"

"No, it's impossible and potentially unsafe," I told her. "Everyone over there is off their fucking rockers if they think this is going to go smoothly enough to get it all done that fast."

"So why didn't you just tell them that?" Bennie asked, sipping a glass of red wine and eyeing me over the globe of the glass.

"Because they're throwing money at me to get it done." I lifted a shoulder and sipped my Prosecco. And I was going to get it done if it killed me. I'd be damned if I'd sacrifice my reputation for money. But I did want the money.

"So it can be done," Bennie said, jabbing a red-nailed finger onto the tabletop. "You wouldn't still be involved if it was really impossible."

I sighed. "It can probably be done. But it'll be tight, and it will depend on the capabilities of a guy I think is probably way out of his comfort zone here."

"The hot one? What's his name?"

CeeCee was waiting for me to answer, but my attention was caught by a group entering the restaurant behind her. A group that included the bane of my existence. "Will Cruz," I said, under my breath.

"Right," CeeCee said, sounding like she'd just been given the answer to *Final Jeopardy* and was about to be handed thousands of dollars. "Will Cruz!"

As CeeCee practically screamed his name, Will's head snapped around and he caught my eyes. His expression changed from surprise to a kind of knowing look that sent a shiver through me, completely without my permission.

He held my eyes until I managed to rip my gaze away, but by then he'd clearly seen me and also knew I was talking about him, since CeeCee had cackled his name to the entire restaurant. He was with Ghost, Aubrey, Wiley, and the two new people who'd come up today. Monroe and Brainiac. No idea what their actual names might have been. Callsigns were easy to remember, at least.

The group attracted attention as they made their way to the table they must have reserved in the far corner, where they all settled. Locals watched as the newcomers moved through our midst and sat. Each of them was striking for different reasons, and though they were out-of-towners, they moved in a way that spoke of authority and confidence. I guessed that must have come from the years they'd spent in the military.

On Will, it was almost painfully sexy, and Ghost and the new guy, Brainiac, weren't hard to look at either. As we watched them settle in, Bennie blew out a little breath and giggled. "This is going to be an interesting year."

"Nothing this cool has happened in Kasper Ridge since... man, ever," CeeCee added.

"Can we just order?" I snapped, forcing myself to turn my back on the group already laughing loudly and chattering behind us. I'd watched the blonde, Monroe, sink into the seat next to Will and lay a proprietary hand on his shoulder as she whispered something into his ear. Were they a thing? Why did it bother me if they were?

Shit. This was going to be a really long job.

Chapter 13
Telephone: No One's Favorite Game

WILL

I needed to talk to Ghost about the new plan and the need for almost double the original budget, but I knew a reunion dinner at the Surly Fox with Brainiac and Monroe wasn't the time, and he'd been on the phone all afternoon.

I hadn't expected to see Lucy here, though it was kind of a nice surprise. She was dressed up again, her hair piled on top of her head with a few dark strands hanging down, her lips painted a dark wine color. Someone at her table had said my name the second we'd walked through the door, and seeing her sitting there, knowing she must have been talking about me, gave me a little thrill. I smiled at her and gave her a nod, but she turned away, and now it felt like she was refusing to look at me.

Two could play that game.

"Remember that bar back in Atsugi?" Monroe was asking me, her hand on my shoulder.

"No one really remembers it," I joked.

"You picked up an entire squadron in that place, Monroe," Brainiac said from her other side. "I bet it was memorable for you."

"Good times," Monroe quipped, grinning.

"I knew fighter pilots were players," Aubrey said, grinning.

"Monroe earned the reputation for us all," I told her. Though in all honesty, I hadn't ever been much for one-night stands, not even in the service when women tended to congregate around the O-Clubs and bars near base. I didn't date much, though I had the sense there were plenty of willing participants if I decided I wanted to. I'd had a few serious girlfriends, most of whom didn't enjoy my tendency to take extended vacations overseas at the Navy's whim, so none of them had lasted.

"It was hard to resist," Monroe purred. "Being a female fighter pilot puts you into what we call a target-rich environment."

"I suppose it would," Aubrey commented. "That's so seriously badass, I can't even imagine."

"Oh, you would have fit in just fine," Ghost assured her.

"You should have seen her put Ghost on his ass the day I got here," Wiley told us, hugging Aubrey into his side. "That's my kickass girlfriend."

"You a little scared of her, man?" Brainiac asked, leaning in toward Wiley.

Wiley laughed as Aubrey turned to him wide-eyed. Then

he put a hand to his mouth and in a stage whisper admitted, "yeah, a little."

Aubrey jammed her elbow into his side and everyone laughed.

I tried to enjoy the banter—it was so much like the old days, with the addition of Aubrey and Wiley, of course—but it was hard to focus with Lucy Dale sitting across the restaurant ignoring me so pointedly I could feel it. Nerves forced my hand to my head, where I shoved my fingers through my hair.

"Your hair looks perfect, Fake Tom. Like always," Monroe said, catching the motion.

My hair had been one thing the guys had always teased me about. When I'd arrived at flight school, it had been perhaps a bit...over-styled. I'd always liked product, and maybe I'd had kind of an Ice Man from *Top Gun* thing going on. Okay, maybe I'd had a lot of *Top Gun* things going on, come to think of it. But that was the life I wanted to live. Eventually, I'd grown out of the styling fixation, but shoving my hand through my hair to keep things arranged was a nervous habit I couldn't seem to shake.

Truth was, I was having trouble keeping myself from reliving the moments on the back patio with Lucy earlier. I'd actually considered leaning in to kiss her, but had come back into my rational mind just in time. I'd relived that moment, with a bit of embellishment, in the shower before dinner, and things were getting a little tense down below as my mind took me through it yet again.

Monroe was narrowing her eyes at me as I gave her a smile and dropped my hand from my hair, then she followed my gaze across the space to Lucy. "Aha, I get it," she said. "That's the little hottie that was at the resort this morning when we pulled in. Almost didn't recognize her without the hard hat. What's the deal there?"

"No deal," I bit out quickly, hoping no one else had over-heard. I didn't need anyone believing I was focused on anything but pulling off this reno.

"There could be a deal," Ghost told the table, "but Fake Tom has agreed that it'd be better to keep his hands off the help in this particular situation."

The help. That would definitely steam Lucy Dale. She thought she was in charge. And based on her experience, and the way she handled me, maybe she should have been.

"How's the renovation looking?" Aubrey asked after we'd placed our orders. "Archie says there's some delay?"

I glanced between them. Being up here was like playing a constant game of telephone. Anything you said to one person would surely get passed to everyone else, just in a different form than you hoped.

"No delay," I said, keeping my eyes on Ghost. "Just a reshuf-fling of plans and budgets."

"Budgets?" Ghost said, his eyes narrowing.

I hadn't wanted to get into this tonight. And not here. But now he was asking, so I explained that doubling the crew and work would double the budget, forcing us to spend money he'd targeted for next summer now.

Ghost didn't respond for a minute, his eyes dropping to his lap. Finally he looked up, and the haunted look he'd worn right after the mishap that had ended his career was back. It sent a shiver through me. "Can't do it," he said, his voice almost a whis-per. "We just can't do it."

"Not a problem," I said quickly, my mouth ahead of my brain. "I'll cover the advance." I'd considered this already and had dug through my own accounts to see if I could swing it. I could. Barely.

Ghost was already shaking his head, but I knew it was what

I had to do. I had to make this job work, even on my own dime, and I had to make it incredible.

"When things are running, you'll pay me back," I told him.

"I don't know—"

"You don't need to. We all have faith in you. In this plan," I said with more confidence than I felt. I'd do just about anything to keep that haunted look off Ghost's face, and even more than that to keep from going back home to tell Dad I was exactly what he thought I was—less than him.

"Let him," Aubrey suggested. "We're all in this together."

"One hundred percent," Monroe said. "In fact, let's get some money coming in sooner rather than later."

"We're not even close to opening," Ghost said, sounding discouraged.

"We've got the yurts," Aubrey piped up. So far, she hadn't had luck getting guests to take her up on the idea of glamping out behind a construction zone, and she and Wiley had actually been living in one of the yurts since they were just sitting there.

"We'll get your yurts filled," Monroe said, squaring her shoulders and giving us the grin that had convinced us too many times to do things we shouldn't. Monroe was a salesman at heart, and an excellent planner of shenanigans. "Let's open up your bar, Coyote."

Wiley's eyebrows shot up. "I mean, yeah, I'm ready. Just need another bartender, maybe."

"You've got me," Aubrey said, leaning into his shoulder.

"That'll work for beer and wine," he said, looking skeptical. Aubrey frowned and jabbed him in the arm.

"We'll make it a sneak peek, get locals up there to put eyes on the place after all this time. Maybe do a weekly event?" Monroe looked around the table.

Ghost's face had cleared and he smiled, nodding. "One

thing we are ready for is drinking," he agreed. "Yeah, let's do it. Can you make it happen?"

Monroe preened. "Of course I can." She stood and walked across the restaurant to the woman at the hostess stand as we all watched. Lucy's table watched her as well, but my eyes were drawn to Lucy as if by some kind of magnetic force. She looked amazing, her blue eyes aglow and her cheeks pink.

"What's she doing?" Brainiac asked the table. Monroe was being directed to another man who stood behind the bar, the owner, maybe? After a quick word with him, she returned to the table, a confident smile on her lips.

A few minutes later, the man had stepped to the center of the small restaurant and looked around, calling out, "Ladies and gentlemen, I'm sorry to interrupt your meals, but may I have your attention, please?"

The restaurant quieted as people turned to see what was going on.

"I have the honor of being the first to invite you all to preview the soon-to-be-opened Kasper Ridge Resort. The owners are here tonight, and they've asked me to let you know about a sneak peek cocktail event at the resort bar next Friday night. Anyone who shows their dinner receipt from tonight will get one free cocktail at the fully refurbished resort bar!" That announcement inspired cheers and applause from the diners.

"Six o'clock next Friday," the owner concluded. "See you there! And come here for dinner afterwards - we'll stay open an hour later to accommodate!"

We all turned to gape at Monroe.

"A week from now?" Ghost asked, color draining from his face.

She shrugged. "It's just the bar and the lobby that they'll see. And if the lobby's not done, it'll add to the intrigue."

She was right. It was brilliant. And a weekly event would

hopefully put a bit of cash back in Ghost's pocket, and that would help us all.

I sipped my beer, glancing to my side to find Lucy Dale staring at me from across the space. When she saw that she had my attention, she mouthed, "What the fuck?"

I lifted my glass in her direction and turned back around to eat.

Chapter 14
Riding with Jensen...

LUCY

I nviting the general public into a construction zone was a recipe for disaster.

And it was also kind of brilliant, based on the reactions of my friends.

"Oh my god, we're so going to that," CeeCee said, clapping her hands in front of her as her big brown eyes widened at us.

Bennie looked less excited. "The beginning of the end," she groaned.

Bennie was not a fan of tourists, but they were pretty much CeeCee's lifeblood. She ran the adventure outfitter in Kasper

Ridge, renting and selling everything from mountain bikes to climbing gear.

"We'll get eyes on Lucy's job," CeeCee pointed out. "And we'll get to see the hunk she works with up close and personal. Maybe give him the sniff check."

"He does not need a sniff check," I told her, my spine straightening. CeeCee had a thing about the way men smelled, and she swore she could tell you everything you needed to know about a prospect just by smelling him. I could just imagine her walking a circle around Will, sniffing him. It was not what I needed to solidify my position of authority at work right now.

"Every prospect needs a sniff check," CeeCee said.

"I'll agree there," Bennie said. "Remember Doug Hayden?"

"He was twelve," I reminded them. "He was not a serious prospect."

"When you were eleven he was," CeeCee said. "And he failed the sniff check. And now look at him."

Doug Hayden had gone into his family business, becoming a butcher like his father. I'd bumped into him a few times around town, and he did have a particular... scent to him.

"You mean, 'now smell him,'" Bennie said, laughing as she finished off her wine.

"I bet Will Cruz smells goooood," CeeCee said, drawing out her statement and leaning into her hand, braced with her elbow on the table. She made a dreamy expression and something inside me wholeheartedly agreed with her. I already knew Will Cruz smelled good. But that was not going to help us get this job done on schedule, and if anything, it was one more distraction threatening our success.

"Can we talk about something else?" I asked, spearing a potato cube from my plate.

"Sure," Bennie agreed. "What should we wear to the hotel opening next Friday?"

I sighed. The resort was the biggest thing happening in Kasper Ridge in years. There was no escaping it.

* * *

A week later, I found myself in the passenger seat of CeeCee's brother's Uber while the girls chattered in the back.

"You didn't want to take the night off, see the place yourself?" I asked Jensen, who happened to be the only Uber driver in town.

"Are you kidding?" he said, turning to me with a huge grin. "This will be my best night of the year, I bet."

He was probably right. Since the guy had a monopoly on sober rides around here, it was easy enough to overlook the fact that he drove a beat-up Grand Prix that smelled faintly of cow manure—a side effect of his second job as a freelance gardener.

"Can I offer you ladies a water? A mint?" He reached to the back seat and popped open a cooler that opened from the middle, its contents hidden behind the seat back and stored in some kind of built-in cooling unit he'd installed in the trunk.

"Jensen," CeeCee said, "There's a squirrel in there."

"He's completely wrapped in plastic. Very sanitary," Jensen said quickly.

"Um..." Bennie said. "Dare we ask why?"

"The plastic keeps any potential bacteria from—"

"I meant, why do you have a squirrel?" Bennie clarified.

"You can sell those guys for lots on eBay if you dress them up and pose them. This one was already stiff in that pose. Doesn't he look like he's fishing?"

The squirrel in question did have one tiny arm extended as if he was casting a rod, and there was an expectant expression on his face.

"Where did you get this critter, Jensen?" CeeCee asked her brother, a distinct air of disapproval in her voice.

"He was just on the side of the road," Jensen said, explaining this as if picking up roadkill was equivalent to eating a doughnut at the office or scooping up a dollar bill you came across on a walk. "Totally intact. Don't see that every day."

"I hope no one hits a deer tonight," Bennie said, shutting the cooler again.

We pulled into the resort property, and Jensen guided the Grand Prix through the roundabout and right up to the front doors, where there were several other cars unloading dressed-up passengers. I spotted Ghost at the door, welcoming people, and noticed with surprise that there were several planter boxes of flowers and a couple potted trees around the doors. It made the place look almost impressive.

"You ladies call me once you're done getting all hooted up," Jensen said as we stepped out.

"Jen," his sister said. "Ladies do not get hooted."

"Right," he said. "Drunk and whatnot."

"Fine," she sighed.

Jensen was a good guy. He just marched to the beat of completely different band than most people.

"Glad you could make it, ladies," Ghost said, greeting us. He looked slightly nervous, and it made me a little nervous for him. We all had a lot at stake. I hoped tonight would go well.

"Hi Archie. These are my friends, CeeCee and Bennie." I introduced the girls. "Archie Kasper is the owner of the resort, along with his sister Aubrey."

The girls said their hellos, and Ghost waved us inside.

The lobby had been lit with floor lamps, and there were standing walls strategically erected to block the bulk of the very unfinished space. The mobile walls created a little walkway into the bar, and as with the outdoor entrance, this space had been elevated significantly with the addition of flowers, plants, and even a few plush chairs and a little couch in the corner.

"Nice," CeeCee said. "I feel like I'm stepping back in time."

As we entered the bar with its soaring ceilings, gleaming brass rail, and photographs of celebrities and other famous people adorning the walls, Bennie inhaled a sharp breath. "This is incredible."

It was. I'd been in the bar to interview, but lit up at night and crowded with people, it was like entering a different world, one that was tailored especially for a high-end crowd looking for atmosphere. It did feel like going back in time. Was this what the place had looked like in Papa's day? He'd refused my invitation tonight, but I couldn't wait to bring him to see it soon.

"Lucy!" Wiley called to me from behind the bar as Aubrey worked the far end. Music played from speakers above us, and the old-time ambience was augmented by the swoony voice of some forties singer.

"Hey Wiley," I said. "Let me introduce my friends." I made my intros and we each ordered a drink—Wiley talked us into the Kasper Ridge manhattans, made with the whiskey from his distillery. As the girls and I settled into seats at the bar, I spotted Will across the room. He was flanked by women, which shouldn't have surprised me—it was no shock he was a lady magnet. But one of them was that blonde, Monroe. Her hand was on his arm again, her fingers wrapped around his bicep in a proprietary way as she told some kind of story, leaning into the group and talking in that animated way confident gorgeous women seemed to master at birth.

"There's your guy," CeeCee said, following my gaze. "Ew, are they together?"

"I have no idea," I said, my stomach churning uncomfortably at the thought. There was no real reason for me to care, though I couldn't help but wonder maybe they'd been a thing at one time. Or if they still were. "We don't talk about our personal lives at work."

"I'd like to get personal with him," Bennie said. "Look at that hair. Those biceps."

Will looked better than ever. His thick dark blond hair was perfectly styled in a casual messy look, and he wore a soft blue long-sleeved shirt that looked like it was probably cashmere. His muscular legs were sheathed in dark denim with just the right amount of snugness to accentuate what might have been the most perfect ass I'd seen on a man...ever.

"We're colleagues," I said lamely, just as Will turned his head and caught me staring at him across the increasingly crowded space. I wrenched my eyes away a second too late, my blood heating. "Shit."

"Why Lucy, you're blushing," CeeCee said, sipping her drink. "I think you might have a little thing for your boss." She raised an eyebrow and pinned me with a look that demanded an answer.

"He is not my boss," I bit out.

"Well whatever he is, he's coming this way," Bennie said. "These are really good," she added, taking a healthy drink from her Manhattan.

"Take it easy, those are all alcohol," I said, trying to ignore the fact that I could actually feel Will drawing nearer thanks to whatever weird connection my body had decided to attach to him.

"Lucy, you made it." Will's deep voice boomed from behind me, and I turned on my stool to find him just a foot away, all that handsome glory close enough to touch. I could smell him too, that tropical manly thing infusing the air all around us. If I could make a candle that smelled like Will, I'd call it "Sexy Pineapple" or "Tropical Manhood." Or something.

Shit. I was losing it.

I clamped down on every vibrating nerve cell and took a deep breath, getting my reaction to him under control. It was purely chemical. Scientific. Evolutionary. Women were built to react to virile men. It had nothing to do with either of us personally. Especially not with him.

I was fairly certain I did not even like the guy.

"I did make it," I said, pointlessly confirming my presence. "This is CeeCee and this is Bennie." I shoved Bennie in front of me to block the Will-magnet screwing up my body chemistry, but she smoothly stepped to the side.

He greeted my friends, but then turned the full force of his gaze back to me. "What do you think?"

He'd been doing this all week—asking me my opinion on things that had nothing to do with the job, telling me about the plans for the resort. He was acting as if we were friends or buddies or... something. It made it even harder to keep my escalating reactions to him under control.

"Yeah, it looks amazing," I said.

CeeCee stepped closer to Will, a quizzical look on her face. He glanced at her, but then turned back to me.

"Good crowd," he said, and my mind froze as I watched CeeCee lean in close and give him a very loud sniff. His head snapped to catch her in the act, and she stepped back, offering a sheepish grin. Will didn't comment, pressing his lips together for a brief second and raising an eyebrow and then turning my way again.

Heat was surging through me, and I had the uncomfortable urge to squirm around on my stool to relieve some of the rising tension in my body, but I wasn't going to give into whatever this irritating reaction to Will was.

So he was handsome.

So he'd begun actually asking my professional opinion on things at work. It didn't mean anything. It was work.

Mind over matter. I could do this.

"It is a good crowd," I said, unable to control my physical person and offer scintillating or even logical conversation at the same time.

CeeCee stepped close to him again, her head appearing around the side of his muscled shoulder as she grinned at me and nodded, and then shot me a thumbs up.

She mouthed "smells goooooood."

I already knew that Will smelled good. I'd had the misfortune of catching whiffs of him at work when the breeze turned the right way and carried his island-woodsy scent in my direction. I still worried he had no idea what he was doing in terms of rugged terrain construction, but now at least he was taking some advice on board, so I could potentially respect him. But it was still a bad idea to let myself like him too much. He was like a pretty doll, meant to stay in its box on the shelf. I was not going to touch the pretty doll.

"Did I show you the cigar room and wine cellar Wiley's been working on?" he asked me, leaning in close to be heard over the rising crowd and music in the bar. That heavenly masculine scent hit me full force again and whatever rational thoughts were left within me melted just a tiny bit more. God, I wanted to touch him.

"Er, um, no." I pushed my urges aside too late to sound like I spoke English fluently.

"Let's go," he said, offering me a hand.

My body reacted before I could stop it, and the next thing I knew, I was being led from the bar, one of Will's big hands in mine and the other on the center of my low back, my mind nowhere to be found. CeeCee and Bennie stayed right where they were, leaving me to battle my monsters alone.

"It's right back here," Will stepped up to a shelf set into the wall at the side of the bar and pressed something I didn't see.

The bookshelf swung inward, revealing a hidden space. "Cool, right?"

"I had no idea this was here," I said, my mind finally returning, thanks to the surprising discovery. The room behind the shelf smelled a little musty, but it was clean, and when Will hit a light switch, it illuminated cases and humidors clearly meant for cigars, and a set of steps leading downward along a curve. "This is incredible."

Will shot me a smile that incinerated whatever was left of my panties, and he took my hand again, leading me down the stairs. It was darker in the wine cellar, but the shelves were stocked floor to ceiling with dusty bottles that had clearly been left here a long time, probably forgotten when the resort closed.

"These must be worth a fortune," I said.

"Right?" he agreed. He still held my hand, and something about the quiet and close space had us standing very near to one another. I let out a breath I didn't realize I'd been holding as Will released my hand and turned to face me.

His eyes found mine in the dim light, and the wide smile dropped from his face, replaced by something darker, something that held some kind of intent. His eyes dropped to my lips as I took a careful breath, and his chin tilted downward slightly, those blue eyes darkening.

If I didn't know better, I'd have thought Will Cruz intended to kiss me. And if I didn't know I absolutely could not allow that to happen, I'd have thought I would probably let him.

He raised a hand, tracing the edge of his thumb down the side of my jaw, his mouth opening just a bit as I hissed in a breath at his touch.

"Is this okay?" he asked.

I nodded, desperate for him to keep going, to see what else he might do. If my mind had been out of control before, it had gone on an extended vacation now. I leaned into the touch and Will's other hand found my waist.

This shouldn't be happening. But it was. And I knew right then I wasn't going to stop him. I wanted him too much.

"I really want to kiss you, Lucy," he said, his voice like velvet. "It's all I can think about."

I couldn't answer him. But even without words, I did. My head tipped back, my eyes fell shut, and in the next instant, those soft firm lips were brushing mine as Will's hard body moved closer, pressing gently against me.

My arms wrapped his muscled back, and I opened my mouth to him, breathing him in, tasting him, and finding that he was absolutely everything I imagined and so much more. The kiss was soft and languorous, and Will filled my senses entirely —taste, touch, scent—he was everything I needed in that moment and I felt myself giving in to something I hadn't realized how badly I wanted.

And then my mind returned to my body in a sudden snap.

"Shit," I said, stepping back. "We can't do this. You can't kiss me like that."

Will's hand released me and went to his perfect hair. "I think you kissed me, Miss Dale. And if you want me to kiss you differently, just tell me how you like it."

I shook my head. "I did not. You kissed me."

He grinned and I wanted to throw myself at him. "Maybe I did."

"You definitely did."

"I think you liked it."

"I..." I couldn't deny it. He had surely felt it. But it wasn't the right move when I needed to make sure this guy understood my position here. I might have been a woman, but I knew exactly what needed to happen to get this resort ready to go. "It can't happen again."

"It could," Will said, his voice holding a teasing note as he smiled at me. "If you wanted it to."

"Well, I don't," I huffed, probably veering into she-doth-protest-too-much territory. "Besides, what would your girlfriend have to say about what happened the other day? Or about you kissing me?" I thought about the possessive way Monroe put her hands on Will whenever he was near.

"Girlfriend? What, Monroe?" He laughed in a way that told me she was definitely not his girlfriend. "No, she's just a buddy."

Well, that answered that, at least. I blew out a breath and turned, beginning my ascent up the stairs. I needed away from him, out of this close space, and back to my right mind. "Never mind!" I called over my shoulder.

"Lucy, I—"

"Seriously, it's a bad idea. We work together." I faced him as he topped the stairs into the cigar room. "It was just a spur of the moment thing, won't happen again."

"Okay." Neither his voice or his face seemed to indicate agreement, but the word was right.

"Okay." I said the same hollow word and turned to exit, feeling upset and confused in a way I hadn't in years. And not just because I couldn't actually find the door out.

"Here," Will said, reaching around me to push a hidden button on the wall. As the door swung toward me, he gently pulled me back and I was hit again by the scent of him coupled with a wave of desire so strong I was positive I was in deep trouble.

"Thanks." I sped out of the room without facing him again, returned to my stool and downed what was left of my drink, signaling Wiley for another as my friends gaped at me.

It was going to be a long summer.

Chapter 15
Kissing Construction Forepeople

WILL

I stood in the dim light and relative hush of the cigar room for a long moment after Lucy rushed out, my head spinning.

She was right. Of course she was. She was practical and smart and completely right that getting involved on a job was a recipe for disaster. Or at least for some seriously uncomfortable moments if things didn't work out. And with me, romantically, things always had an end date.

Because what the hell was the definition of working out?

I thought about my parents, about the way they seemed to

fit so naturally, to navigate around each other's worlds in a way that just felt like it was meant to be that way. They'd had rough times, sure. But now? Whatever they had, it seemed so unattainable and impossible—especially when every effort I'd ever made toward pursuing that ultimate fit with a partner began like this. An illicit grope, a stolen kiss. A quick interlude. A one-night stand, maybe.

It was one more way I guessed I wasn't made like my dad. He wasn't just good at his job, he was good at his marriage. I couldn't seem to find a woman who could look past my perfect hair and whatever else they saw on the outside long enough to figure out if there was anything worth sticking around for on the inside.

And I wanted Lucy to see more. I wanted that in a way that was a little bit concerning, if I was honest.

Shit. I needed to put that aside and keep my head on work.

I blew out a long breath, put a hand through my hair, and shut the door to the cigar room as I rejoined the party.

The bar was packed. People were laughing and drinking, music played in the background, and Wiley and Aubrey were flying around behind the bar like they'd choreographed the whole thing ahead of time.

One more couple that seemed to navigate one another naturally.

I pushed through the crowd and headed for Monroe's blond head, which I could see above most of the people packed in around her. She was tall to start with, but she also favored ridiculous shoes. It had always made her easy to find.

"There you are," she said, her hand landing reassuringly on my forearm as I slid in next to her at the bar. I tried not to look to my left, but I'd seen Lucy perched on the stool with her friends, and even the sight of her made my heart tick up a beat or two.

"Having fun?" I asked her, looking between her and

Brainiac. Monroe wore an easy grin, but Brainiac looked like this event might actually be paining him. "You okay, man?"

He shrugged. "Crowds. You know." He winced as a man bumped his shoulder and he scooted closer to us. "Just not really my thing."

Brainiac had always kept himself a bit apart from the rest of us. When we'd been in the squadron together, I'd assumed it was because he was older than the rest of us, a higher rank too. But even now, I got the same feeling—that he was just a few steps from being actually present, that there was always a bit more going on in his head than he was letting on. It was probably where his call sign came from.

"So what went on in the closet over there?" Monroe asked, jabbing me with a lacquered nail and giving me a raised eyebrow.

"You saw that, huh?"

"I see everything," she said.

"It's nothing," I lied. "Just a quick—"

"Fuck?" Her eyes lit up.

"No." My voice held a warning note. Monroe liked to get involved, and that would cause problems here. I wanted her to stay away from Lucy Dale. "A quick chat about construction."

She smiled at me in a way that told me she wasn't buying it. "Was it good?" Her voice was low, suggestive.

I rolled my eyes. "Maybe, but that was the end of it. We work together."

Brainiac nodded once, seeming to agree that this was the right thing to say.

"But you like her." Monroe was not going to quit.

"Doesn't matter."

Before I knew it, my tall and very irritating blond friend was using her butt and back to subtly maneuver us backwards along the bar, closer and closer to Lucy and her friends. She kept her hand clamped around my forearm, dragging me along as people moved out of the way for the tall blonde bulldozer giving them little choice and pretending she had no idea what she was doing.

"Sorry," I mouthed to a group that had just been forced to let us by.

Ghost was talking to Lucy and her friends, and Monroe positioned us just next to them so I could hear almost every word over the music and the crowd.

"Oh hi," Monroe said, turning and addressing the small group in a way that could not have been less subtle.

I stood behind her, feeling like a complete tool. Lucy's eyes moved from Monroe to me and back again, sending a shot of liquid heat through my veins.

"You guys met, right?" Ghost said, addressing Monroe and Brainiac. "Lucy, CeeCee, and Bennie have lived up here their whole lives. And get this"—Ghost punched me in the shoulder when I tried to pretend I was extremely interested in fishing the lime wedge out of my drink—"Lucy's grandfather was good friends with Uncle Marvin."

"Well that's interesting," Monroe said, her voice exaggerated. She was enjoying my discomfort and I had no doubt she was going to continue her twisted attempts at matchmaking until I made it exceptionally clear that I would kill her if she didn't stop. "Tell us more, Lucy," she drawled.

I glanced at Lucy, stuffing down a chuckle at the irritated look she shot Monroe.

"Papa grew up here," Lucy said. "And his father actually managed the original incarnation of this hotel."

"You're kidding," Ghost said.

"I'm not. Papa grew up playing here with Marvin. And when Marvin came back to rebuild and run the place, Papa spent a lot of time with him. Your uncle actually came by our place a couple times before he died."

Ghost straightened, his eyes widening. "Any idea why?"

The hunt. Ghost's mind was always circling around that ridiculous treasure hunt. I didn't believe there was treasure up here, not the hidden kind at least. But it made Ghost happy, so I kept quiet.

Lucy shook her head. "Just visiting, I'm sure."

"Long shot here," Ghost said, pulling something from his pocket. "But I don't suppose you would have any idea what this goes to? Or if maybe your grandfather might know?" He put the big iron key he'd shown me onto the bar in front of the women.

"Ooh," CeeCee said. "It's so cool looking. Can I?" She moved to pick it up and Ghost nodded.

All three women examined the key, Monroe leaning in to see it too.

Bennie took it from CeeCee, turned it over in her hands and then handed it back to Ghost. "I know what it fits."

Every head in our small group turned to look at her.

"I think it's a key to Lost Lonely Park."

"And what is that?" Monroe asked before Ghost could get a word in.

"It's a private park nestled between about eight huge houses over on the other side of the highway. Kind of a little secret oasis for the rich folks up there in those big old houses," Bennie said. "One of my friends had a relative that lived in one of them, and we played there once when I was a kid. Every resident has a key, and no one else is supposed to go in."

Ghost stared at the key in his hand as if it unlocked the mysteries of the universe. "We have to go. Can you show me where?" He pulled out his phone and opened a map. Ghost was obsessed. But I figured if he was focused on this, it kept his mind from darker subjects.

Bennie pointed out the location, a little green spot on the

app. "There's one gate you can try that isn't in someone's yard. It's here." She indicated a spot on the east side of the tiny park.

"Why do you want to go to Lost Lonely?" CeeCee asked. "It's just a park."

Ghost shook his head, tucking the key back into his pocket. "I don't know why, but I think Uncle Marvin wants me to. Thanks," he said before turning and pressing through the crowd to the back of the bar where he pulled his sister near and whispered into her ear. I watched her face light up as she glanced our way.

"I get the feeling we're going to the park tomorrow," I told Monroe. As long as the hunt didn't get in the way of getting the construction done on schedule, I guessed it couldn't hurt anything.

"This is part of Ghost's treasure hunt?" she asked.

"Yep. He's obsessed." I spoke to her, but my eyes found Lucy's face. She'd returned to conversation with her friends, ignoring me in a way that felt intentional.

"I think you are too," Monroe said, following my gaze.

Chapter 16
Believing in What's Real. Like Sasquatch.

LUCY

My ears were still ringing when I laid down to sleep after our night at the Kasper Ridge Resort bar. The place had been packed, which I knew was good for Archie Kasper and the longevity of the resort in general. I just wasn't sure how I felt about it.

The people up here were curious about the place, and it was hard to blame them. Kasper Ridge had always been kind of a secret kept in the open. It was the biggest hotel for miles around, the only ski resort this far south back in its day. But it had also been a hideaway for the reclusive and the eccentric. Papa told me stories about the celebrities that used to come here to escape the pressures and visibility of Hollywood or New York, and the images lining the walls of the bar had proved him right. Sports stars, movie stars, musicians, politicians, and even mobsters had stayed at Kasper Ridge in its heyday. And if tonight was anything to go on, the resort might beckon those types again before long.

As I closed my eyes, I tried to focus on the prospects that the place would bring our small town. Money, of course, and that was good for everything from the local grocery to the restaurants. But it would also bring tourists—regular people stopping through for a week or two and then returning to their lives.

The thought made me sad, and I tried to force myself not to think about Will, about the fact that he was undoubtedly just stopping through, albeit for a bit longer. I didn't want to care.

But whenever I let my guard down, I found myself reliving the way his hands had felt on my body, that stolen kiss in the close intimacy of the wine cellar. I could still hear the distant thump of the music matching the sound of my blood racing, could still smell Will's cedar and island scent mingling with the dusty aged air of the cellar around us. The feel of Will's hands on me had branded me—I could still sense them and almost believed they might have left some kind of indelible imprint where he'd held me.

And the kiss . . . it was different than others I'd experienced. Tender. Searing. And it should never have happened. Not only because it wasn't the right thing to happen between two people who had at least six months of hard work ahead of them and who didn't need to complicate their relationship.

That kiss shouldn't have happened because I knew that from this point forward, every kiss in my life would be compared to this one.

It had been slow and sweet, but there was an aching need

buried within it, and when Will's full lips had met mine, something inside me had erupted with want, with emptiness. And the last thing I needed was to turn to city-boy Will Cruz to fill some vacancy within me.

But all the practical thinking in the world didn't stop me from dreaming about him that night, about strong shoulders, thick tousled hair, and eyes that made me long for things I didn't even know existed before he'd touched me. When I woke up, I felt achy and needy, and even activating my battery-powered friend didn't relieve the uncomfortable awareness Will's recent kiss had awakened.

Dammit. I didn't need any of this.

I arrived at work wearing more armor than usual, stepping out of my truck to find Mateo already directing the crew on the west side of the resort, where we'd begun reinforcing the existing structure and marking out the addition we were putting on to accommodate the new patio and sitting areas.

"Morning boss," he said, and Mateo's warm familiarity and reassuring presence made me feel slightly more grounded.

"Morning Mateo," I answered, looking around with satisfaction at the work being done. Systematic, practical, reliable. This was how I operated. I believed in things I could see and feel, things I could control. Whatever was happening deep inside me in response to Will? It wasn't real. And I was going to forget all about it.

I wasn't even marginally successful in my efforts not to think about Will Cruz that morning, no matter how determined I was. I found myself glancing up any time I thought I heard him approaching, and even wandered over to the east side of the resort with a flimsy question about pavers that I was finally forced to admit was just an excuse to see him.

Crap. I wanted to see him.

But more than that, I wanted him to see me.

And I didn't know why.

"Morning, Lucy," Will said when he spotted me coming, carrying two heavy paving stones in my arms. "Let me grab those for you." He reached for the stones.

"I've got it," I said. I didn't need help carrying bricks.

Will raised his hands and took a step back, but the smile stayed in place. "Okay, okay, Firecracker. You've got it." That name again. I should have told him to cut it out, but part of me actually liked it. As if I had a callsign too, like I was part of something.

I set the pavers down between us. "I have a question."

"I've got answers," he said, and I tried to not to enjoy the pointless banter that always seemed to spring up between us.

"I bet you do."

"If you want to go back to the wine cellar, I could give you a few more." His words were suggestive, but his tone was easy and warm. I glanced up at his eyes, which flashed with mischief.

"That didn't happen, remember?" Hearing him mention the kiss sent fire blazing through me again.

"I do remember," he said, the smile turning less jolly and sexier. "I remembered it all night."

I did not need to know that. Thinking of Will thinking of me while he was alone in his bed did nothing to help my own growing and inappropriate attraction. I forced down the desire to step closer to him, to see if he might kiss me again. There were men all around us, local men who knew my reputation and who expected me to conduct myself like the foreman they reported to, not like a love-starved teenager.

"We work together, Will. And what happened last night . . ." Dammit, I could feel a blush climbing my cheeks.

"Was really nice," he finished for me.

"Nice?" My mouth asked before my mind could stop it. I hoped it had been more than nice. Of course if he'd thought about it all night, I wasn't alone in feeling that way. I shook my head to clear it, to try to jolt it back on track. "No, it doesn't matter. It never happened," I said, putting my hands on my hips, mostly to stop myself from doing something stupid with them like fisting the front of his soft blue chambray shirt and demanding he kiss me again. "And it will not happen again."

"Right," he agreed, one side of his sexy mouth lifting like he knew exactly what I was thinking. "Unless you want it to," he said, clearly enjoying this and still standing way too close.

"Look, I came over here with an actual question for you."

"Right. Ask the question." He crossed his arms and waited, the smile never fading. God, he was beautiful. It was so annoying.

"How are we laying these pavers? Parallel or perpendicular?" I arranged the stones one way and then moved them for him to consider the other arrangement.

"I like them offset," he said. "What do you think?"

"You're the boss," I reminded him, hoping it might help remind me that the wild mambo happening inside me was totally inappropriate in a work situation. Jumping this man, wrestling him to the ground and demanding he satisfy me sexually would not be professional. At all.

He grinned and chuckled. "Right. I am the boss. So they'll go perpendicular."

"Fine. Good. Thanks." I straightened, feeling suddenly lost now that the question had been answered. I hated this version of myself. I was put together and confident, but a touch from Will in a dark closet had me confused and bumbling. Needy. Wanting.

"Good then," he said, watching me in a way that made me think he knew exactly the effect he had on me.

"Right," I said. This was not going especially well. I leaned over to pick the stones up again, but Will beat me to it, lifting them easily and holding them against his wide chest. The muscles in his biceps bulged, straining the fabric of his shirt as he hefted the pavers. "I'll carry these back for you."

"There's no need, I—"

"Is it wrong to want to spend just a minute or two with you?"

"It is if—"

"Go to dinner with me, Lucy."

"What? No. Didn't you hear me say this was—"

"I heard you say a bunch of things I don't think you really believe. About how we work together and how we should be professional. But I also heard what you said last night when I kissed you. I'd like to hear more from that part of you. The part that kissed me back."

I glanced around wildly, worried someone might overhear the words that were sending my body into overdrive, but no one was close enough to hear. "It was a mistake. I'd had a drink, and—"

"Forgive me if I don't believe you're the kind of woman who gets drunk and has meaningless flings in wine cellars."

"You don't know me, Will." My mind was spinning. He couldn't ask me out. It was totally over and above the level of professionalism that a worksite demanded, so far from appropriate I couldn't even process it. And god, I wanted to say yes.

"That would be the point of having dinner," he said, setting the pavers down on the pile the crew had put next to the cleared and leveled site where they'd be laid. "To get to know you better."

I stared at him, my emotions and my mind at war within me.

"Lucy." His voice dropped and the way he fixed me in that ocean blue gaze felt intimate, private, like the rest of the world didn't exist—only us. "Let's have dinner. It doesn't have to mean anything. It's just dinner."

But it would mean something, wouldn't it? "I don't think—"

"Look, Firecracker. You have to eat, I have to eat. Let's just eat together. One time. If it's terrible, I won't ever ask again."

It wouldn't be terrible, and we both knew it. It was what dinner might lead to that worried me. And what would happen after that, when Will decided to return to Los Angeles, when he remembered that tiny mountain towns and small-town women were not his thing. He was temporary here, and this was my home, my whole life. I was afraid if I let myself get involved with Will, those things might not feel like enough once he was gone.

But I wanted him. All of him. At least once before he left.

"Dinner," I said, not really meaning to agree but not willful enough to refuse what I knew I wanted. Maybe he'd prove himself so irritating over dinner that I'd be able to put aside the raging physical attraction I had to him. Or maybe I could let my body have what it thought it wanted, have the fling, and then my mind could get back in the driver's seat. Either way, I'd be able to get back to what mattered. "Fine. When?"

"Tomorrow," he suggested, his smile widening.

Good. The sooner he was out of my system, the better. "Where?"

"You have suggestions? I only know of the Fox."

"There's the Surly Fox, Chambers, or the Trellis. Chambers is a little nicer than the Fox, and the Trellis is fancy. Steak and stuff." And no matter where we went, someone would see us. This town was too small for secrets. I didn't like being the subject of gossip, but then again, everyone in town knew something about the project at the resort. It should be easy enough to explain away a casual dinner with a coworker.

"Chambers?" he suggested.

"Good." I was glad he hadn't chosen the Trellis. A fancy dinner would only confuse things more.

"Six?"

"Fine. I'll meet you there."

He shot me that smile again, and then turned to head back to his side of the build. I stared after him, watching the way his body moved—graceful and fluid, but leaving no doubt about his masculinity. I didn't want to notice the tight roundness of his backside in those jeans, or the way the muscles of his back and shoulders filled out the shirt draped over them.

"So you have a crush on the boss, huh?" Mateo appeared at my side without me noticing him, and his deep voice made me jump.

"Of course not." I brushed my hands down my jeans, as if I could wipe away the pull I felt to Will's retreating form.

"Of course not," Mateo agreed, but he shot me a knowing grin as he turned and headed back to the edge of the patio he was preparing to put down, a stack of stones in his arms.

I sighed. If I'd hoped to keep whatever this thing was a secret from the men I worked with, it was clear they already suspected something. Hopefully, they knew me well enough to know nothing would impact my focus on the job.

I'd have dinner with Will Sunday night and get whatever this was out of my system, one way or another.

Chapter 17
Winning A Moose's Approval

WILL

"I thought we agreed you were going to keep your greasy meathooks off our contractor," Ghost said, giving me a sideways glance from behind the wheel of his SUV. We were on a Sunday morning outing to visit Lost Lonely Park. Aubrey was in the back seat, and I wasn't quite sure why Ghost had insisted I come along.

"We did agree," I said. "But . . ." I let that hang because I couldn't explain quite why I'd pushed things. There were no rational reasons why I'd cornered Lucy in the wine cellar and kissed her, or why I'd insisted until she'd agreed to go out with me.

"You do realize that the entire future of the resort pretty much rests in her hands, right? We need to keep her happy or we're screwed, FT."

When they started abbreviating my call sign back in the day, it wasn't a good thing, and Ghost using FT now was no better.

"Yeah, I get it." I didn't know what else to say. On one hand, Ghost was my friend, and I knew he wasn't going to stop me from pursuing something if it seemed like I was serious about it. On the other hand, the whole point of me being here was to prove to myself—and eventually to Dad—that one screwup didn't define me, that I was good at my job. And he was right, messing around with our foreman could have disastrous consequences.

"Maybe he can keep her happy," Aubrey said, "by screwing her." She waited for the laugh. When it didn't come, she went on. "The heart wants what it wants. I can attest to that. And maybe if Lucy and Will get together, things will go even better for the resort. Look at me and Wiley."

"I'd rather not." Ghost frowned at the winding road ahead of us.

"I think you guys would make a cute couple," Aubrey added, causing Ghost's frown to deepen further.

I was trying to figure out how to make promises I couldn't keep to Ghost—that I wouldn't screw things up, that Lucy wouldn't decide she hated me and leave, that everything would be fine no matter what happened between Lucy and me—but I didn't have to because we pulled up along a narrow empty street just then.

Huge green trees towered over the little splash of asphalt, and an iron gate was set at the end, so covered in vines and unruly branches that it was hard to make out the ironwork scrolled sign at the top. But we already knew it said "Lost Lonely Park."

"Such a sad name for a park," Aubrey said as the three of us approached the gate.

Unlike so much of the terrain up here, which was wide and open and felt like it went on for miles, even the air around the park entrance felt close and guarded. Huge houses hulked on either side of the narrow street, their landscaping and fences just visible behind the screen of trees at the edges of the road.

We peered through the few parts of the gate that weren't totally overgrown to see a somewhat rugged open space inside. There were more trees, but there was also a patch of manicured lawn, a few paved trails winding away from it, and a concrete bench off to one side. The park was empty, and while the morning sunshine had washed the landscape we'd passed on the way here, this place felt like it lived in a state of permanent dusk.

"Let's give it a try," Ghost said, pulling the old iron key from his jeans.

"Even if it works, what do we do then?" I asked, picturing us all standing around inside the park. There was something foreboding about the place and I didn't relish the thought of lingering there.

"I guess we'll see," Ghost said as the key turned and the gate gave a rusty clank that seemed to echo through the trees around us.

"That's it!" Aubrey whisper-shouted, pumping her little fist. I was less excited. This meant we had to go in, and something about the park gave me a bad feeling.

Ghost pushed the gate inward, but it gave only an inch or two, thanks to the decades of vines binding it in place. We all pulled at them for a moment, trying to separate the twisted vegetation from the iron, but the lock might as well have held fast. The gate was not opening like this. Maybe it was for the best, though I doubted Ghost would give up when he'd gotten this close. Even I found myself wanting to see it through, no matter how ridiculous the hunt was or how much entering this park felt like breaking a law.

"I have an idea," Ghost said, jogging back to the car. He returned with the seatbelt cutter he must have kept in the glove compartment. With the tool in hand, he made quick work of the clinging vines, and the old gate sighed as it opened inward to allow us access.

"Okay," Aubrey said, stepping into the quiet hush of the park.

There was no one around as Ghost and I followed Aubrey out to the center of the grass, and dappled sunlight showed bright flickers in a few spots on the emerald green lawn. Otherwise, it felt as if we'd entered some kind of sanctuary, and the forms of the giant houses that flanked the park seemed to be standing guard.

"What do we look for?" I asked.

Ghost shrugged. "No idea. This is my first time hunting treasure too."

"Let's walk the fence line," Aubrey suggested. "Maybe there's something tucked into it or some kind of marking or something?"

We split up, each of us moving along the fence that separated the park from the properties around it. The silence inside the space was eerie, and I found myself tiptoeing, trying not to disturb the hush that was beginning to settle even into my mind, laying a quiet blanket of calm atop every whirling and dizzy thought that had been racing through me since coming to Colorado.

The fence was old but sturdy, woven through with roots and branches, and in a few places, homeowners had built another fence just outside this one to demarcate their own properties. It was interesting and impressive, but I wasn't finding anything that screamed "treasure hunt material."

I did, however, hear some screaming.

"Just what do you think you're doing?" A shrieking voice came from the other side of the park and I turned to find a tiny old woman in flannel and denim railing a fist at Ghost. At her side was a massive animal, which I thought might be a dog, but there was a chance it was something closer to a lion. It raised its massive head and let out a menacing growl from between jagged teeth. The old woman was excessively loud, considering the quiet of the space, and it felt like any second she'd have every homeowner around rushing out to see who was trespassing. But the dog was what had ice stiffening my veins.

Ghost gave a worried look to the dog and then addressed the tiny woman at its side as it continued to growl. "Sorry, ma'am, we're just looking for something. Didn't mean to disturb you."

"This park is private property," she went on, her wrinkled little face reddening. "Moose told me y'all were in here and he doesn't like strangers." The dog—Moose, apparently—let out a low "whoof" at the mention of his name. He dropped to his massive haunches, saliva dripping from his wrinkly jowls.

"How'd you get in here anyway? Did Arnold Adams have another wild party I didn't get invited to?" She shot a fiery gaze at the edge of the park, where I assumed Arnold must live, and Moose gave a deep snarl of shared irritation.

"Um, no," Aubrey piped up, her eyes on the dog at the woman's feet. "We have a key. Hey, what kind of dog is that?"

"The kind that eats trespassers," the woman said. "A key, you say?"

Ghost held up the iron key for the lady to see, and she squinted at it suspiciously.

"Where in god's creation did you get that?" she asked. "We

haven't given out keys like that for ages." Her anger seemed to have morphed into curiosity, and her tone had changed too. "Who are you people anyway?" Moose made a noise that sounded a bit like a question, flopping his giant head down as he collapsed to the ground, rolling to one side. It felt like both the dog and his master had decided we were no threat. I felt my muscles relax slightly.

"I'm Archie Kasper," Ghost said. "My uncle used to live up here, at the Kasper Mountain Resort? I'm renovating the place. This is my sister, Aubrey, and a friend of mine, Will."

The woman looked between us, focusing on Aubrey and Ghost with an unwavering scrutiny before looking down at the dog. "They say they're Kaspers, Moose. What do you think?"

The enormous dog climbed to its feet and sniffed at my friends, ignoring me completely.

"I don't like dogs," Aubrey whispered in a low tone, her whole body going rigid as Moose padded around her, sniffing.

"Don't tell him that," the old woman suggested. "He don't much like people, if you want the truth."

"Fantastic," Aubrey said.

Moose dropped back to the ground and rolled to his side again, clearly finished with his investigation.

"You do look a bit like Marvin, I guess," the woman said.

"You knew Uncle Marvin?" Ghost asked. The hope in his voice had me interested in the answer too.

"Everyone up here knew him." The woman shrugged. "He was a good man. He and his wife were both good people."

"We never met our aunt," Aubrey said, a hint of sadness in her voice.

The woman didn't respond to that, seemingly lost in her own head for a moment as she gazed at us. "Show me the key once more," she said, taking it from Ghost as he held it out to her. She turned it over in her hands, a little smile playing at her lips and her eyes clouding a bit. She squinted and looked up at Ghost. "I honestly didn't think I'd ever see one of these old things again."

"Would you like to keep it?" Ghost asked her, surprising me.

"No," the woman said, handing it back. "It's yours. That's Lola's gate over there, and this is probably the only key left to it. Since Lola was your aunt, you better keep it. And if you'd like to use the park, you can. I'll let the others know."

Aubrey and Ghost exchanged a disappointed look. Though the woman was kind now, this wasn't exactly treasure. "Thanks," Aubrey said softly.

"Could you wait here a minute?" The woman asked, looking between us. "I have something for you. But I can't remember quite where I put it. Might take a little bit."

A little flicker of excitement jumped to life in me, and I saw Ghost go practically rigid with it. "Of course," he said.

"Keep an eye on Moose," she said, and turned to go, leaving us with the enormous dog. Moose didn't seem to mind. He watched her depart through huge, saggy, doleful eyes, and then let out a low huff before seeming to go to sleep.

"She knew Uncle Marvin," Aubrey said.

"And our aunt. Lola," Ghost said.

"You never met Lola?" I asked.

Ghost shook his head. "Uncle Marvin didn't talk about her. She'd been gone a while by the time Aubrey and I first came up here. I don't think he really ever got over losing her."

"I wish I knew more about her," Aubrey said. "I've always had the sense there was a good love story there. Movie stuff."

"Well, she must have been a nice person if they named a gate after her," I said.

The siblings nodded, looking around the park with what was probably a new appreciation, knowing their family had been here at some point.

The woman took the better part of an hour to find whatever it was she had for Archie. Moose snored loudly, and we all ended up wandering around the park, exploring a bit as the dog's low snuffles echoed through silence around us.

"Here it is," the woman said, rushing back toward Ghost from the gate that must have led to her own property. Moose lumbered to his feet at the reappearance of his owner.

Ghost moved toward her from the side of the park where he'd been walking, his eyes fixed on the envelope she held in her hands.

"Thanks," he said, taking it from her.

"What's in it?" The woman asked.

"You don't know?" I asked her.

"Marvin made me swear I wouldn't open it. He told me you'd come looking for it someday. He said you'd show me Lola's key to prove it was you." Maybe Marvin had been less nuts than I'd suspected.

"Wow," Aubrey said, her voice a whisper.

"So what's in it?" the woman asked again.

Ghost seemed to ponder whether he should open it in front of her, but then clearly gave into the idea. He slipped open the white envelope and pulled out another piece of paper, this one more yellow and wrinkled than the envelope itself.

"Part of the map," Ghost said, holding it out for us to see.

It looked like a corner, but this piece was devoid of any real markings at all. No roads, no mountains. Nothing appeared on the old scrap except a symbol on one corner that looked like two cursive letters woven together. An 'A' and an 'L.'

"Well, I don't know what the hell you're supposed to do with that," the woman said, looking disappointed. "If I'd known that was all it was, I wouldn't have bothered putting it in the safe."

"Sorry," Aubrey told her. "Thank you for keeping it."

"Meh." The woman seemed to have lost interest in us. "If anyone else bothers you, just show 'em the key and tell them you've already talked to Moose. They'll leave you alone."

"Thanks very much," Ghost said, but the woman was already leaving, trudging back toward her fence with Moose at her heels.

Her gate clanged shut, and we were alone in the quiet park again.

"Well, what do we do now?" Aubrey asked.

"I haven't got a clue," Ghost answered.

"I've got a date," I told them. "Let's head back."

Archie rolled his eyes, but he led the way back to the car and back to the resort, where I showered and got ready to meet Lucy Dale. I hoped she hadn't had second thoughts and decided to stand me up—though part of me thought things might be simpler if she did.

Chapter 18
Accidental Flirting

LUCY

"I hope your friends appreciate you getting dressed up like this for them. You're probably more than most folks in this little mountain town can handle," Papa said, giving me a warm smile as I kissed his cheek before leaving to meet Will.

I might have let him believe I was going to meet Bennie and CeeCee, mostly because it was easier than answering the thirty questions Papa would ask me about Will. And I doubted he would think highly of my decision to go out with my boss.

Only, was it even a decision?

I'd decided firmly to stay away from the sleek out-of-town playboy with the perfect hair. But then . . . somehow I'd found myself kissing him one day and agreeing to a date after that. Now, here I was, in a tight-fitting black sundress, sky-high sandals, and my head a complete mess.

"I'll be back in a couple hours," I promised him. "Shall I bring you a burger?"

Papa gave me a toothy grin. "You do love me best."

"Of course I do. Fries?"

"Do you really need to ask? Oh, and a milkshake please."

He nodded with satisfaction and lifted the book of puzzles back to his lap. Papa was always working a crossword or a sudoku. He'd read somewhere that the work kept his brain young.

I climbed into my truck and pointed it down the highway to Chambers, a restaurant about ten miles down the road where I was meeting Will.

When I entered the dark space, it took a few seconds for my eyes to adjust. There was a bar off to one side, and a seating area just behind the hostess stand.

"Help you, Luce?" The hostess tonight was Bennie's younger sister Abigail, who looked cute with her hair slicked back in a ponytail and a crisp white shirt. Her baby face beamed as she picked up a single menu. "Dinner for one?"

A little rash of frustration washed through me. Even the fourteen-year-olds in this town didn't expect me to have a date.

"Actually, I'm meeting someone," I told her, unable to keep my chin from lifting just a little.

Abigail's wide eyes grew even bigger. "Not the hot guy who just came in here and said he's meeting someone." Her voice was a hush.

"That sounds like him," I told her, a little tone of victory in my voice that I was not proud about but couldn't help.

"Oh wow," Abigail said, forgetting her professional demeanor for a moment as she looked at me with something like awe. "He's so good-looking. Is he one of the fighter pilots everyone is talking about?"

"He is," I told her. "He won't be in town long. We're just friends."

"That's too bad." She sighed as if I'd just squashed all her girlish dreams. "He's over here."

I followed Abigail across the space to the table in the far corner where Will sat. He glanced up and those deep blue eyes crinkled at the corners as he smiled.

"Lucy." Will stood and pulled a chair out for me, the one next to where he'd been sitting. Left to my own devices, I would have chosen the chair across from him to keep some distance, but I didn't want to be rude. And I'd have been lying to myself if I didn't admit that being near enough to get the occasional waft of his cologne was okay with me.

"Enjoy your meal," Abigail said, standing next to the table just a beat longer than necessary once we were both seated.

"Thank you," Will and I both said at once, and Abigail turned to leave.

"I'm glad you came," Will said. His voice was warm and low, and it rolled through me like a summer storm, sending unwanted shivers through my body.

"You thought I wouldn't?"

"I wasn't sure. I hoped you would."

"I don't make a habit of standing people up."

"Thought you might make an exception for me," he said, the joke not quite reaching his eyes.

The waitress arrived before I had to answer, and I was glad.

Seeing this suave man look anything less than confident elicited a strange reaction in my chest, made me want to comfort him. I swallowed hard and ordered a glass of Pinot noir.

"Tell me about your day," Will suggested, leaning in. His words and everything about his body language invited me to share, to open up. I wasn't sure anyone had ever looked so eager to hear whatever I had to say. It was hard to remain guarded, but I needed to try.

"Let's see," I said. "Friday night I went to this bar opening at an old resort a couple of Navy hotshots are trying to refurbish."

"Yeah?" He grinned. "How was that?"

"I made poor decisions."

"Did you?"

"Definitely. I allowed myself to be seduced into a private corner and then I kissed a co-worker." As the words left my mouth, I heard my own voice. Low, playful. I was flirting.

And I did not flirt.

"Poor decision? You sure about that? Was he a bad kisser?"

This was my chance to put a stop to all of this. Tell him it was awful. Tell him I only came here tonight to reaffirm my commitment to remaining professional.

"Not even close," I heard myself say.

"So he was a good kisser? Would you assign any superlatives to the kiss?"

"Superlatives?"

"You know, like 'extraordinary,' 'fantastic,' 'transporting,' that sort of thing."

He was enjoying every second of this. And as our wine arrived, I realized I liked the banter too.

"Let's go with 'good.'"

"That's not very imaginative." Will actually looked disappointed, his full lips turning down slightly. He lifted his glass. "To more impressive adjectives in the future."

I lifted my glass, feeling myself smiling, even against my better judgment. I shouldn't be encouraging this. Hell, I shouldn't even be here. But I was. And I realized that something inside me didn't want to hold back. It was too hard.

I liked Will. For whatever stupid reasons, I really liked him and his cocky attitude and his annoyingly beautiful face. I'd let myself enjoy tonight, and all I'd have to do was remember that if this was really going to be anything, it was a fling.

"So you had that soul-shaking kiss on Friday night," Will said.

"Kinda putting words in my mouth there."

His eyes dropped to my lips, as if he was thinking of other things he might put in my mouth, and a line of fire shot through my core.

"Please, proceed." He sipped his wine, those lake blue eyes never leaving my face.

"Saturday I had to work," I said.

"Your boss must be an asshole."

I lifted an eyebrow. Will was technically my boss, but it rubbed me the wrong way to hear him assert it like this. "He definitely is," I agreed. "Saturday night I spent with Papa watching the Rockies play, and now I'm here."

"Papa?"

"My grandfather. I live with him. Have for most of my life. It's his business I took over."

"So you always planned to be a mountain contractor? Take over his business?" Will's open interest made me feel seen in a way I wasn't sure I had been in a while. Everyone up here already knew my whole story, it was nice to talk to someone who didn't assume they knew everything about me.

I took another long sip of my wine. "Not really. I almost finished college but Papa got hurt on a job so I came home. I'd thought about it before—taking over the business. I helped out as a kid, and all through high school, but I guess I was still open to the idea of finding another path. Going somewhere less small and confining. But I didn't. I came home. The rest is history." I shrugged as if this little piece of information was as meaningless as the weather, but Will didn't let me get away with it.

"What would you have done otherwise?" He asked.

"I was thinking of going to law school," I said, admitting something I hadn't told anyone since I'd come back. Even Bennie and CeeCee didn't know I'd been accepted at Berkeley. "My grades were good, and I'd already been accepted. I guess I would have been a lawyer."

Will nodded at this. "I could see you as a lawyer. Tough, fair. It fits."

"But I like being here," I said, putting the memory aside. I'd made peace with my choices. "This is home."

"I like it here too," he said, his voice just a bit lower. Heat flooded my core again.

Our food arrived then, and I was glad for the distraction. Having Will so close at my side was doing things to my chemistry and my self-control.

"What did you do today?" I asked him, hoping to shift the focus from me.

Will chuckled and smiled at me. "I was helping Ghost with the next piece of his big treasure hunt."

"So that's for real?"

"I guess so."

"What's the treasure?"

"I think that's the point of the hunt."

"Why in the world would an old man set something like this up in the first place? Why not just leave his nephew and niece whatever he had in the will?"

Will shrugged. "More fun this way? Did you know the old guy?"

"I never met him. Papa knew him well. They used to play cards together. And when they were kids they were best friends."

"Seriously?"

I nodded, remembering what Papa had told me about the old man with the shock of white hair sticking up atop his head. "He was an eccentric, that was sure. And Papa said he could tell a story like no one else he'd ever met."

"Oh yeah? That's cool. I wonder if you know something that could help them figure out this hunt."

"I don't remember much that will help them." I took a bite of my soup, and Will ate some of his meal. The silence between us wasn't uncomfortable, but it was laden with a tingling tension that zapped between us. "Tell me about today."

Will smiled, taking a sip of his wine before he spoke. I found myself leaning in, becoming more invested in both the treasure hunt and Will. "So Ghost had this key that they found earlier, and it was your friend Bennie who told him what it fit."

"For the private park, right?"

"Yep. Lost Lonely park. So we went there this morning. Almost got chased out by this lady and a huge dog."

"You met Moose!" I laughed. Everyone in town knew Moose. He was too big to pass without notice.

"Right. So first she was all mad about us trespassing and everything, but then Ghost showed her the key and she said it was a key to Lola's Gate, and that Lola was their aunt."

"Oh, that makes sense," I said, remembering Papa talking about Lola now. "So that was it? Where do you go from there? It sounds like a dead end."

Will shook his head. "When she figured out who Ghost and Aubrey were, she went back into her house and came out with an envelope that had part of the map in it."

"There's an actual map?"

One side of Will's smile ticked up higher. "Cool, right? So this was just a corner of it. Nothing on it at all except this weird symbol that's like two cursive letters together. An A and an L."

That rung a bell for some reason. "Really? Can you show me?" I dug in my bag for a pen and handed it to Will, along with a receipt.

"I'm not a talented artist," he said, but he bent over the paper and got to work, a little wrinkle appearing between his brows. "Like this," he said, holding the paper out to me.

Recognition dawned. Papa had a symbol like that on a long wooden box he kept in his office. It hadn't been there when I'd been a kid, or I'd know what was inside because I was snoopy like that. But now I wondered.

"Huh," I said. "I might be able to help."

Will handed me the pen back and I told him about the box.

"Ghost will be so excited," he said. "If it's okay if I tell him. But for tonight, let's not think about the treasure hunt, okay? Tell me more about you."

I still wasn't sure getting to know Will better was a great idea, but I was past arguing. His attention made me feel warm, seen. Wanted. "Well, feel free to tell Ghost about the box if you want. Maybe it's nothing, but the symbols match."

We sat for a quiet moment, each watching the other until I had to pull my gaze away.

"Tell me about growing up in the mountains," he said.

"Maybe I'd rather hear about flying jets."

"There's time for that on our next date," he said as a cloud passed through his eyes. Interesting.

"That's quite an assumption."

"Not really," he said.

"Yes it is."

"Here's an assumption: You find me charming and irresistible."

"I do?"

He frowned, but the playful glint remained in his eyes. "Don't you?"

Dammit, I did.

I sighed. "It might take a few more days to figure out."

"I'm free tomorrow night," he said, grinning.

And that was how I found myself on not just one date with someone I shouldn't have even considered going out with, but agreeing to a second date too. Before the first was even over.

At the end of our meal, Will walked me out to my truck, graciously carrying Papa's food for me.

"Thank you for dinner," I said, feeling warm and full and my veins zinging with something that had nothing to do with the food or wine. Will stood just inches from me at the side of the truck, and I knew if I leaned my body back against it, he'd close the space and touch me again. "You didn't have to buy Papa's dinner."

"I was happy to. I look forward to seeing you tomorrow," he said, his low voice a promise in the darkness around us.

A shiver went through me and I distracted myself by unlocking the truck with the fob in my hand.

Will stepped just a bit closer, lifting one hand to my cheek. His warm fingers made my body tense in anticipation. He paused, maybe waiting to see if I was going to protest, and then he leaned forward, brushing his lips over mine softly.

It wasn't a kiss, not really. And as he stepped back to let me open the truck door, I was surprised to realize how much I wanted more.

"See you tomorrow," I said, feeling off balance.

Will handed me the food and then shut the door behind me after I'd climbed in. He stood there watching as I backed out and pulled away.

He was thoughtful and attentive, handsome and sexy. He

was so close to perfect it was frightening. As I drove home, I replayed the soft near-kiss over and over.

Not only did I want more, I realized I was willing to put aside my fear and uncertainty to have it.

Chapter 19
Meetings will Solve Everything

WILL

"**A** box? What kind of box? Tell me more. Can we see it?" Ghost was practically dancing in front of me. I'd returned to the resort and found everyone hanging out in the bar after my date with Lucy. I'd told them about the box Lucy mentioned in an effort to get them to stop quizzing me about my feelings.

I definitely had feelings. I just wasn't sure what to label them, and I definitely didn't want to explore them with Monroe and Brainiac, the Kaspers and Wiley.

"She said it's wooden and long."

Monroe stifled a laugh.

"Get your mind out of the gutter," Brainiac quipped.

"Think we can see it? Can we go over there?" Ghost was still jumping back and forth on his feet, and I realized he might have been hanging out in the bar a little too long to be heading anywhere.

"She lives with her grandfather, and I doubt he'd be excited about late night visitors on a Sunday. It can wait." I nodded to Wiley, who held a glass and a bottle of Half Cat raised to me with a questioning look. He poured me a couple fingers and I joined the others, pulling up a stool at the bar.

Ghost sighed and leaned in a bit, lowering his voice so the others didn't hear. "It might not be able to wait long, man."

I frowned at him. "Meaning what?"

He took another gulp of whiskey and gave me a frank look. "I'm pretty much gambling here. Whatever's at the end of this hunt better be a shitload of cash. Because we're running on fumes here, man."

I didn't like hearing that. I'd known it was true—hell, my own finances weren't as solid as they'd been when I arrived, thanks to the condition and budget of Kasper Ridge—but I didn't want to think about it. Especially not now, when I was still encased in a Lucy Dale bubble of possibility. "We'll figure it out. The Friday nights will help, right?"

Ghost rubbed a hand over his face, making his dark red hair stand on end as his fingers raked through it. "No. Maybe. I don't know. They could. The first one went really well, actually. I just wish I had a little more cushion to work with."

"But we'll have guests in soon, right? Monroe is starting to take bookings for November."

"Did I hear my name?" Monroe leaned across the bar. For some reason she was back there with Wiley, getting a tour of the bottles he had lined up. Aubrey was on his other side, looking annoyed at Monroe's attentions. Monroe tended to have that effect on women.

"I was just reminding Ghost that we'd have this place raking in cash soon, since you're on the job setting up bookings for snow season," I told her.

"Right," she said, confirming nothing. "Yeah, not yet."

"Why not?"

"We need to talk timelines first, so I know what I'm really promising them."

"We've done that." Frustration bubbled within me.

"Just want to doublecheck. Hard to believe things are going to be ready in a couple months, that's all." Monroe shrugged like this was not a big deal.

"So you're all sitting here, second-guessing my timeline?" Had they been hanging around, discussing how I was completely incompetent? Were they worried I couldn't manage the job? A familiar insecurity threatened to rise within me.

"No," Brainiac said, interjecting from next to Ghost. "It's not like that. We all just want to be conservative here, that's all. We've got a lot at stake."

"I know that," I bit out. "I have a lot at stake too. Which is why the schedule is aggressive. And why I'm pushing toward getting things done on time. Ahead of schedule, even. And what exactly do you have at stake, anyway, Brainiac?"

Brainiac's mouth clamped shut and he dropped my gaze, leaning back in his chair and lifting a glass to his lips.

"Let's sit down tomorrow with Lucy too," Ghost suggested. It was a rational idea, but for some reason it sent my emotions totally haywire. Would everyone in my professional life always doubt me? Was this just the way it was going to be forever? I needed them to believe in me. I needed someone to. I had thought this job was my chance to prove myself, but now it felt like Ghost had about as much belief in me as my dad did.

"How about you trust me to handle my shit?" I fumed.

"It's not about trust," Ghost said, sounding weary.

"It's about all of us being in this together," Aubrey said. "And helping each other get things done. Let's have a regular meeting Monday mornings. We can check progress on all the things."

"Smart," Brainiac said.

Wiley wrapped an arm around Aubrey's shoulders and tugged her into his side. "She is."

"Fine," I sighed, the fight leaving me. They were right. It was a huge project, and construction wasn't the only part of it. "What time?"

"Nine," Ghost said. "And see if Lucy can bring that box."

"Okay. I will." I tossed down the rest of my whiskey and stood. "I'm gonna head up." I had some things to think about, and the quiet and privacy of my dilapidated hotel room was beckoning me.

As I climbed the stairs, I pulled my phone from my pocket and texted Lucy Dale.

Me: I knew you were probably thinking about me, so thought I'd say hi. I had fun tonight.

Lucy: Full of yourself much?

Me: Maybe a bit.

Lucy: Understatement.

I unlocked my room and stepped inside, happy for the silence that greeted me. I slid into an armchair and watched to see if Lucy would say anything else, but the screen stayed silent.

Me: Just wanted to let you know Ghost is calling for a meeting Monday mornings at nine.

Lucy: Oh good. Meetings. That should help progress.

Me: Is that sarcasm? Or you really like meetings?

Lucy: Take a guess.

Me: Yeah, me too. Hey, wondered if you could bring that box you mentioned. Would your grandfather mind?

Lucy: I already asked him about it. He's bringing it himself. I think he just wants to see the resort.

Me: I'll give him the grand tour. Thanks. Ghost will be excited.

Lucy: So will Papa.

Me: We still on for tomorrow night? I have an idea.

Lucy: Why am I worried?

Me: You'll like it. Just bring some stuff to change into after work. We're staying here.

Three dots danced across the screen, disappeared, and then started again. I realized, a beat too late, that suggesting a date at a hotel might send the wrong signal.

Me: I mean, I have a date planned here. Not in a hotel room.

Shit. That was not smooth.

The dots continued to dance and I tried again.

Me: Brainiac told me tonight they've got the projector working in the movie theater. I thought we could watch a movie.

Lucy: Oh. Yes. Okay.

Me: See you tomorrow morning.

I waited, but Lucy didn't answer. After a while, I brushed my teeth and climbed into bed, feeling worn out. It hurt to imagine that Ghost didn't have faith in me—it felt a little like distrust, and that made me uneasy.

* * *

Monday morning dawned bright and crisp, the sun spreading through the trees and reflecting off the mountains to the west, painting their shoulders pink and orange. I'd gotten up early and hiked the trail that essentially circled the resort, trying to get my head straight.

It had worked. By the time I came back in view of Kasper Ridge at a jog, I was too sweaty and worn out to continue beating myself up about things. Until I saw Lucy in the parking lot, anyway.

Just as I started to get my breath back, her white truck pulled past me and she parked and hopped out, looking sexy as ever in denim jeans and a Kasper Ridge Construction T-shirt. I slowed my pace, coming to rest with my hands on my knees, my chest heaving in the thin mountain air.

"Out for a run?" she asked, one eyebrow climbing as if this was amusing to her. She strolled toward me, the sun highlighting the red in her dark hair, pulled back into a complicated braid, which she'd said was the only way she could keep her hair out of her way and still get the hardhat to sit right. I loved it.

"I went for a hike," I told her, straightening up and adjusting the ball cap on my head. "It turned into a run at the end. The downhill part."

She nodded. "That's a good trail. Papa used to like to take me out there when I was a kid. See any elk or bears?"

A little twist of surprise made my heart rate tick up again. I hadn't even thought about running into wild animals—I'd been so inside my own head. But Ghost had definitely mentioned them. "Thankfully, no."

"They wouldn't bother you," Lucy said, "usually."

"Hadn't really thought about it, but Ghost says there are mountain lions up here too."

"There are," Lucy confirmed. "You'll probably never see one, but they'll see you. They're stealthy and you're probably a little bigger than anything they'd want to take on. If the resort has outdoor cameras, you'll probably catch them looking around at night. They're curious."

For some reason the idea of lions prowling the grounds at night gave me the willies. But I didn't want Lucy to see it, so I changed the subject.

"Is your grandfather coming by today?"

"I think he's planning to come later in the week."

Ghost would have to wait. He'd be bummed, but I kind of thought we needed to focus on the resort before the crazy treasure hunt, anyway. "I'll let Ghost know. He's looking forward to it."

"Papa is too." Lucy stood there for a moment, smiling and looking at me, and I watched as her eyes dropped to my mouth as I took a swig from the bottle I carried, then roamed down to my throat as I swallowed. A light pink blush rose in her cheeks and she cleared her throat when she met my eyes again and realized I'd seen her checking me out.

"I'm gonna head in and shower," I said. "See you out back in fifteen minutes. Don't forget the big Monday meeting."

"I'm ready," she said, not meeting my eyes now. "See you." She turned and walked around the side of the parking lot toward the spot where her crew was beginning to gather for the day.

I went inside to shower, feeling unreasonably happy for no reason I could pinpoint. I was just glad to see Lucy, even more happy that Lucy seemed glad to see me.

Chapter 20
What Happens in the Hard Hat...

LUCY

I n my experience, meetings often got in the way of actually getting things accomplished. However, the efficiency with which Ghost ran the meeting Monday morning was impressive, and I guessed it must have been a result of his military background.

"Great. So we've handled inventory and ordering, initial guest reservations and getting kitchen operations up and running along with housekeeping for essential services starting this winter. Now, all of that is assuming this construction schedule is feasible." Ghost looked pointedly at Will.

"We've basically doubled resources so that we can complete all of the outdoor work this summer. We cut the timeline in half. We'll be ready." Will's shoulders were back and he looked relaxed and confident. But Ghost's eyes moved to me.

"You agree?" He asked.

"It's riskier overall," I admitted. "But since we're not stealing resources from the operation on the west side to complete the east patio, I don't think there will be an issue. It will accelerate your ability to serve guests. It was a good call." I forced myself not to look at Will as I said this. This was the entire reason not to get involved with people you worked with. Now I felt like everyone here would think I was just agreeing with him because I was attracted to him.

"And twice as costly," Ghost said. "We'd budgeted to complete the west side, then planned to use operating income to complete the east side next summer. I'm worried that even with additional investment, this could stretch us too thin if something goes wrong. What if we took the men and resources being used on the east patio now and pushed them west? Maybe we could decrease the time it takes to get that done and move some resources inside to the rooms instead?"

"No," Will said. "The outdoor areas are weather dependent, as you know, and they're the key to getting the ski season launched. Guest rooms can be done in almost any weather, and we'll have the third-floor guest rooms done by November since the demo up there is finished. That was in Lucy's original plan." Will glanced at me as he said this, and warmth bloomed in my belly at the support.

"Do we still have money to do those rooms if we keep pushing on the patio?"

Will frowned and his back straightened as he drove a finger into the table. "Hey Ghost? You brought me up here because I actually know what I'm doing. And I'm confident enough in the plan that I financed half of the current work myself. Just let me do the job, okay? We'll get it done." He delivered this in a perfectly calm voice, but the tension laced between the words was clear.

"We'll get it done," I assured Archie. "Will's plan is solid." I wondered if the others at the table could sense my concern for Will, could see that I wasn't just defending him because the plan was solid, but because I was beginning to feel things for him I shouldn't have been feeling.

Archie breathed out a long sigh, and the others around the table in the large suite where he'd set up his operation visibly relaxed. "Okay," he said. We all waited for him to add more, but that was it.

Finally Will stood. "We should get back to work." He still sounded tense. I followed him out to the hallway and to the top of the curved staircase, barely able to keep up with him.

"Hey," I said as he reached the bottom, clearly intending to ignore me the whole time. He seemed unreasonably upset. "Hey, wait a second."

He turned, and his expression was grim, his full lips pressed into a tight line. "I don't need you defending me, Lucy. I've got everything under control."

I lifted my hands, taking a step back. "I was just trying to help."

"I don't need help," he said, and the words came out in a hiss.

"Okay," I said. I almost apologized, though I didn't feel sorry in the least. Confused? Sure. A little pissed off myself? Definitely. I was about to tell him I didn't think there was any point to me staying after work this evening when he spoke again.

"Shit." His eyes found mine and then dropped. "Shit. I'm sorry. I appreciate you helping me out. Ghost respects you, and your word carries a lot of weight."

I rubbed my neck, worried I might have whiplash.

"This is a kind of loaded situation, that's all. I came up here because I was sick of working for my dad, having him treat me like a bumbling kid who couldn't manage being in charge. And to have Ghost question me after I've sunk everything I have into supporting him . . . It just kind of triggered me, I guess."

"I guess," I said, understanding softening my own irritation. I was relieved to understand why he'd snapped.

"I really am sorry. I'm so glad you're here, that I have your experience to depend on. I couldn't do this without you."

I smiled, tempted to agree with him out loud, but content to acknowledge that he was right mentally instead. "Thanks."

"And for the record? Whatever happens while we're wearing hard hats and talking budget and schedule has nothing to do with whatever might happen later on, okay?" It was as if Will could sense my hesitation, like he knew my inner conflicts hadn't evaporated.

I didn't answer, still undecided about how wise it was to agree to another date with someone I worked so closely with in a situation that was even more complicated than I'd originally thought. But I looked up into those deep blue eyes and felt my insides heat and my resistance melt.

"I'll see you outside," Will said. "And then later on, I'll meet you right here. Okay?"

Since the first time Will had touched me, it was clear my body was in charge where he was concerned. And even though I didn't speak, my head was nodding and I felt myself smiling. I wanted to spend time with Will. Not as his foreman, not as a colleague. I wanted so much more than that.

I knew my body was going to lead me there anyway. Even if it was complicated.

* * *

That evening I said goodbye to my crew, making busy work for myself until the last of them had departed for the evening. I didn't want them to see me meeting Will. I was less concerned about Ghost, Aubrey, and the others. I had a feeling they were a bit like Will's family, since they all lived together here at the resort. I wasn't going to tell them I was interested in Will, but I wasn't going to hide from them either.

I cleaned up in the lobby bathroom, splashing some water on my face and letting my hair down after managing a quick washcloth bath in the sink. It wasn't ideal, but it was enough to make me feel less construction worker and more woman on a date.

I stepped out into the lobby, wearing cigarette pants, pumps, and a flowy tank top with a little cardigan pulled over it. Will stood at the base of the stairs, and when he caught sight of me, a sexy smile spread across his face.

"Wow," he said. "I don't know how you managed that in a half-functional bathroom, but you look incredible."

"You look nice too," I said, feeling a blush crawl up my cheeks. How was it I could order full crews of burly men around all day and still find myself embarrassed at one compliment from this one?

Will wore fitted dark jeans and an Oxford shirt tucked into his waist, showing off broad shoulders and narrow hips. His sleeves were rolled partway up his forearms, and something about the casual ease—and the muscular shape of his arms— made me swoon a little. And I was not a girl who swooned.

"Shall we?" Will asked, stepping to my side.

"Yes," I said, distracted by the hand Will dropped to my low back to guide me toward the door at the far west side of the lobby.

He led me down a darkened hallway, which I knew would eventually lead to the restaurant, arcade, and movie theater.

This was basically the entertainment wing, so it wasn't high on our list of priorities compared to accommodations.

"Right in here." He opened a wide set of doors and we stepped into a room with a counter at one side. Will walked to the counter and stepped around behind it, lifting an airpop machine to the surface. "Popcorn?" He asked.

"Sure," I said. Will had clearly set this up ahead of time, and he looked a little bashful getting it going. My chest warmed even more.

"Eventually, we'll have the movie theater popcorn machine here," he explained. "This is just a stop-gap measure." He turned on the machine, and the sound filled the space with noise, making it impossible to talk.

The area had clearly been a movie theater in the past, and I'd never had the chance to explore it. We were in the old lobby, which was wallpapered in a flocked red and white paper, and empty movie poster frames spaced evenly along the walls. The carpet—what was left of it—was a rich burgundy color, and the counter where Will was making popcorn reminded me of the bar out front. It was solid wood, sturdy and ornate.

"Here you go." Will handed me popcorn in a large tub, and then pulled a bottle of red wine and two glasses from beneath the counter. "Water bottle inside," he said, inclining his head toward the large double doors at the other side of the space.

"What movie are we going to see?" I asked.

"It's a classic," he said. "And a surprise."

I smiled, a lightness inside me I didn't often feel. Before Sunday evening, when was the last time I'd been on a date? Or been with someone as willing to be playful as Will? He definitely had a chip on his shoulder in the construction arena, but once we were away from that job, there was something so easygoing about him, like he was more than willing to laugh at himself. It was refreshing.

Inside the movie theater, a few rows of velvet-upholstered chairs were in pretty poor shape, and one entire row was missing up front. It was there that Will had set up a couple camp chairs and a low table between them, and he invited me to sit down.

"I'll be right back," he said, and he disappeared back up the aisle. I turned as he exited and watched as he appeared in the little projection booth up high. He gave me a wave, and then an old fashioned reel player flickered to life, an image dancing on the screen in front of me, jumping and cracking before settling into a steady roll.

Will returned and settled back into the chair at my side, and then handed me a glass of wine and grinned as the credits for the movie began to roll.

"Disney?" I asked, a sense of nostalgia washing through me. I hadn't seen one of the original Disney films since I was very young.

"It's what they had on hand," he said. "*Snow White.*"

"I love it." I settled into my chair and smiled, feeling strangely pampered by this entire setup. Sure it was a dusty and dilapidated space, and I was sitting in a rickety camp chair, but Will had gone to all this effort for me, and it felt good. In the past, no one had gone to any real effort to make me feel special. I'd been on dates, had boyfriends, but it felt like it had all been surface level.

I settled back and ate my popcorn, doing my best not to inhale deeper to try to catch Will's scent over the butter smell coming from the tub in my hands.

"Mind if I—" Will pushed the little table behind us—neither of us was using it anyway—and scooted his chair closer to reach into the tub for popcorn.

We watched the movie, drinking wine and eating popcorn, and occasionally our hands brushed together in the tub as we both reached in. It wasn't intentional, but it was curiously erotic. Each time we touched, a little thrill shot through me, and I wanted something more, something I couldn't quite put my finger on, though my body had several ideas.

Toward the end of the movie, it happened again, and I might have accidentally let out a little gasp when Will's hand lingered, his fingers brushing mine with intention. In the darkness, I felt him turn toward me, felt his eyes on my face in the glow from the movie. And when I turned to look at him, I knew something had shifted.

Chapter 21
Action with Snow White

WILL

I removed my hand from the popcorn tub, keeping Lucy's fingers intertwined with mine, and carefully set the tub on the ground. Then I gave a little tug on Lucy's hand, and without a word, she lifted out of her chair and moved closer, following my lead. I settled her onto my lap, her back pressed up against me, my arms around her. For a moment I wondered if the chair would hold us both, but it seemed sturdy enough.

"Is this okay?" I whispered into the soft waves of dark hair at her neck.

"I wouldn't have moved if it wasn't," she said. She wasn't

being argumentative. She was being Lucy, and the fact she was completely in control of her decisions and her actions at all times was hot as hell.

Her warm body was fitted against mine, her soft round ass pressed up against my thrumming erection. I knew she could probably feel it beneath her, but she didn't seem to care, and the tease of having her right there, touching me . . . it was killing me in the best way.

I lifted a hand and moved the hair from her shoulder, exposing her neck, a zing shooting through me and straight to my dick when she let out a breathy little moan. I let the tips of my fingers trail across that delicate skin, from just behind her ear, along the curve of her soft neck, down across her shoulder and back up, and Lucy's breathing came faster.

Snow White was singing on screen, the soft, high-pitched melody weaving around us and creating some kind of magical alternate reality. One where Lucy Dale sat on my lap. One where I placed soft kisses along her neck in the dark. An alternate reality where she turned in my arms with another little moan and kissed me, her arms lacing around my neck, her lips hard on mine.

I'd laid a blanket out in front of us, partially to cover the somewhat destroyed floor of the old theater, and just in case we got cold. But now, it was the perfect place to lay Lucy down. We slipped from the chair and she didn't need any coaxing to slide onto her back, her arms still around my neck as I lowered myself to her side.

"More," she whispered, pulling me until I'd pressed myself along her length, practically laying on top of her. The temptation of her soft capable body was almost painful, every one of my nerve endings screaming with the need to touch her, to feel her. And her fingers were gripping my back, kneading the muscles there, pulling my shirt from the waist of my pants as her mouth opened to mine, over and over.

The movie was forgotten as I slipped the cardigan from Lucy's shoulders, kissing each of them and lingering on the soft skin I found. She moaned and pushed at me, and for a moment I thought she was asking me to stop, so with a frustrated grunt I pulled away. But she used the space to pull her tank top over her head and give me a wicked smile.

"That's better," she said in a voice that made every inch of me throb for her. "Take off your shirt, Will."

She was giving me orders.

I fucking loved it.

"Yes ma'am," I breathed, whipping the shirt over my head in one quick motion.

"Fuck," she said, her eyes on my chest.

Yes. I really, really wanted that.

But I would never push someone somewhere they didn't want to go. And I was fairly confident by now that Lucy would let me know exactly what she was comfortable with. And even if it killed me, I wouldn't take it an inch further than that.

Her eyes roamed my bare skin and a lusty look came into her eyes as her palms found my pecs and slid down over my abs.

"You're fucking glorious," she whispered. "Better than I imagined."

"You imagined what I would look like without my shirt on?"

"Don't get arrogant about it."

"Too late," I said, leaning down to worship the exposed skin of her abdomen, to place soft kisses up to the lacy cups of the black bra she wore, to cup each of her small, perfect breasts with a palm. "Amazing," I told her, loving the way she fit in my hands. "These are amazing."

I went to push one cup down, dying to take her in my mouth, but she stopped me with a hand. "Don't do that," she said, sending my frustration spiking again. We were stopping here?

"Oh," I managed, beginning to pull myself from her body.

"No, stay there. I just mean—here, just take it off." She arched her back and unclipped the bra as I watched, pulling it from her body to expose both of her perfect breasts for me.

I should have said words, but I was beyond them, my body taking complete control as I leaned back down, making the most of every second with Lucy beneath me. I dropped my lips to one of her peaked nipples, my fingers playing with the other as her breathing came faster.

Her hands roamed, eventually sliding into the waistband of my jeans and then working around the front to unbutton them. She pushed, and I pulled them off and then helped her out of hers.

"You're gorgeous," she said, as I knelt in only my boxer briefs, sliding her pants from her beautiful legs. They were muscular and curved, strong and gorgeous. I looked up into her face to find her eyes glued to my erection, clearly visible in its eagerness as it jutted out inside my briefs, the head straining out of the waistband to be free.

I grinned at her. "I could say the same about you," I slid my hands up her thighs, bending down again to lick softly across her navel.

"Lower," she commanded.

I didn't waste any time, kneeling between her legs and dipping my head to exhale a hot breath over her silk panties, pleased when she groaned as the warmth penetrated her core.

"Will," she moaned.

Her name on my lips was so sweet and sensual, it nearly robbed me of all control.

I slid the panties aside and let myself taste her, then dropped lower and licked up her soft wetness. She moaned again and I positioned myself more comfortably, adding one hand to the effort. I kissed, licked, and sucked, coaxing her clit from hidden to swollen and throbbing, egged on by her breathy moans and her hands fisting in my hair. I was struggling for control but I wasn't about to stop.

As she began to shake, the pressure on my head grew firmer, and Lucy Dale took her orgasm with ferocity, essentially riding my face and letting out an unselfconscious sound that drove me crazy. I wanted to bury myself in this woman and never come out, I wanted to hear her screaming my name over and over again for the rest of my life.

Or at least for the rest of tonight.

Both thoughts were somewhat terrifying, but I was too far gone to care.

I held Lucy for a long minute, her breathing slowly normal-izing, but my own breath was still coming hard. I wanted her, but I wasn't going to push. Tonight could be only about her and it would still rank as one of the best nights of my life.

With Snow White still singing, Lucy began to move again, her hands exploring my body. Her hands found my shoulders and she pushed me onto my back with a wicked grin, climbing on to straddle me as my heart rate ratcheted up again in antic-ipation.

She worked her body down mine, stopping at my waist where her hands quickly removed my boxer briefs, freeing my aching erection. I was completely vulnerable to her whims, and I didn't think there was anything better in the world.

Lucy took me between her small hands, and then gripped me firmly and stroked until I thought I'd lose my mind. I fought for control as she watched me, clearly knowing exactly what she was doing to me and loving it.

"I'm not gonna last if you keep that up," I told her, barely able to form words. Her fingers were wrapped around my shaft, her other hand doing something mysterious and insane to my balls and the spot just behind them that I thought might send me off the deep end permanently.

And that would be just fine with me.

"No?" She asked, giving me that wicked smile again.

I shook my head, groaning as the dwarves on the screen sang some maniacal song that seemed almost like it must be part of the torture Lucy had devised.

"What if I do this?" She asked, scooting lower and letting her tongue circle my crown.

The wet heat had my body spiking and I was so close to exploding I honestly didn't know if I could stop it.

Shit. I needed distraction. I forced my mind to think about my father. About Markie. About Markie's stupid dog Buzz, who was some kind of ill-conceived pit bull and daschund mix I would have said was impossible. Buzz was a total asshole, and every time Markie brought him to a job site, he'd hump my leg like I was the hottest thing he'd ever seen. If I tried to pet him he growled at me. It was like I was only good for one thing in his tiny little dog mind.

Thinking of Buzz bought me a little time, but when Lucy's mouth descended onto me, and I was enveloped in the sweet heat of her lips again, it took everything I had not to hold her there and fuck her silly. I groaned, just about to give in to the fact that I wasn't going to get to actually have her tonight. But then she stopped.

She stepped off of me, removed her panties, and reached for her purse, pulling out a condom and holding it up. "Would it be okay with you if—" she began. She didn't have time to finish checking for my consent, because I'd grabbed the condom from her and ripped open the packet.

"Patience," she said, taking it back from me and retaking her position straddling me. She was naked and glorious, and she took her sweet time rolling the condom onto me as I fought for control at every tiny touch of her body against mine.

"I'm really struggling with patience right now," I told her.

She gave me the most evil grin I'd ever been subjected to, and then positioned one hand on my shoulder, her eyes never leaving mine. She reached between us, her hand gripping me again, and fed just the tip of me into the hottest, tightest, wettest wonderland I'd ever imagined.

"Oh fuck," I groaned. How had I so completely lost control of this situation? Lucy could do anything to me right now and I'd be utterly powerless. Between her hands and her mouth and her curvy perfect body on top of mine, you'd have thought she was the bigger of us, the one capable of overpowering the other.

Lucy lowered herself onto me, centimeter by centimeter, and it took everything I had not to explode the second she was finally seated, my entire length throbbing with need inside her hot tight channel. She didn't move immediately. Her eyes were closed and her lips curved into a satisfied smile, and she pressed her hands into my shoulders, pushing herself up until her back arched. Her head fell back and those incredible tits jutted before her.

I reached my hands up to cup them, and Lucy sucked in a breath, finally revealing that this was affecting her too. She pressed harder on my shoulders and slid herself up my length, then lowered slowly down again.

"Oh god," I moaned. "You're going to kill me."

Lucy ignored me, focused wholly on the torturous motion of her hips, sliding languorously up and down my length as every muscle inside her body seemed to be gripping me in an iron vise.

I used my thumbs to flick her nipples, causing her to hiss in a breath, and then I gave each one a gentle pinch and she groaned. I pinched a tiny bit harder, and Lucy cried out, increasing her speed and motion right where I needed it.

Finally, she was fucking me properly, at a speed and ferocity I could really get behind, and I was seconds from coming, but there was no way I was going to let go before she did.

Luckily, Lucy was close. She was letting out a cry with every thrust now, and her chest was heaving. "Oh god, oh god, oh fuck, oh . . . Will!" She practically screamed my name as she exploded around me, and the pulsing of her body was all it took to draw my pent-up orgasm from me with a violence that surprised me.

I held her to me, keeping myself buried deeply inside her as I shuddered through the longest orgasm I'd ever experienced. At one point I actually feared I might lose consciousness.

Finally, she collapsed on top of me and I loosened my grip, but only a fraction. I didn't want to let her go.

"Shit," she whispered in my ear, and fear bloomed within me on the chance that wasn't a happy expletive. "I think that was the best sex I've ever had," she said, and the fear was instantly replaced with satisfaction.

But then she said, "what the hell will I do when you leave?" It was whispered, almost more to herself than to me. I wasn't sure what to make of it. I had no plans to leave.

"I'm right here," I said.

And she nodded against me, wrapping her arms around me.

Chapter 22
Voyage to Mandoon

LUCY

Now I'd done it.

I'd let myself have the thing I knew I should stay far, far away from if I wanted to retain my dignity, my sanity . . . and my heart. Will Cruz was a walking orgasm. I'd known it from the very beginning, and now I'd proved it to myself, and absolutely no good could come of it.

He'd held me close and filled every one of my senses, and for a long time, I'd set aside my best judgment and let him. But slowly, as my rational mind began to function again, a hard knot formed in my chest. I didn't want to admit that I knew what it was, but it was hard to ignore. Somewhere between working together, dinner, and Snow White, I'd begun to fall for Will.

That week at work, I did my best to be professional, but I felt like there was a spotlight on us, like every guy on my crew could see that something had happened between us, that I'd crossed a line. When Will had found me alone Tuesday morning and kissed my cheek, I'd melted at first, but then jumped away, glancing around.

"You can't touch me here," I told him. "Where people might see."

"But I can touch you later?" he asked, his smile melting my defenses as usual. "When we're alone."

"We'll see," I had told him, but I knew there was no point pretending I was going to say no now.

And when Papa asked to ride in with me Thursday morning, the long slender wooden box tucked under his arm, I knew he'd see right through me the second he saw us together.

"This is good," Papa said, gazing out the window as I navigated the curvy mountain road toward the resort. "I can check your progress, see if there's anything I might help out with."

"That would be great," I told him, meaning it. Even though I didn't really need Papa's oversight anymore, it was always good to have a seasoned veteran of this kind of project offer suggestions. And while I did not enjoy suggestions from just anyone with a tape measure and a bit of construction experience, Papa understood this environment better than anyone. Maybe better than me.

We parked in my usual spot and Papa met me at the front of the truck, his hardhat sending something in my heart spiraling down a series of memories from when I'd been a little girl, when it was Papa who ran the company. "Show me what you're up to," he said.

I led my grandfather around the side of the resort where the patio was being paved around the huge concrete pilings we'd poured to support the overhang that extended half of the distance. We walked around the perimeter, and I pointed out the enormous fire pit, the outdoor restaurant patio, and finally came to the far east side where the fence would separate the terraced hot tubs from the more open parts of the patio.

"This is impressive," Papa said, taking in the enormous space. "A lot of area here to level."

"It was a task, that's for sure." My cheeks glowed under his praise.

"Good choice with the pavers, I think. They'll wear well." Papa nodded in satisfaction. "How's the inside stuff coming?"

"Next phase," I told him. "We've got all the focus out here while the weather's good, but we'll move in to refurbishing the lobby, lounge, restaurant and common areas next, along with the guest rooms on the third floor."

"Good. Away from the noise." Papa nodded again and I knew I was doing what he would have done, which made me proud. I was just about to show him the old bowling alley and movie theater when Will strode out the back doors.

"Hey Lucy," he said, coming to a stop several feet from me but still sending shivers of warmth wicking across my skin.

"Will. I want to introduce my grandfather, Ernie Dale. He built Kasper Ridge Construction from the ground up, taught me everything I know."

"Nice to meet you sir," Will said, extending a hand to Papa, who shook it heartily.

"You too, son." He glanced between us, his sharp eyes narrowing. "You the one who's been keeping Lucy busy up here then?"

That was a little ambiguous, and I frowned at Papa, hoping he wasn't going to ambush me now. He hadn't asked who I'd been seeing the couple nights I'd been out, and I'd assumed he thought I was with the girls.

"Um . . ." I didn't like to lie, but I was about to throw out something silly about how he had it all wrong when Will spoke.

"No sir. Lucy doesn't need me giving her directions. I'm mostly just trying to follow along so I can learn something, and stay out of her way. She's the expert."

Warmth spread through me at his words, and Papa chuckled deep in his chest.

"Don't stay out of her way too much," Papa said. "It's been a while since Luce found anyone worth her time."

He was talking in riddles, but it was clear he knew there was something more here than a co-working relationship. He seemed to approve, which made me happy. Or at least if he didn't, he wasn't going to embarrass me about it at work.

"No sir," Will said, grinning and then shooting me a quick wink. If Papa hadn't already been pretty sure we were more than just colleagues, the wink sealed it.

"Should I go get the box? Where's Marvin's nephew?" Papa looked around for Ghost as the noise of construction around us began to ramp up for the day.

"Inside, sir," Will said. "Here, we can go through the lobby and you can check it out on the way. Lucy said you used to hang out here with Marvin?"

Papa shot Will a huge smile as we headed inside through the maintenance door. The sliding glass doors would be installed in the next month all along the back of the building, but they were on order so for now the gaping holes where the old doors had been removed were boarded up.

"My dad used to manage this place," Papa told Will. "But it wasn't like this all those years ago."

"That's what I heard. I'll go get Ghost," Will said, catching my eye as Papa looked around the darkened space. We'd come around the sweeping staircases to stand in the middle of the main lobby area, and Papa was shaking his head and whistling a deep low note.

"Let's get the box," I said, ushering him forward toward the front door.

He nodded and hastened his step, but moments later we were back inside, Papa gazing around like a charmed child.

"Hi there," Ghost said, hurrying down the stairs and stretching out a hand. "Mr. Dale?"

"Yup," Papa said, shaking Ghost's hand with a smile. "And you're Marvin's nephew for sure. That dark red hair and blue eyes give you away."

I'd only seen pictures of Marvin Kasper with white hair, and all the photos were black and white. It was strange to think he'd looked anything like Archie.

"I am, sir. Good to meet you. Would you want to come sit for a bit? We can get some coffee in the bar."

Papa nodded eagerly and followed Archie toward the door to the bar. Inside, he stopped short.

"Holy fried bananas," he whispered, chuckling again. "It's like Marvin is still here, holding court." He gazed around at the photos on the walls, taking in the long shined brass rail and the glazed windows up front letting sunlight spill in to light the room with a hazy glow.

"We cleaned up the bar first, hoping to start pulling a bit of income as we rebuild," Archie explained, going around behind the bar to start the coffee machine.

"Well you've done a bang-up job," Papa told him, settling himself onto a stool. "Though your uncle would be a bit disappointed that Rufus didn't get to come back."

I swiveled my head to look at my grandfather. "Rufus? Who is Rufus?"

He chuckled, his eyes aglow. "The old bear that used to

stand up there." He pointed to an alcove above the bookshelf that hid the cigar room, where there was an empty space that could easily hold a painting or a sculpture. Or a bear, I guessed.

"Oh, the bear," Archie looked guilty for a minute. "I saw him up in the storage room. Kinda freaky."

"He lives right there," Papa stated, pointing at the space again. "Marvin would insist on it. You were here as a kid," Papa went on, narrowing his eyes at Archie. "You don't remember Rufus?"

"I guess I do. I didn't know he had a name."

"There were others," Papa said, seeming to think for a moment. "They all have names."

Archie looked chagrined. "There's a whole herd of taxidermy animals up there."

Papa nodded as if everything he believed about life had just been confirmed. "And you'll bring 'em all out when you're finished up with the refurb."

Archie did not confirm this for him. To his credit, he didn't deny it outright, either.

Papa placed the long wooden box on the bar, and Will and Archie both leaned in to examine the engraved marking on the top.

"This is just like the one on the piece of map we have," he said. "Did Lucy tell you about the map?"

"She did," he said. "And you promised me coffee."

Will laughed and caught my eye over Papa's head, sending me a warm look that made my toes tingle.

"I did," Archie said, turning to pour a mug for Papa. "Cream? Sugar?"

"Black as the devil's soul, thanks." Papa accepted the mug happily. This was the most social interaction he'd had all week, and I could see that he was in no hurry to rush things. I glanced at my watch, a little worried about what might be going on outside, but Mateo was an experienced crew lead. He'd have things moving along according to plan.

"So this is the box Marvin left with me," Papa said, his big grizzled hand resting on top of the box, which was about as long as his arm, and just as wide. "He asked me not to open it, so I haven't."

Archie's eyes were glowing as he listened.

"Where's Aubrey?" Will asked.

"She and Wiley went to Denver this morning for supplies," Archie told us. "She said to go ahead."

Papa nodded as if this made perfect sense to him.

"Can we open it now?" I asked, curiosity getting the best of me.

"Please," Archie said.

Papa carefully unlatched the little gold latch to one side of the lid, and then lifted the lid carefully back. Inside, the box was lined with red velvet, and nestled into the fabric were several long white rolls of paper.

"More maps?" Will asked. He sounded disappointed.

"I don't think so," I said, catching a glimpse of some kind of artwork inside the end of one of the rolls. "Let's see."

I carefully lifted one of the rolls from the box and slid off the dried up old rubber band keeping it rolled. It resisted flattening, but I smoothed it on the bar top and Archie and Will held down the bottom.

"Voyage to Mandoon." I read the words across the top of the poster, as we took in the rest. It was clearly an old movie ad, showing a buxom woman and a man in an adventurer's hat standing in an embrace next to a jungle with a river running past. I could imagine something like it in a magazine in the 1950s or up outside an old theater.

"It's a movie poster?" Archie said, his voice a question. "Is that what all of these are?" He sounded a little disappointed.

We unrolled all the posters, weighting the curling edges with glasses from the bar, and then we walked the length of the bar, looking at them all. There were nine of them, each one a different film, but all of them pretty old. I hadn't heard of any of the films.

"Do you know these movies?" Archie asked Papa.

"Saw a couple of 'em back in the day," Papa said.

"Any idea why my uncle asked you to keep these for him?" Exhaustion laced Archie's question. Clearly, he'd hoped for something more, and I felt a little sorry for him.

"Not a clue, son." Papa sounded equally disappointed. "He liked movies, your uncle. Always entertaining movie stars up here when the place was open, you know." He pointed around at the black and white photos on the walls.

"Yeah," Archie said.

"Do you think we're supposed to work something out from the titles?" Will asked.

"Maybe," Archie said. "I'll get them all and we can work on it." He took pictures of each one with his phone.

"You want to hold onto the box?" Papa asked. I wondered if it was hard for him to give up—it was the last connection he had to Marvin.

"Would that be okay?" Archie asked him.

"Sure," Papa said. "I've got no use for it." He stood up from his stool, drained his coffee, and turned to look at me. "Guess I'd better get on back and let you get to work."

He turned to face Will. "You treat her good," he said in a low tone. "Or you'll have me to answer to."

I stared at my grandfather. Clearly, he couldn't resist a second longer. I loved that he was protective, but I was old enough to take care of myself. "Papa!"

Archie's eyebrows went up, but Will maintained a serious expression.

"I will sir," he said. "Thanks so much for coming today. Good to meet you."

"You too," Papa said. He turned to face Archie again. "Both of you boys. Don't be strangers, now. And get Rufus back up where he belongs if you don't want your uncle haunting you."

"If he haunted us, he could tell us what this hunt was all about at least," Archie said.

I felt bad for him as I walked Papa back out to the truck to take him home. Archie had a lot riding on the resort, not the least of which was his personal finances, I guessed. Will had hinted that Archie had some other things going on too, and I wondered how much it would affect him if this didn't all turn out like he wanted. I hoped he'd be okay.

"Nice kid," Papa said as we pulled onto the highway. "Think he's gonna stick around?"

"Which one?" I asked.

"The one you like. The pretty one with the hair. Will."

I lifted a shoulder and wished my stomach didn't thrill at just the mention of his name. "I doubt it," I said, hoping somehow I was wrong.

Chapter 23
Making Poor Choices is a Choice

WILL

Wh-hen Lucy returned, we were both so busy I barely had a chance to say anything to her all day. I caught her watching me once when we were both near the center doors of the resort, but as soon as I met her eye, she hurried away in the other direction.

Was Lucy avoiding me? Playing hard to get, maybe? Or did she think we'd made a mistake?

She left for the day without saying goodbye, and a little flicker of worry began to waver inside me. Had it been a mistake getting involved with her? She wasn't exactly an open book. I needed this project to succeed, and now I was worried I'd just thrown the proverbial wrench into the system.

But as much as I needed this job to go well, I was even more worried about things with Lucy. I had feelings where she was concerned, and while I wasn't quite ready to look at them closely, I knew I couldn't just shut them off either.

I met the others in the bar that night for a drink before dinner, and was impressed to see that Ghost had already found frames for the movie posters, which were hanging around the room beneath Marvin's photos.

"Got these up quick," I told him, swiveling on a stool to face the poster advertising 'Amazon Cruise,' another movie I'd never heard of.

"Thought there was a chance they'd mean something to someone when we open the bar tomorrow night. Maybe they can help us pick up the thread." He took a sip of his drink, staring at the poster. "Right now we're at a dead end."

I sighed and swigged my own drink. Dead end felt like the right expression. "At least construction out back is on schedule," I said, to remind us both that not everything was going wrong. And to remind Ghost that we weren't here for a crazy treasure hunt. We were here to launch this resort.

"Good." Ghost gave me an evaluative look. "And Lucy?"

"What are you asking me?"

"Things between you are . . ."

"I have no idea. Good? Or maybe nonexistent?"

"How could either be true?" Ghost turned his stool back to the bar, glancing around at the others, who were deep in conversation at the other end.

"I don't know. Things were really good earlier this week. I took her to the movie, and then . . ." I didn't kiss and tell, but was pretty sure Ghost got my meaning.

"Got it. Go on."

"But all week, we've been crazed managing the build, and today she took off without even saying goodbye. I think she thinks it was a mistake."

"Thinking what she thinks is always going to be a problem."

"From the guy who's clearly an expert on relationships."

"Hey, I've had relationships," Ghost said. "I just don't have one right now. I've got enough on my plate."

He definitely did. "And things for you are good?" I looked up at him quickly, then back down to my drink. We didn't talk openly about Ghost's mishap, the one that had ended his military career, but we all knew it weighed on him.

"I'm good. I mean, that's always gonna be there. But I'm good. And this resort, this project, even the hunt. It's like Uncle Marvin knew I needed something to focus on. I just hope it's not all some wild goose chase."

"The prize needs to be worth the hunt." I hoped Ghost was right about his uncle, but part of me worried maybe he'd just been a crazy old man. Maybe none of it made any real sense, and maybe there was no treasure.

"Right. And these posters . . ." Ghost trailed off and spun around again to look at the wall of old movie ads. "Not like it would have helped, but where's 'Casablanca?' 'Gone with the Wind?' Something I actually know about. Why these?"

"And have we even heard of these actors?" I asked. "Harry Maloney and Annie Lowe. Arthur Lenske and Juliette Hannigan. This one says, 'featuring Annette Arnold and Annie Lowe.'"

"Annie Lowe got a lot of work back in the day, I guess," Ghost said.

"Do you think that's it? Maybe it's not the movies, maybe it's the actors we're supposed to pay attention to."

Ghost scooted off his stool and I followed. Together we

walked the row of posters looking for common names. Annie Lowe was in quite a few, but not all of them.

"So maybe it's the mysterious Annie," I said. "But she's not in all of them."

"Who is Annie Lowe?" Ghost whispered, almost to himself.

Aubrey, who had left the others to stand along the row of posters, staring at them, pulled out her phone. "Annie Lowe was a popular Hollywood actress with a promising career, cut short by her mysterious disappearance in 1961. Ms. Lowe never resurfaced in Hollywood, and there was wide speculation about what might have happened to her. Some believed foul play might have been involved and a brief investigation into her then-fiancé, Rudy Fusterberg, was deemed inconclusive."

"Very mysterious," Monroe said.

"But not very helpful," Ghost said.

Brainiac had been quiet through all this, and now he turned to us. "The only way to see where we need to go next is to lay out all the potential avenues for exploration. We'll begin with the actual titles. I can write a quick program that can look for any ways they might fit together to spell words or sentences that might make sense."

We exchanged surprised looks. This was the Brainiac I remembered, but he'd been surprisingly reserved since arriving.

"We should also look at the actors, and any other names that appear on these posters. See if we can find commonalities, other movies the same people were in, or maybe they went to the same high school. Anything that links them. Aubrey, can you handle that?"

"Sure," she said, grinning. "I'm excellent at online stalking."

Wiley shot her a disturbed frown at this proclamation.

"We should also investigate the settings and plots of the films, maybe there's something there." Brainiac went on.

"I can do that, I guess," I told him. I still wasn't convinced this wasn't just a distraction, but at least Brainiac seemed to have a plan for attacking it.

"But the build comes first," Ghost said. "We all need to remember that. As much as I want to figure this thing out, we have to focus on making the resort operational and profitable in the real world. Which means bookings, Monroe . . . and Brainiac, can you start looking at the mountain? See how the lift looks and figure out what we need to open a run or two this season?"

"You're kidding," I said, not meaning to be quite so blunt.

"Just curious," Ghost said, a little defensive. "Might be impossible. But it's worth checking out."

"I'll take a look," Brainiac said.

"And in the background, we can keep working on Uncle Marvin's hunt," he said.

* * *

That night, I lay in my room staring at the cracked ceiling, letting my mind wander over whatever it wanted, and Lucy's face kept creeping back into my thoughts. Her expressive mouth, her fierce gaze.

I loved her face. I wanted to know more about what went on behind those lively blue eyes, and Lucy was hard to read. We hadn't actually talked much on our date, I realized. Snow White had done most of the vocalizing, at least until the end.

I reached for my phone.

Me: You up?

Lucy: Barely. Everything okay?

Me: Yeah, sorry. Get some sleep.

Three dots danced for a moment and then disappeared, and I was about to put the phone back down when a text popped up.

Lucy: I'm awake.

An invitation? I sat up, excited to talk to her, even by text.

Me: How'd things go today? I didn't get to see you before you left.

Lucy: Sorry, I wanted to get home to check on Papa. He was pretty tired after visiting this morning. He's having some bad days lately.

Me: That's hard. You think it's anything serious? Suddenly I felt guilty for assuming all of Lucy's actions had to do with me. Of course she was concerned if Papa was having a hard time.

Lucy: Not sure. He's all I've really got. And sometimes I forget he's almost 90.

I wasn't sure how to respond. I'd never been close with my grandparents.

Me: I think you're lucky to have whatever time you get with him. You're smart to take advantage of it.

Lucy: Your family...?

Me: We aren't like yours. Not super close.

I thought of the expectation I felt whenever I was around my dad, the disappointment that I brought him. I wanted to mention it, but didn't know how to bring it up. I'd talked to her a little bit about Dad. Maybe she didn't need to see that side of me anyway.

Lucy: I'm sorry.

Me: Are you going to drop by the bar tomorrow after work? I waited for her answer, hoping she would say yes, but preparing myself for her to say she'd need to be with her grandfather, or that she didn't think she could make it for some other reason.

Lucy: Last time I did that, I made poor choices.

Me: I know you aren't talking about me.

Lucy: I am.

I let that sink in. She thought I was a poor choice. But she'd gone out with me. There had to be something to that.

Me: So you would not make the same choice again? If, say, I invited you to help me choose a bottle of wine from the cellar tomorrow?

Lucy: Actually, I have a history of poor decision making. I probably would accept.

A thrill shot through me and I felt my lips pull into a grin.

Me: Good. I will definitely need to find some wine.

Lucy: I wish I was better at saying no.

Me: Ouch.

Lucy didn't respond again for a moment, and I let that last text sink in a bit. On the one hand, I was clearly so charming she couldn't resist me. On the other, she wished she could. Why?

Lucy: I'm just trying to protect myself.

Me: I'm not going to hurt you. I wasn't sure if I should be offended that she assumed things between us were destined to fail, that they'd end badly. Why would she even bother with me if she'd already decided?

Lucy: You might not hurt me on purpose.

Me: I think you miss out on some good things always planning for the worst.

Lucy: But then I'm not surprised when the worst comes.

Me: I'm going to work on distracting you from that fatalistic mindset. You can go ahead and prepare for the worst, but I'm going to show you

the best of everything between now and then. If you'll let me.

Lucy: I shouldn't.

Me: But you will?

It took a while for her to reply, but eventually she did, and while it wasn't the exact answer I wanted, it was an answer.

Lucy: Good night Will.

Me: Sweet dreams, Firecracker.

I had plans to make.

Chapter 24
Touring the Facility (and Cake)

LUCY

The bar at Kasper Ridge was even more packed than it had been the week before. Word was getting out, and everyone in a fifty-mile radius of the resort wanted to put eyes on the place. News about the hunt had gotten out too, and there was even an article about it in the *Kasper Ridge Review* (so at least four people had seen it.)

"Do you think this is going to be like that Forrest Fen thing?" CeeCee asked as we sat at the bar, martinis in front of us. I was trying to focus on my friends, but I kept searching the bar for Will, wanting to see him more than I should.

"What the hell are you talking about?" Bennie asked, her eyes lingering on the movie posters lining the walls.

"That treasure hunt a while back. Some rich old art collector hid an actual treasure chest and then published a poem, challenging people to go find it." CeeCee's eyes sparkled as she told us about it. "A bunch of people died, and the guy who finally found the treasure ended up getting sued or something."

"Um. Fun," Bennie said, nothing in her face agreeing with the word "fun."

"Can you imagine?" I asked. "Random people out here combing these mountains for gold?"

"Yeah, if you thought one city boy running the show was bad, what if every nut in the Los Angeles basin came up here looking for riches?" Bennie laughed, but that was because she didn't see Will standing right behind her. I'd seen him come in, but hadn't managed to warn her because I was too busy noticing how utterly amazing he looked.

His eyes met mine and he cocked his head to one side. "Who is the city boy running the show in this scenario, Luce?"

Busted. I smiled my best get-out-of-jail smile and got to my feet. "Didn't you need help picking out some wine or something?"

CeeCee and Bennie were staring at us shamelessly—they knew there was something going on, but I had to be selective about what I told them since neither one was good at keeping a secret.

Will glanced at my friends, but then reached for my hand and gave a little nod of his head. "If you're up for it."

"She is," Bennie said breathlessly.

I heard CeeCee giggle as Will led me toward the bookshelf that hid the cigar room, and as we passed through it and it swung shut again, almost all the noise from the bar faded. Will didn't say anything but I could feel his eyes on me as I turned and descended the stairs down to the wine cellar. As I neared the bottom of the curved iron staircase, the air around me took on a warm golden glow, and when I stepped down into the small space, I was surprised to see a small table set for two, fake flames gleaming in little candles in the center of the table. Faux candles flickered all around, set into the wine racks and onto shelves everywhere I looked.

Two silver domes covered plates set at each place at the table, and a silver wine chiller stood to one side, a bottle waiting inside.

"Looks like you've already chosen the wine for tonight." My voice was a little breathy as I processed the fact that Will had done all this for me.

"Well, the first bottle maybe," Will said, pulling out one chair for me.

I sat, trying to keep my rational mind in place, faced with this wildly romantic setting. No one had ever done anything like this for me before. And if you'd asked me, I'd have said I didn't want it. I'd spent so much of my adult life trying to be taken seriously by men, trying to prove I could operate in the masculine-driven world of construction, I tended to shy away from thinking about things like wine and roses. Sure, I liked a pretty dress and some devastating lipstick now and then, but I used those things to keep the men I worked with a little bit off balance. This was something else entirely.

This was romantic.

And my heart was racing.

"Do you like it?" Will asked, lifting the silver dome from my plate. There were three small plates inside, one with a dainty pile of tuna and avocado molded into a little tower, one with a small filet and a side of broccoli glistening in the light, and one with a delicate chocolate cake holding up a dollop of creme shaped like a star.

"Dinner?" I asked, surprised.

"I doubted you'd had time to eat, and I wanted to impress you. You know, in case you think I'm just some city boy up here trying to run the show." His sexy lips lifted in a half smile.

"I might have said that at one point," I admitted. "But I mean, this dinner . . . this is pretty city."

"You don't like it?" He sounded worried suddenly

"Are you kidding? This is what people up here drive four hours to Denver to get. Where did it come from?"

"Ghost is trying out chefs. I put in an order."

I lifted my fork and tasted the tuna appetizer. It was cool and tangy, some kind of citric sauce complementing the avocado perfectly. "Hire him," I breathed.

"It's a her."

"Even better!"

Will poured wine for me to taste and when I nodded my acceptance, he poured a glass for each of us. The sounds of the bar above were a distant hum in the background, and it felt like we were alone in a cave together. In a way, I supposed we were. A shiver ran through me as I met his eyes.

"You said something the other night," Will started, looking uncertain. "About me leaving."

"I did." I felt my spine stiffen in preparedness. This was where he told me his plans to stay through the end of construction. Or to make sure things were on track and then go. Or maybe he'd tell me he was going to stay forever, but he wouldn't. People who weren't born up here didn't stay here.

"Why do you expect me to leave?" He sounded legitimately curious, as if this was surprising to him.

"Do you plan to stay forever?"

"Is that part of the deal? Anyone you get involved with has to vow to never leave Kasper Ridge?"

I took a sip of my wine, heat rising in my cheeks. "When you put it that way, it sounds ridiculous."

"Is that what you expect, though?"

I put down my glass, meeting Will's eyes. "In my experience, people—especially worldly people with some education and experience of other places—don't tend to decide to put down roots in Kasper Ridge."

Will made a noise like he was considering this idea.

I swallowed hard. "I'll just ask you, then. What is your plan?"

A little smile flickered across his face and he took a sip of his wine, swirling the glass at eye level as if he was considering it. Or considering his answer.

"Tonight?" His smile was mischievous and hot as he purred the word.

"I'm trying to ask a serious question."

He shrugged. "I hadn't planned that far ahead. I'm here to do a job, and you're right if you're thinking that a job inevitably comes to an end at some point. You already knew that."

Something inside me deflated, but I managed to keep the light smile on my face. It was too late. I was already involved here, and he was absolutely leaving. At some point, the investment I'd accidentally made in this man would leave me hurting and alone. Just as it had several times before when I was too young to even consider that families moved, people left. Junior high. High school. Only I had a feeling that with Will, it would hurt much, much more.

"I'm not a big believer in making plans too far out," he went on. "Because things change. Things can happen that we don't expect."

"Right."

"You don't sound convinced."

"Of what? Of the fact that you're not answering the question?"

"You want me to tell you that I'll stay here forever with you?" The way he said it made me feel slightly ridiculous.

I put my glass down a little too hard, and wine splashed over the top. "Of course not. We just met. I would never expect anything like that."

Will offered me his napkin to wipe my wet hand, but I ignored him. I was irritated, angry, confused . . . mostly because he was pointing out how ridiculous my own expectations were. I focused on drying my hand with my own napkin, keeping my eyes firmly on my own body and away from his deep blue gaze.

"Hey," he said. "Lucy," he said more forcefully when I didn't look up at him.

"What?" I asked, exasperated—mostly at myself for letting this conversation ruffle me. Why did I care so much what this guy did? Why had I let myself become so invested in him?

"I'm not going anywhere. Not now, not in the foreseeable future. So can we just take things one day at a time?"

When I didn't answer, he went on.

"Here's the thing. I know I don't know you well. But there is something about you that is so intriguing, so compelling. You're like no woman I've ever met before, and when I'm not with you, I'm thinking about you. I'm trying to figure you out."

"You are?" The words were out before I could stop them. His honesty was screwing with my defenses.

"I am. I'm trying to figure out how you manage to own every room you walk into, garnering immediate respect from everyone in it. I'm trying to understand how someone so confident and forceful can have skin and lips that are so ridiculously soft I can't stop thinking about touching them again. And I keep wondering what I can do to hear that little noise you make again."

My face was on fire, and my pulse was racing. "Noise?" I gulped.

Will nodded, and the look in his eyes, lit by the flickering candles, was pure devilry. He was talking about sex.

"But before I can figure any of that out, you have to promise me something."

I took a long drink of wine. This entire situation felt completely out of control—but it was like being on a roller coaster: exhilarating and unpredictable. "Okay."

"Stop trying to plan everything. Just take the ride. Let's see where we end up. It'll be fun, Lucy Dale, I promise."

I let out a long sigh. I wanted to take the ride. I wanted to, but... "We work together. This whole thing is so far out of my usual comfort zone. I mean, I have rules, and—"

"Let them go."

"I think I already have." Even as I said these words I felt the last of my defenses fall.

"Good." He sat back in his chair and lifted his fork and knife, cutting a piece of steak and eating it as I watched.

He was a puzzle I wanted to solve too. I wanted to know everything about him. "Tell me about flying," I said, figuring it was a good place to start.

He grinned. "Flying a jet was like being hand-picked by God to go cloud surfing, and getting to be one of only a few people in the whole world to do it."

"Fun, huh?"

"And terrifying. It was fun, definitely. Thrilling. But there was a lot riding on it too."

"Of course. You're going pretty fast in a pricey plane."

"Well yes. But expectations, too. The squadron, the mission.

The CO. My dad." Will's eyes dropped at the mention of his father.

"Your dad? How was he involved?"

"He was in the Navy too. Also a pilot. Decorated and admired. Dad's a fucking hero."

Aha. A little door opened into Will's psyche, and I got a glimpse of what made him tick. It explained a lot. "So you followed in his footsteps?"

"Only in circumstance. I am not the hero he was. In his eyes I'm mediocre at best. At pretty much everything."

"And you hate that. You want him to be proud." It was like I suddenly had a view inside Will Cruz.

"Is that so unusual?" His eyes met mine again, challenging me.

"No. Of course not."

Will leaned back in his chair and frowned into his glass. "Maybe we could talk about something else."

"Sure," I said, realizing that Will's dad was his sore spot. I didn't want to push. I wanted to distract him instead.

For a few moments we ate in silence, the weight of Will's concerns about his dad pressing in on us. When he finally looked up again, I caught his eye and gave him a wicked grin.

"What?" he asked.

"I was just thinking that maybe I'd be able to do a better job helping with this renovation if I'd seen more of the accommodations here at the resort."

One side of Will's full lips hitched up. "Is that right?"

"For instance, maybe I should see your room."

Will grinned, and then his eyes dropped to the table. "Okay, but we're taking these." He scooped both chocolate cakes onto one plate and pointed at a wine bottle resting on a dusty shelf. "Grab that."

Laughing, we climbed the steps and sneaked out the cigar

room through the bar and to the sweeping staircase in the lobby. If anyone saw us fly past, I didn't care. I was too busy thinking about what would happen next.

"Follow me," Will said, and I rushed after him up the stairs.

I was going to live for today. It wasn't my style, and I tended to like to plan. But not planning had gotten me here, and here felt pretty damned good.

Chapter 25
Firecracker Goes Bang

WILL

It was as if a switch had flipped inside Lucy after I told her about my father. In that instant, she seemed to put aside all her hesitation and uncertainty—I watched the determination come into her gorgeous blue eyes. And there was no way in hell I was going to let that go to waste by insisting that we talk more about Dad.

Even if it had felt liberating to confess all of that to her.

I'd never told a woman about my complicated relationship with my father before. Why would I? I wasn't sure why I'd told

Lucy, except that she'd asked directly, but if this was the result of making myself vulnerable...

"I mean, I saw the third floor in the west wing, but this is worse. Do we call this shabby chic?" she asked, following me down the hallway where wallpaper hung in strips from the walls and the carpet was pulled up in sections at one side.

"I think we call it partially destroyed. But with a lot of promise."

"It does have promise, actually." Lucy's voice sounded unguarded at my side, honest and open in a way I rarely heard.

"It's going to be amazing one day."

"You'll make sure of it, Will." We'd come to my door, and those words had me pushing her back against it with my hips, caging her with my body so that I could capture her mouth in mine, even as I held a plate in each hand.

God, I wanted to believe her. I wanted to be as sure as she sounded in that moment that this would be the job I'd get right, that I would finally prove myself, that I'd be good enough for once.

"Show me your room," she said, her voice breathy and deep.

I put down the plates on the floor and unlocked my door. We stumbled inside together, my arms around Lucy so she wouldn't fall.

I'd actually had a couple pieces of furniture delivered, figuring I'd always find use for a quality couch and a good bed, along with the coffee table and leather chairs I'd added. The furniture that had come with my luxury accommodations at Kasper Ridge was falling apart, and while that was part of the charm and mystery of the place—I wanted to come back each day to something that felt a little more like home. A little more finished.

Lucy gazed around as I switched on the lamp between the leather club chairs. I watched her eyes take in the desk near the window, the long clean lines of the couch, and then stop at the doorway to the bedroom.

"This room is huge," she said, and she trailed her fingers along my arm as she moved to the plate-glass window, peering out into the darkness at what would one day be an impressive ski mountain. "We need to light this hillside," she said.

"It's in the plan."

She glanced at me, her eyes shining. "It is, you're right."

I went out to get the plates, and then set them down on the long counter at one side of the room, and moved to take the wine bottle from Lucy's hands. She put it onto the low table at her side and captured my hands, pulling my arms around her so that we were both looking out into the dark wilderness, her back against my chest.

"This place is going to be incredible," she said, sounding dreamy.

"It already is," I murmured, pressing my face against the soft skin at the curve of her neck.

She let her head drop back, giving me access to her throat and pressing her perfect breasts forward, begging my hands to cup them, pulling her against me more firmly.

I teased little circles on her flesh with my mouth, loving the sweet scent of her and the little breathy moans she made as my hands roamed her body. She pushed herself back against me, grinding against my erection.

She spun around after a moment, her hands dropping to my waist as her eyes danced with fire and lust. Lucy pulled my shirt from my jeans and then stepped close to push it off over my head before reaching for her own blouse.

"My job, Firecracker," I said.

She lifted her arms over her head, and I took a moment to let my hands trace down their lengths as her head tipped back and she let out another breathy moan that set me on fire. I lifted the shirt over her head, exposing her beauty and sending lust pulsing through me.

As her arms wrapped around my neck, her flesh pressing to mine, I kissed her softly. Her mouth was warm and pliant, and as I deepened the kiss, her lips parted and her tongue darted out, teasing and inviting me in. She took a step back, hissing as her warm flesh met the cool glass of the window, and I used the firm solidity of it to press into her harder.

I ended the kiss, pulling my head back for just a moment to gaze at her, to revel in her beauty. She was so unselfconscious, so sure of herself as she leaned back against the glass, watching me. It drove me wild. I'd been with women—enough to have the confidence I needed in this department—but none of them had been this self-possessed, this wholeheartedly confident of their own appeal and sexuality.

Lucy was a revelation in so many ways.

I dropped to my knees, letting my hands slide down her sides and peeling off her leggings as I slipped lower.

She moaned as I let a hot breath wash over the front of her panties, and then she reached down and pushed them out of the way, clearly telling me what she wanted. Again.

I nearly lost it right there as she stepped out of hers shoes and the clothing pooled at her feet.

My hands held her soft hips as I pressed my face close to her. Her scent alone had me struggling for control. I could have let go right there and called it one of the most satisfying experiences of my life. But she deserved so much more than that.

Starting with soft kisses and moving slowly deeper and firmer, I explored Lucy in a way I'd been imagining since the night I'd gotten a taste in the movie theater. The sounds she made were a soundtrack I hadn't even dared to imagine, so primal and needy that my brain was completely unleashed from my body, everything in me connected only to her, to her next response.

Her hands were in my hair, and her body was shuddering against the glass as she cried out, and when she added my name to the litany of words streaming from her mouth as she came, I felt like I'd won the Olympics and the World Cup combined, like I'd secured the top spot at Top Gun, or like my father had finally told me he was proud of me. It was everything. Everything.

Lucy's body went lax, her hands relaxing in my hair and moving to cup my cheeks as she slid down the window, coming to rest in my arms.

"That," she said, sounding breathy and spent, "was fucking amazing."

I scooped her up and stood, carrying her like a princess to the bedroom. I placed her carefully to one side of the bed, and peeled down the duvet on the other and then tucked her in, shucking off my pants and climbing in next to her, my head propped on my hand.

"Don't get all relaxed," she said, smiling up at me. "This isn't over."

"I'm definitely not what I'd call 'relaxed,'" I assured her. "Just giving you a break."

She shook her head against the pillows and reached for me, pulling me on top of her and kissing me, long and slow. I could feel every inch of her silky skin against my body, and when her hand slid between us, cupping my length, I thought it would be fine with me if this turned out to be my very last moment on earth.

Lucy stroked me as I kissed her, and the sensation rocketed through me, transporting me again to that incredible parallel universe where I was winning. At everything.

I rolled off of her to pull a condom from the nightstand, and as I knelt over her, she took charge again, guiding me exactly where she needed me to be.

Being welcomed into the soft heat of Lucy's body was like coming home—if home was a fucking erotic fantasy you didn't even know you were allowed to have. It was absolutely everything I'd ever be capable of dreaming about.

I moved slowly into her, reveling in the open surprise of her mouth, in the dreamy look in her eyes as she watched me over her. Her hands gripped my back, and I took my cues from the way she kneaded my flesh, from the way her moans came faster, more urgently.

I could feel her gripping my length deep inside her, and when that grip became a fluttering pulse, I lost it completely.

"Lucy," I said, hoping to signal that I was coming. But it was too late, Lucy was already crying out my name, her arms gripping me as she came.

My own release chased hers, and I thrust through it, gently at first—honoring her orgasm—but then faster and harder, needing to move. And when light exploded behind my eyes, my body following programming so basic and primal I couldn't begin to understand it, I had a fleeting thought about this being the very best of everything. About never letting it go. A word like 'love' flashed through my mind too, but I'd never put too much stock in ideas generated in the heat of a release.

Still, it had never happened before.

"These resort happy hours are really phenomenal," Lucy said, laughing. "I think they're gonna take off."

"Not everyone gets the behind the scenes tour, though." I let myself collapse to one side of her, wrapping myself around her warm, firm body and nestling my face into her hair.

"You'd have to charge for it. Like, a lot."

I lifted my head to narrow my eyes at her. "I'm not sure I like what you're implying, Ms. Dale."

She laughed. "I didn't mean to imply that you were a gentleman of the night, sorry. But I mean, if this construction thing doesn't work out..."

"I think whatever just happened had more to do with you than me," I told her. "Or the combination of us together."

She was quiet a moment. "It's not always that... that... ?"

"Never," I assured her. "Only with you."

She sighed, and then turned her head to look at me. "I never know if I should believe you."

That wasn't what I wanted to hear. "What? Why not?"

"Everything about you screams 'playboy' to me. And the things you say... they're just so... good."

"You think I'm feeding you lines?" I lifted my head again, propping my elbow to support my head. I didn't like this. I didn't want Lucy to think she was some fling, some dalliance in a line of women. I might not have been about to promise her this was forever, but I didn't like her thinking it was merely convenient either.

"I just don't know. I'm so far beyond my comfort zone. I've already broken all the rules I've made to keep myself safe. I'm out in unmarked territory here. And I just have this sense that you've got a bit more experience than I do."

"Luce," I said, desperately wanting her to have faith in me, to trust me. "This isn't some routine I run through regularly. With you, actually, I feel like I'm going completely on instinct." I paused, not sure how much more I should say.

Her eyes were on mine, hungry, pleading for something else.

"I'm not sure I've ever felt quite like this," I said, knowing I should be careful. Nothing here was certain. "This doesn't feel like a fling. It feels like... like something I'd like to explore. Something real."

Her beautiful eyes squeezed shut and then found mine again. "Are you looking for something real, Will?"

My heart squeezed at the vulnerability in her gaze. "I wasn't looking for anything when I came up here. But I'm so glad I found you."

Lucy watched me for another long breath, as if she was trying to make up her mind about something. And then she slipped her arms around my neck and kissed me, long and soft and sweet. And it was all the answer I needed right then.

Chapter 26
It's Gotta Be the Hair

LUCY

I texted the girls that night and stayed with Will, slipping out the following morning like a college girl doing the walk of shame—something I actually never did in college. It was my goal in life not to be ashamed of my actions. And when I got home the following morning, slipping in before Papa was out of bed, I sat down at the counter and thought about that.

I wasn't ashamed of the time I'd spent with Will. I wasn't ashamed of whatever this thing that was happening between us. Because as much as I'd tried to keep him at arm's length, it was becoming too hard.

We worked together. He was technically my boss. But I no longer worried that he underestimated me because I was a woman. If anything, his open admiration for my capabilities was part of what drove my attraction to him.

And that hair.

And the smile that made me feel like all that mattered in the world was getting to see it again. And the way he smelled. And pretty much everything about Will Cruz.

"You're smiling. Coffee that good?" Papa asked me, shuffling into the kitchen and sitting heavily in the chair across from me. "Will you get me some? Let's see if it makes me happy."

I stood and went to pour another cup. "You're not happy today?"

"I feel off."

I tried not to let those three words set off my internal alarms. "Off?" I asked, placing the steaming cup in front of my grandfather.

"It's nothing, Luce. How are you? Up pretty early on a Saturday." He gave me a wicked grin and I realized that I wasn't as sneaky as I thought I was. He clearly knew I hadn't been home last night.

I dropped my gaze to my coffee as I sat across from him.

"I should have called you. It was late by the time I knew I wasn't coming back, though. I didn't want to wake you."

"You're a grown woman, Lucy. You don't owe me a thing." The words were right, but the delivery was weak. Worry began to fizz in my stomach.

"Well, I'm sorry. I'll call next time."

Papa's eyes met mine. "Think there will be a next time, then? You like this guy?"

"I wish I didn't. Life would be a lot easier."

"Lot more dull if all you did was hang out here with me."

"That's not true. You're the most active eighty-eight-year-old man I know."

"Because the other eighty-eight year old men are dead." Papa delivered this line matter-of-factly, but it belied the sadness he'd often expressed at the reality that many of his friends had passed. I hated thinking about this, but I knew our days were numbered.

"That isn't true. Your poker club is almost all men over eighty."

"And Alice Henkins. Don't forget that old bat."

"Not nice."

"Just sayin."

I wasn't sure how to respond to that. "You feel okay though? Just a little sad today?"

"You don't need to worry about me, Lucy." Papa sipped his coffee and deftly redirected my thoughts. "You like this guy." It wasn't a question this time.

"I shouldn't."

"But you do." Papa nodded with what looked like satisfaction, his mouth a firm line and his eyes blinking slowly. "That's good. He's handsome. Successful."

"And most likely leaving."

Papa put down his mug a little too hard, sending a wash of coffee splashing down the side to pool around the bottom of the mug on the table. "If you're only planning to date men who live in Kasper Ridge, it's gonna be a pretty short list. Want me to write it up for you?"

I made a face at him. "I'm just saying. It's a temporary thing. A fling."

"Just a fling. Because neither one of you could possibly change your plans."

"I'm not leaving Kasper Ridge." We'd had this discussion. My life was here. With him. He'd raised me when no one else had been around to do it, and now he needed me. I wouldn't abandon him. Plus, I had a business here. One on the brink of a success that would carry me for years ahead. And the men who worked for me depended on me.

"Right."

"And Will isn't from here. He'll go back to the city at some point."

"And it's a long trip by wagon train to visit California." Papa shook his head grimly and sipped his coffee.

"I get it," I told him. "I'm just being realistic."

"You're just refusing to see the possibility," he corrected. "Lucy, let me tell you the one thing I know about life."

Papa knew quite a lot about life, but I allowed him to continue.

"You head out on a path. It might be the best path in the world, full of plans and reasons and all kinds of justifications that make it seem just right. And then you run into someone. And guess what? That person is on a great path too. But neither one of you planned to run into the other. And sometimes, it turns out that your paths don't just cross, they intertwine. Because you decide it should be that way." He traced a finger through the spilled coffee and looked up at me. "Your life isn't predestined. You decide. And you get to change your decisions based on new information."

I understood what he was saying, but there was more to it than a simple decision. And there wasn't a scenario possible where I left Kasper Ridge.

"Don't get so wrapped up in planning that you miss all the great things that happen along the way." Papa leaned back in his chair, and let out a tired sigh. His skin looked pale, and his shoulders hunched in a way I wasn't used to.

I lifted a hand to his forehead and he waved me off.

"I'm fine. Just off."

"Off worries me."

"Well, I'm old. Statistically, I'm probably gonna die at some point. And so are you, actually. Just later, I hope. See if you can do some living first, okay?"

I stared at him, worry and fear swirling with the elation I'd felt at the time I'd spent with Will the night before. "I'll try," I promised him as he rose and shuffled out to his big recliner in front of the television. "And you're not dying today," I added. He hated it when I fawned over him, but I'd need to make sure he got plenty of rest and fluids this weekend.

* * *

Papa remained quiet all weekend, and while nothing happened to make me think I needed to take him to the doctor, I was still worried when I headed to the resort Monday.

Will and I had texted all weekend, checking in and saying hello, mostly—but it had felt intimate, special. When I found him waiting for me outside the resort Monday, a little glow of happiness inside me burned brighter.

"Good morning," he said, opening the door to my truck and helping me down.

I glanced around to see if any of my crew was nearby. Mateo already suspected there was something going on, and while I wasn't necessarily hiding it, I didn't need them all whispering to one another either. No one lingered nearby.

"Hi," I said, my voice sounding more dreamy and singsong than I remembered it.

Will kissed my cheek and whispered in my ear. "I thought about you all weekend. I missed you."

A thrill shot through me, and my mind reeled back to Friday night, my back pressed against the cold dark window in his room as his mouth explored me. "I missed you too," I admitted.

"Have dinner with me tonight?" he asked, and the hopeful smile on his face made my heart twist around inside my chest.

"Here?"

"Or in town."

I thought about Papa, felt the little spike of worry that had dogged me all weekend. "Why don't you come over?"

"Will your grandfather mind?"

I shook my head. "He'd love to see you. He's been in a funk. Maybe it'll help to have someone to talk to besides me."

Will's panty-melting smile spread across his sculpted lips. "If you're sure that's okay."

"I don't really cook," I told him. "It'll be something simple. Or we'll order in."

"I wouldn't be coming for the food," he said, a timbre in his voice that sent a shiver through me.

"With Papa there, we might not get to do that, either."

He straightened. "I'm happy to spend time with you. Period. No expectations, Lucy."

"Okay." As I finished getting my things out of the truck, I tried not to entertain the thoughts building in my mind. That this felt like something different than a fling. That I still thought it was dangerous because my heart was definitely involved. That I wasn't going to stop it.

I locked the truck and walked with Will inside the darkened lobby and up the stairs to Ghost and Aubrey's suite, where we met on Monday mornings. The crew had gotten started early, but I'd texted Will that I would be there in time for the meeting. I wanted to make sure Papa ate breakfast.

"So things are on schedule?" Archie asked as I finished explaining where the outdoor progress stood.

"I don't want to jinx it, but we're ahead of schedule," I said.

"That's why some of my crew is moving inside," Will said,

surprising me. He'd thrown this idea my way, but we hadn't discussed it. "If Lucy agrees, that is."

The little glow in me burned even hotter. He wasn't steam-rolling me. He wasn't taking over. He was asking for my go-ahead.

"Sounds like we can spare them," I agreed. "And that'll give us a jump on the lobby and common areas."

The interior work was essentially cosmetic. The structural engineers had suggested a few supporting beams be put in here and there, but the resort was sound for the most part.

"What about the receiving drive out front?" Aubrey asked.

I saw Will's mouth move as if he was going to answer, but then he turned to look at me.

"That's the next outdoor phase once the patio is complete out back. I think we'll be there in the next two weeks."

She nodded and grinned at her brother. "This is really happening!"

"It is," he agreed, though Archie didn't look as delighted as his sister. "And what about the movie posters? Anyone come up with anything?" The hunt was becoming equivalent to the reno-vation in these meetings. If things weren't on track, I'd worry about the distraction.

"They were all produced in the same six-year span," Brainiac said, speaking for the first time all morning. "And the single commonality, besides Annie Lowe being in most of them, is the company that did the production, Mountaintop Films."

"What's their story?" Aubrey asked, leaning in.

"Not quite sure," Brainiac said. "Internet records are sketchy and inconsistent. Looks like it wasn't a big operation. Maybe one guy, maybe a couple."

"Names? Anything we can follow from here?" Archie asked.

"I'll keep digging."

Archie nodded, his face grim. "Did you hire that chef, Monroe?" We'd all agreed that the food produced Friday night was incredible, and that we needed to hire the chef who'd produced it all right away.

"Uh, no," she said, one painted nail raised to her lips. She tilted her head to one side and blinked at Archie. If I didn't know how smart she was, I'd potentially be buying her blond bombshell act. She was good at it. "Not sure she's really available for a job this big."

"Well for now it's only Friday night bar food and a few special events," he pointed out. "Is she working somewhere else? Maybe we can't afford her."

"It's more about her qualifications," Monroe said, straightening up. "She's not a trained chef."

"Not sure it matters," Will said. "The dinner she made for us Friday was incredible." He glanced at me for assent and I nodded my agreement.

"Plus, you brought her up here to do events," Monroe went on, watching Archie's face.

"I haven't hired a . . ." he trailed off, understanding dawning. "Wait, you?"

She grinned and tipped her head to one side.

"You made that food?" Brainiac asked, sounding as surprised as Will and Archie looked.

"I dabble," she said.

I tried to ignore the unfairness that a woman who looked like Monroe could be both a kickass fighter pilot and a fantastic chef, and focused on the conversation around the table.

"You're hired!" Aubrey shouted.

"She was already hired," Wiley pointed out.

"So the thing is, I've never done big scale stuff like actual restaurant work," Monroe said. "Just events."

"So you handle events. Maybe you create the menus? Then

we bring in someone else to run the restaurant kitchen?" Archie suggested.

"Okay," Monroe said slowly. "I guess that makes sense."

"Who knew you could cook like that?" Brainiac said, almost to himself.

"Well, I did," Monroe said, shrugging.

The meeting broke up, and I followed Will out to the hallway and to the top of the stairs, just a step behind him when he came to a full stop at the landing. He was staring at a man who'd just stepped into the lobby. Even in the relative darkness of the building's interior, it was easy to see the resemblance between them.

"Shit," Will breathed, just as the man glanced up.

"There you are, Will." He sounded put out somehow that he hadn't known where Will was from the second he arrived. An immediate dislike rose in me.

My suspicions about exactly who he was were confirmed when Will's body went rigid beside me. "Dad. Hi. What are you doing here?"

Chapter 27
Adult Supervision

WILL

"Things are on schedule out in LA," Dad said, in answer to my question. "Figured I'd come up and see what you guys are up to. A bunch of J-Os running some fancy resort? That was something I had to see to believe."

Dad never seemed able to move his mind out of military speak. We hadn't been junior officers for years, but to Dad, we were always a bunch of kids under his command.

"Oh." I didn't have warm words to welcome my father, and

he'd caught me on a morning when it had felt as if everything in the world was going exactly my way. But here he was, ready to cast his judging eye over everything I'd been cheerful about just moments before.

Lucy, as if sensing my discomfort, placed her hand on my forearm and gave it a little squeeze. I glanced at her, the calm crystal of her eyes centering me, and pulled myself together.

"Dad, I'd like you to meet the foreman we hired to oversee the resort renovation, Lucy Dale. Her company is the best in Kasper Ridge." I said this as we descended the stairs and came to a stop in front of my father, who stood in the center of the open space as if he owned the place. And as always, was disappointed.

"Well, Miss Dale, it's a pleasure to meet you. Hope you're not pushing my son around too much." Dad smirked like he'd just made a charming joke, and extended a hand to Lucy.

"It's nice to meet you," she said, shaking his hand and standing taller somehow. "Actually, it's nice to work with someone with as much experience as Will has. I think my mountain construction background and his years of working every aspect of jobs really complement one another. He's a professional, for sure."

Lucy's words made me want to scoop her up and carry her to my bed again, but that wouldn't have been quite the right move in this exact situation. They also warmed me with pride. Dad had never spoken that way about me, and we'd worked together for years.

Dad considered Lucy with his steady gaze for a moment longer than I would have liked, and then turned his look to me. "That right?" he said, clearly amused that someone would offer such glowing praise to his hopeless son. My stomach churned.

"Yes sir. We're ahead of schedule, actually. And if we want

to hang on to our lead, I'd better get back to it. Nice meeting you." Lucy smiled at Dad and turned to go, shooting me a sympathetic look over her shoulder. She knew enough to know that this reunion wasn't necessarily going to be pleasant.

"Cute little thing," Dad said, when Lucy was out the door.

"She's the most capable foreman up here," I said, feeling steam begin to accumulate under my collar. I had been far too relaxed to prepare properly to defend against Dad's brand of bullshit today.

He laughed at this, which only served to steam me up more.

"Show me around, son." Dad clapped me on the back, and I tried to tamp down the frustration I felt that he'd dropped in without notice, that he thought he was still the senior officer, that he could bend everything in the world to meet his own needs.

I'd just gotten a handle on my emotions when a burst of laughter floated down from upstairs, and the voices of my friends grew louder. We turned as Brainiac, Wiley, Ghost, Aubrey, and Monroe came down the stairs, and I noticed my father draw himself taller out of the corner of my eye. As if he was getting himself into attention, ready to address his inferiors.

I sighed and steeled myself. "Hey guys," I called. "Come say hi to Dad."

"Sir!" Brainiac said, surprise clear in his voice.

"Hey, it's Terminator," Ghost called, sounding happy to see Dad.

My friends stood in front of my father, none of them quite able to keep themselves from coming to attention—old habits die hard, after all.

"Good to see you all," Dad said, shaking hands and patting them on the shoulders. "I don't think I've met you. I'm Dan Cruz." He looked at Wiley and Aubrey.

"Wiley Blanchard, sir," Wiley said.

"We call him Coyote," I added, and then felt like a moron when Dad didn't even glance at me.

"And this is my sister, Aubrey," Ghost said.

"You've got quite a crew here," Dad said, putting on his friendliest act. "Will was just about to give me the grand tour."

"Great," Ghost said, sounding like he meant it. I shot him a scowl behind Dad's back. The last thing I needed was all these guys kissing up just because Dad once outranked them. We were all civilians now, and being an asshole in civilian life meant people shouldn't kiss your ass.

Only maybe Dad was only ever an asshole to me.

With that cheery thought in mind, I turned back to my father. "Well, you've seen the lobby."

He chuckled. "Leaves a lot to the imagination," he said. "But I can see the promise."

"Right?" Ghost seemed to take this as his cue to explain exactly how the place would look when we got it open. He led the tour, guiding Dad around as if he was a visiting dignitary while the rest of us followed behind like his faithful servants.

"You could have called, Dad," I pointed out as we wrapped up. "Where are you staying?"

Dad looked between me and Ghost. "This is a hotel, isn't it?"

"No problem, sir," Ghost said, shooting a look at Aubrey, who seemed to know this was her direction to go get another room ready for habitation.

"We've got lots of rooms," she said. "They're not all . . . up-dated yet."

"Aubrey, I've gotten a good night's sleep in places most folks wouldn't be willing to leave their garbage. It'll be fine." He gave her his winning grin and then looked around at the rest of us.

"You've got a big job here, guys. Looks like you're on the right track, though."

It wasn't quite praise, but at least he wasn't cutting us down.

"Thanks, Sir. I sure hope so." Ghost practically saluted.

"You know, at this point you can probably just call me Dan," Dad said.

"Old habits," Brainiac said. "We can try, Sir. I mean, Dan."

"Great," Dad said. "Well, I've got some work to do—I imagine you all do too. If Will here can show me a spot where I can make some calls and get on top of a few things, I can let you all get back to it. Maybe we can have dinner later? Is there a restaurant around here?"

"There is, Sir," Monroe said, maybe stepping in before one of us volunteered her to cook. "The Surly Fox. Very . . . local."

"Sounds good. Six thirty?" Dad was already ordering everyone around, even though he'd just reminded us himself that we were no longer under his command. Some things never changed.

"Great," Wiley said. "I'll go help Aubrey with your room. You're welcome to work in the bar, Dan. There's a few tables in the back where you can spread out."

"Excellent. Thanks, son." Dad looked at me expectantly.

"Uh, should I help you get your things?" I asked.

"You've got work to do here, don't you? Why don't you get to it? I'll see you later." Of course. If I'd told Dad I needed to get back to work, he'd tell me that a good son and a good host would help a guest with his bags. But suggesting I help with his bags got me chastised for not taking work seriously. I would never win.

"Sounds good." I turned on my heel and headed for the back, my mind suddenly roiling with thoughts I'd pressed securely down when I'd left California.

I'd never live up to his expectations. I could never make him proud.

Why did I even care?

Why the hell was he here?

Lucy caught my eye as I stepped outside, and I wanted desperately to run to her, scoop her into my arms, and bury myself inside her, hopefully erasing everything that had already happened this morning. But fucking Lucy wouldn't make Dad go away. And even if he left now, the weight of his judgment and expectation would linger.

I gave Lucy a quick wave and turned to the east patio, where my crew was beginning to install the stonework that hung on the thick square columns supporting the upper deck, and on the low walls that surrounded the hot tubs.

My phone dinged in my pocket about an hour later, and I pulled it out to see what it was.

Lucy: Everything okay? You don't seem happy to see your dad.

Me: I'm not. And he made plans for me tonight, so I'll have to take raincheck on coming over. The thought of spending the evening with my father instead of with Lucy brought a dark cloud floating over me, despite the bright sunny day.

Lucy: That's okay. See your dad.

Me: Will you come? 6:30 at the Fox.

Lucy: I'll come for a bit. I'm worried about Papa.

My own selfish concerns were muffled as I read these words.

Me: Is he okay?

Lucy: I think so. Just a little off this weekend. Just want to be around if he needs me.

Me: Of course.
Lucy: You'll be okay, right?
Me: He's my dad.
Lucy: That's why I'm asking.
I smiled. She got it.
Me: I'll be fine.

Chapter 28
Susan is Less Great

LUCY

I met Will and the rest of the group at the Surly Fox that evening after swinging by home to change and check on Papa. He assured me he was fine. But his face was pasty, and he didn't appear to have moved from his spot in his favorite chair since I'd left that morning.

"I'll bring you a burger," I told him, but he waved me off. And that was even more concerning. Papa and the burgers from the Fox were one of history's great love affairs.

When I arrived at the restaurant, Mateo and a few of the guys from the crew were seated at the bar. I caught Will's eye and then went to the bar to say hello to my employees. Sure, I saw them every day in hardhats and flannel, but it was nice to get a moment to say hello as a human being.

"All good, guys?" I asked them. Sometimes in the noise and chaos of the construction environment, we didn't really get a chance to catch up.

Mateo gave me a smile that didn't quite reach his eyes. "All good, boss."

I glanced at Tony and Chris, the two guys sitting with him. The looks on their faces didn't scream "all good." I'd known Mateo and Chris since we were kids. Tony was a newer addition to our group, but his family lived here, and he was clearly staying.

I frowned and plopped myself onto the chair at Mateo's side, signaling the bartender for a beer. "Tell me."

"No, Lucy, don't worry, it's nothing." Mateo's weak smile made me worry.

"It's not Lily," I said, hoping that by making this an assertion instead of a question I'd somehow ensure that nothing was wrong with Mateo's adorable daughter. He'd been raising her himself since his wife had died unexpectedly when Lily was only two.

"Lily's great," he assured me, a little glimmer of fatherly pride erasing some of the worry he'd been wearing in his expression before.

"But Susan is less great," Chris said flatly.

"What's going on with Susan?" I asked. I'd met Mateo's girlfriend a few times, and while she wasn't my cup of tea, they seemed solid.

"Bailed," he said without emotion.

"Bitch," Tony added.

"Why?" I asked, the question out before I considered whether it was the right thing to say.

"You tell me," Mateo said, turning to give me a searching look. "Not ready for the whole insta-parent thing I've got going on, not prepared to spend her life with cracked fingers and lips at high altitude, not interested in seeing the same thirty people everywhere for the rest of her days?"

Mateo was reinforcing every worry I already had about the potential for long-lasting love in my hometown. I glanced past him to where Will sat with his father and his friends, the group of outsiders laughing loudly and bringing an atmosphere of fun to our regular mountain cafe that would fizzle back into nothingness when they all decided they'd had enough.

"I'm so sorry," I told him.

He rubbed a hand over his chest, tilting his head to one side as if to stretch his neck. "It's fine."

"It sucks," I said.

"It does," he agreed, and I saw the sadness on his face then, deepening the light green of his eyes, pulling his lips tight. "Lily loved her."

I nodded, hating the thought of tiny Lily sad. "Did you?"

"Maybe. I think so. Maybe not," he said. He let out a mirthless chuckle. "Shit."

"Seriously," Chris chimed in, lifting his glass. "Shit."

Tony lifted his glass and I raised mine. As one, we touched them together to Mateo's, and we all said, "shit," maybe a little more loudly than we'd intended.

I squeezed Mateo's shoulder and stood. "I need to get over there," I said, nodding toward the table holding all the Kasper Ridge Resort people. "But you can call me. Give Lily a kiss for me."

"Will do."

I carried my beer to the table at the far side of the restaurant and greeted everyone. "Sorry to be late. Nice to see you again, Dan."

I slid into the empty chair at Will's side, and his hand found my thigh a second later, as if he needed something to hold onto, to keep him grounded. A tiny thrill sizzled through me at the idea that I might be that for him.

"Nice to see you again, Lucy," Will's father said. "Great atmosphere here. You've lived up here your whole life?"

I nodded. "Except for college, yes."

"Quaint," Dan said, lifting a glass of something amber to his lips and sipping.

Quaint was a word tourists used to describe my home-town. It indicated charm, but also somehow implied it was less than something else. I was just as happy to have those souls head on back to whatever place they came from, wherever they judged to be more than Kasper Ridge. But even as I had this thought, Will's fingers on my leg made me wish it wasn't always true that people left. I didn't like admitting it, but I really wanted him to stay. I was starting to have stupid ideas about things like shared living arrangements, vows. Maybe kids.

"You doing okay?" I asked him as conversation turned to shared stories of the group's military days.

"Mostly," he said. "I just wish he'd given me a little notice."

"Is he staying a while?"

"Leaving in the morning."

"So you'll live." I was glad that Dan wasn't staying indefi-nitely. His presence clearly unsettled Will, who had just begun to cast off the arrogant façade and let me see the sweet capable man behind it.

"I'd do better if you snuck into my room tonight," he said, his fingers inching up my denim-clad thigh under the table.

I felt heat rise over my chest and desire flare deep inside me. "I can't," I told him. "Something's wrong with Papa. I need to keep an eye on him."

Will's hand stopped its exploration. "What's going on? You said he was 'off...'"

"I'm not really sure," I told him, worry making my stomach clench. "But he's definitely not himself."

"Luce, if you need to take him to the doctor or anything, don't worry about—"

"Thanks."

I ordered a burger for Papa, hoping he'd eat it if he smelled it, and waited while they prepared it. I excused myself less than an hour after I'd joined the little group. I wasn't honestly upset I couldn't stay, although I would have liked to hang out, if only to give Will an ally.

Everyone else was talking about their own missteps and funny episodes from their time together in the Navy, but Dan didn't tend to focus on himself. I didn't like the way he almost imperceptibly denigrated his son, but I guessed that me sitting here another hour wouldn't change a pattern that had no doubt evolved over many years.

When I had Papa's dinner in hand, I thanked the group for including me and rose. I would have kissed Will's cheek, but I wasn't sure if his father knew anything about our involvement, and I didn't want to give the man anything else to judge Will about. "I'll see you tomorrow," I told them. "Safe travels, Dan."

Dan stood and kissed my cheek. "It was lovely to meet you." At least the guy had manners. I cast one more glance at Will, who looked coiled to spring as he watched his father say goodbye to me.

* * *

The next night I did stay late at the resort. Will's father had left, and he invited me to have a drink in his room. Papa had seemed about the same that morning, and I wondered if he was depressed, if there was something going on that I didn't know about. I knew I'd need to find out a little more, but Will seemed to need me too.

And if I was honest, I needed some time with him.

I'd quickly grown used to having something of a partner in him, at work and outside of it. Will understood me in some way I hadn't known I'd needed to be understood, and once he'd quit trying to prove himself to me and I'd gotten past his ridiculous good looks, it had become clear that we were a good team. It was nice having someone around who I knew had my back, who cared how I was feeling, and who I could share my thoughts with.

And as much as it was nice . . . it was terrifying. Needing someone set you up to be hurt.

Still, as I knocked on Will's door after changing out of my work clothes, a feeling of delicious anticipation washed through me. It wasn't only to do with the way his touches and his kisses made me feel. It was the way *he* made me feel. Seen, appreciated, understood.

I was so screwed.

When Will opened the door, a noise escaped his throat that was somewhere between a grunt and a moan, and at the same time, he reached for me and pulled me into a kiss that sent heat flooding my body.

He kissed me like a man who wasn't sure of his next step, his next breath, but who knew this one thing might save his life. He kissed me like I was everything.

And when he let go, he gave me a sheepish smile. "I've been needing to do that for days."

The heat and sheer want were crowding my mind and making it hard to talk, so I just took Will's hand and let him lead me to the sidebar next to the couch.

"Wine?" He asked. "Or whiskey."

"Whiskey please."

When we each had a glass, we went out to the patio beyond the glass doors at the side of his suite and took seats staring out into the enormous trees and sweeping indigo sky just visible over the edge of the mountain.

"You doing okay?" I asked him, each of us looking ahead.

He sighed. "Yeah. Dad just makes everything feel less real, if that makes any sense."

"What do you mean?" For a second I wondered if he was talking about us.

"Like nothing I've done matters. Like it's all some cute game I'm playing, because if it isn't his, or done his way . . . I don't know."

"I think he's threatened by you."

Will nearly spit out the mouthful of whiskey he'd just sipped. "Not in this lifetime."

"I can't think why else he'd be constantly undermining you in front of your friends."

Will looked at me then, the line between his eyes deepening. "You think he does that?"

I nodded, wondering how deep into someone else's complicated parental relationship it was okay to poke my finger. "Any time he talks about you, it's with this strange mix of pride and something else. Like ownership or something. And when you talk about things that have nothing to do with him, he inserts himself."

Will's face cleared slightly. "Yeah."

"It's almost like he's proud of you, but doesn't know how to express it, so he tries to own you instead."

He didn't say anything, but his eyes remained on my face, as if he could read more there.

"I'm sorry," I said, realizing I probably had no right to speak. "I spent my life watching other people with their parents. It's not a relationship I'm qualified to talk about, actually."

"I'm sorry, Lucy." His voice conveyed his sympathy—he knew my parents were dead, but I hadn't told him much about it.

"No, I mean. That's not something I'm sad about anymore. I grew up without them. My life is just a different version than yours in terms of family, that's all. But I'm saying I can't judge how your dad feels or what he thinks. I shouldn't try."

"But I think you're right."

"Yeah?"

"Yes. He came up here, expecting to see me failing, I guess. But instead, you and Ghost told him how well things were going, that we were ahead of schedule, that I was actually doing a good job managing this shit."

"You are."

"With your help," he said.

"So he's proud."

"But what you said, about him inserting himself. You're not wrong."

I took a sip of my whiskey letting it slide down my throat with a delicious vanilla burn.

"He wants to invest."

"What?"

"In the resort. He wants to infuse the place with cash so we can get operations running. He thinks it will be a success." Will's tone made it clear he didn't like this idea. I wasn't sure I did either.

"It will be," I assured him. "But do we need him?" The thought of big city money—beyond what Will had already invested himself—coming into play here gave me pause. Would Dan want to bring in his own people? His own equipment? Would he take over?

Would I be out of a job?

Suddenly, I didn't feel like drinking. I set the glass on the low table in front of the railing. "Is Ghost going to let him?"

"He's considering the idea. Dad hasn't made a formal offer yet."

"You have a say too. You've got an equity stake." The thought of Will's dad sweeping in and taking over worried me. A lot.

"But it's ultimately up to Ghost and Aubrey. This is just a job for me, but it's their future."

It was just a job for him. Meaning there was an end point. And if his dad helped, accelerated the process . . . never mind what that might mean for me and the guys who depended on me for work, for security. That meant accelerating the end date on whatever this thing was between me and Will.

"Hey, I have to get back," I said, standing.

Will's face fell, and for a moment I considered staying. I knew being around his father was hard for him, I knew he could use a little shoring up. But I had my own worries too, and even though I'd thought Will and I were both becoming invested in this thing between us, it didn't seem like he was thinking about us when he considered his dad's proposal. He was only looking at it as a job. From a distance. The knowledge put a sick feeling deep inside me.

"I need to check on Papa," I told him. "See you tomorrow."

"Yeah. Okay," Will said, following me to the door. "Goodnight Lucy."

"Bye." I left without turning around, though I wanted to stop and kiss Will again. I made myself go, feeling his eyes on me as I practically fled down the hallway.

Chapter 29
Cruz-Colored Tornado

WILL

I watched Lucy leave with a confusing mix of emotions racing through me. I wanted her to stay. That part wasn't confusing at all. Lucy's very being was like the exact chemical combination I never knew I needed. When she was around, I felt alive. I felt seen and valid, and like a good person.

But it wasn't that.

The confusion, I suspected, was due much more to my father's unannounced visit, and the things he'd said while he was here. His words still echoed through my mind, coming to me over and over on repeat.

"You're doing a good job up here, Will. I'm proud of you. Coming up here was a good business decision. I think it'll pay off for you."

I'm proud of you.

You're doing a good job.

I'd done my best not to show how those words had affected me when he'd said them—in front of Ghost, no less. But I swear to god, hearing the exact words I'd been wishing he'd say since I was five years old was overwhelming.

And the thing was, he didn't even seem to notice.

The man I'd spent my life trying to impress, the guy I'd wished so many times would just tell me I was enough for him had finally told me it was true. And he'd delivered the line as if we were just chatting about the weather. As if he told me every day that he was proud of me.

There was something unsatisfying about finally getting what I thought I'd always wanted, and I couldn't figure out why. Was it because it felt like he was trying to edge in on the great thing I'd found? Because the second he thought I might have gotten a step ahead of him, he threw a huge sum of money at it, trying to take a bigger piece?

Then again, how much more faith in me could I ask for from the man I'd thought would never show any? Not only did he tell me I was doing a good job up here, but he was so impressed he wanted in himself. Dad's love language was cold, hard cash, so for him this was the ultimate declaration of adoration.

Maybe.

Or else he just didn't like that I'd finally found something of my own, something that didn't rely on his reputation.

I wanted to believe the best, but I honestly didn't know what to believe. And if Lucy's face when I mentioned Dad's offer of money was any indication of what might actually be going on, then I should follow my instincts and say no. Only it wasn't up to me at all.

I went to bed early that night, my head full of conflicting thoughts and my arms feeling empty, wishing Lucy had stayed. I didn't sleep well, my dreams full of Dad and Lucy, and bizarre situations where I could never quite do that thing I was meant to do. Fill a swimming pool with punch using a hose that didn't reach far enough. Save the puppies from a burning building, only the tiny mutts were multiplying somehow, and every time I delivered an armload to safety, I'd return to find thousands more waiting for me to rescue them. By the time the dusky gray light of another day drifted through the windows in my bedroom, I was exhausted and also eager to get up.

Because daylight meant work, and work meant Lucy Dale.

Except I had a message from her on my phone.

Lucy: Taking Papa to the doctor. Mateo will run the crew today.

Every bit of worry from the night before grew and multiplied like those damned puppies, filling the vacant spaces in my mind. Papa was really sick . . . I knew Lucy would be upset—she'd been upset already. I wanted to go to her, but the cool tone of her text and the way she'd left the night before gave me pause. Maybe this was something she needed to handle alone.

Me: Okay. Thanks for letting me know. Hope Papa is okay.

I wanted to add more, but I deleted the additional words as soon as I saw them appear on the screen. Did Lucy need to know I'd miss seeing her? That I wished she'd stayed in my arms the night before? That I wanted her there every night? None of it seemed like the right thing to say now, in a text, as she worried about her grandfather.

I shoved my phone into my pocket and headed to the kitchen to find breakfast.

"Fake Tom," Ghost greeted me. He was leaning against one of the long steel counters in the kitchen next to Brainiac, each of them eating toast. "Colonel Cruz sure blew in and out of here like the wind, huh?" He grinned at me, shaking his head.

"More like a fucking tornado," I said, too much of my confusion about Dad coloring my voice.

"Good to see him," Brainiac said. "Kind of still unnerves me, though."

Ghost nodded. "Yeah, I'm always worried he's going to report me to someone, give me some extra shitty duty."

The two of them laughed, but I didn't have any humor where Dad was concerned. "Pretty much the story of my life."

Ghost watched me for a long beat. I could feel his evaluative eyes on my back as I poured myself a cup of coffee. "Think he was serious?" he asked.

I turned and looked at him, finding a seat on the counter opposite him. I was about to answer when Monroe's voice broke in.

"If I'm supposed to be running this kitchen, then counters are for glasses, not asses," said Monroe, coming around the corner with a plate of scrambled eggs and bacon in her hands.

"I'm not an ass," I told her, smiling sweetly. "You love me."

She frowned at me, her light brows drawing together over the eyes that had mesmerized way too many junior officers back in the day. "I don't love you. I tolerate you. And we don't know where that butt has been." She put down the eggs and swatted me off the counter.

Brainiac and Ghost laughed as we followed Monroe to the bar to eat.

"We need to get some tables set up in the restaurant,"

Brainiac complained as we followed the scent of bacon through the big empty lobby.

"No point when we're just gonna rip the place apart soon," I told him.

"Sooner than later if your dad has anything to say about it," Ghost said, sounding like he was entertaining this idea.

"Bacon!" Wiley and Aubrey were already in the bar, restocking and cleaning. We spent more time in the bar than we probably would otherwise, but since it was the only real finished space at the resort, we gravitated to it.

Plus, alcohol.

"So let's talk about that," Aubrey said, lifting a piece of bacon to her lips.

"About bacon?" Monroe asked. "Crispy enough?"

"It's perfect and you know it," Brainiac said, elbowing her at his side. "You're just fishing for compliments."

She smiled and batted her eyes at him, making me wonder yet again if there was anything going on between them.

"Yeah," Ghost said, looking serious as ever. "If Colonel Cruz is for real, that kind of cash and focus up here could get us fully operational within the year. No more phased approach. We could knock it all out at one time."

I nodded. My resistance to this idea was emotional, and I knew it. I didn't have any logical arguments, so I kept it to myself.

"But then we've got Colonel Cruz to answer to," Monroe pointed out. "Which might be just a bit too nostalgic for my liking." And mine.

The others nodded.

"I don't really see how we can say no," Aubrey said. "What's the downside besides you guys being weird about a man you used to have to report to being in charge?"

"It's our place, not his," Ghost said, echoing the thoughts in my own head. It made me feel better that Ghost was the one who said this.

"It would still be ours. He'd just be our main investor." Aubrey reached for another piece of bacon.

"Fake Tom, you've got an equity stake at this point. What do you think?" Ghost asked me.

I blew out a slow breath, searching for words that represented my logical resistance rather than my knee-jerk emotional reaction to the idea. "I've worked with Dad most of my life. The last few years, in this business. So I know how he operates. And while he's a smart businessman, he's also controlling and demanding. He gets an idea of how things should go, and doesn't always want to hear from the people making it happen why that might not be the best plan." It was a fair assessment, and I had managed to keep it logical, not emotional.

"He's a micromanager," Brainiac suggested.

I nodded.

"And the size of his investment would pretty much put him in charge," Aubrey said, tilting her head to one side.

"I guess the question is, can we do this without him?" Monroe asked us.

"That's a good question," Ghost said. "I'm gonna think about it some more." He looked at me. "Don't say anything to Lucy. I don't want her to worry she might be out of a job."

My heart rate picked up a beat. "Shit. I already did." Was that why she'd left so quickly?

Ghost frowned at me, but his disappointed look was nothing compared to the one I'd grown up with.

"Sorry, man." I thought about his words for a moment. "But she wouldn't be out of a job, would she?"

He shrugged. "Your dad was talking about bringing in men and equipment. I guess it just depends on his plan."

Dad was already taking over. Suddenly it felt like everything I'd left LA to escape was coming here. Perfect.

I finished my breakfast in silence and carried the plate back to the kitchen after telling the others I'd see them later. For now, at least, I was in charge, and I had a project to run.

Just as I stepped out onto the back patio, the already frenzied activity, sunlight, and fresh air making me feel more optimistic, my phone vibrated in my pocket.

Dad: You're doing good work up there, Will. Give me a call. I've got a job down here that could use you at the helm.

I shoved my phone back into my pocket.

I couldn't think about Dad right now.

And yet, the things he'd said in the last twenty-four hours were pretty much all I could think about for the rest of the day. Why did he wait until I'd finally found something of my own to say everything I'd ever wanted to hear from him?

I'd finally found a place I belonged, a place where I felt capable and in control. I wasn't going to give it up just to go back to what I'd had before. But part of me wondered how it might be different now, with Dad's support and faith in me in place of that lingering disappointment I'd felt for so long. Hadn't proving myself to him been the impetus to come here in the first place. Had I accomplished my goal? Was it time to go back?

But Lucy Dale was here. In LA there was just a job.

Chapter 30
Broccoli for Papa

LUCY

"I eat fine." Papa was frowning at the salad I'd put in front of him at dinner. "I know how to eat. I've been doing it for almost ninety years, Lucy."

"The doctor said—"

"I heard that quack."

"Then you need to eat better and take vitamins." I stood over him, my arms crossed. He was behaving like a toddler.

The doctor had given him a B12 shot after explaining that vitamin deficiencies were very common in older adults, and discussing how they can contribute to a host of other issues. In

Papa's case, they were causing some mental fog and depression that had me worried about dementia, and I was eager to see things improve.

So he was taking vitamins and eating better, even if it killed me.

"Lucy, salads are lettuce." Papa was holding a sliver of beet aloft on his fork and inspecting it as though it might leap off the tines and attach itself to his face. "Not whatever the hell this is."

"That's a beet."

"Not meant to eat."

"It is."

"Prove it." He held the fork out to me.

I took the fork and ate the beet while Papa made a face.

That was about all I could take. I dropped into the chair across from him. "You don't want to eat it? Fine. Don't eat it. I give up."

Papa dropped the fork and watched me for a long beat during which exhaustion and worry swelled within me until I actually thought I might cry. "I'll eat it," he said quietly, picking the fork back up and tucking another beet between his lips. "I'll eat the whole thing."

"Good." I sniffed, still on the verge of tears, which was infuriating. I didn't cry. I'd made a policy of that when I was a kid. If I let myself cry, I'd be in tears all the time. There was usually something worth crying about when you were an orphan, but I decided a long time ago that self-pity was a bad look on me.

"I'm okay, Lucy. The doctor said so."

"I know. I'm glad. It's not just you I'm upset about, I guess. But I am worried about you."

"You looked like you might cry about this beet here." He pointed to his mouth.

"It's not about the beet. It's everything."

"I'll eat all this other crap too. Even this stringy lettuce stuff I hate."

"Good."

"So while I eat this delicious and nutritious food, you tell me why you look like you might cry. Is it that out of towner at the resort?"

I shook my head, feeling like it was everything and nothing all at once. But then I thought about it more. "I don't know. Maybe? I'm all turned around."

"That's a man, if I've ever heard a woman talk about one. When your Mimi was mad at me, that was the kind of thing she said." He took a bite of arugula. "And she'd approve of all this, you know." He pointed at his salad again.

I nodded. I missed Mimi. She took care of us both. And as I watched Papa eat and tried to make sense of the confusing feelings inside me, I realized that taking care of people was a thankless and exhausting job. I should have shown my grandmother more gratitude.

"So tell me what he did. If it's real bad, I'll load up my shotgun and head over there."

I chuckled, feeling my heart lift a little at Papa's loyalty. "Definitely nothing shotgun-worthy, but thank you."

"What then?"

"I don't even know. I mean. I do, kind of. His moneybags father rolled in yesterday and proposed to bankroll the whole renovation, for one thing." The worry I'd felt about the security of my job, my company rose in me again.

"So that's a good thing. Maybe."

"Not if it means bringing his own crews and equipment in. That means I'm letting people go. Again. While I scramble for a job that can save the company. There's not enough construction up here to go around, and this job was my peace of mind for at least the next two years." I thought about all the good people I employed, about Mateo, Tony and Chris, and their absolute faith in me. I didn't want to let them down.

Papa nodded. He knew the difficulties of running this business better than anyone.

"But I guess it'd probably be the best thing for the Kaspers, to get the place open as soon as possible." I hated the idea—all that big city bravado rolling into town. I also hated the thought of Will bowing down to his dad, playing second fiddle as his father clearly seemed to expect.

"Kind of rocks the boat, I guess." Papa ate a banana pepper ring and made a face. "That does not belong in salad."

"Fine. No more banana peppers." The turmoil inside me was threatening to erupt.

"That was not a banana."

I dropped my head onto my arms.

"So you don't want the big bossy dad guy up here. I get that. I bet no one else does either."

"He's got the money." My voice came out muffled from between my arms.

"Marvin had money. Archie just needs to find it."

I lifted my head and squinted at Papa. He believed there was actually a fortune hidden somewhere? "Do you know where Marvin put it?"

He shook his head. "Nope. He was pretty broke when he died, actually."

"Well, that's helpful."

"But he wouldn't have set up a treasure hunt to nothing."

"So far we've got movie posters. But you knew that."

Papa nodded. "You guys get Rufus out of retirement yet?"

I tilted my head. "Eat your vegetables. You're still not making any sense."

"The bear."

"Oh. No. I don't think 'tasteful taxidermy' is really the

aesthetic Archie is going for." I wrinkled my nose thinking about the smelly old stuffed bear in the storage space at the lodge. I'd seen him when I'd done my initial assessments, and he looked like a terrifying mangy artifact.

"Rufus was important to Marvin. Just saying."

I sighed.

"Listen, Luce. I'm going to eat all of this, okay?" He pointed at his salad. "The doctor gave me that shot, and you got me these here vitamins." He held up the bottle of multivitamins we'd bought on the way home. "I'm going to do all the things, so you don't have to worry about me. Why don't you go over to the resort and see that young man of yours?"

I did want to see Will. The last words he'd said were still ringing in my head—that this place was just a job for him. I wished I didn't care so much, that I hadn't let myself get so invested. But now the idea of him leaving was one I hated.

I pulled my phone from where I'd left it in my purse when we'd gotten home from the drug store and texted Will. I hadn't spoken to him all day after texting him that I was taking the day off, and we hadn't left things well the night before. I knew we had a few things to talk about too.

Lucy: Busy tonight? Want to grab a drink?

Will responded almost immediately.

Will: Yes. Here? Moose?

I should have told him to meet me at the Moose. I knew exactly what would happen if we met at the resort. What, with all the bedrooms that place had . . .

Lucy: I'll come there. Bar?

Will: See you there.

"Okay," I told Papa. "To bed at a reasonable hour."

"Yes, Mom."

"I'll see you in the morning. We're having fruit for breakfast. And vitamins."

Papa made a face and then waved his hands at me as if to shoo me away.

* * *

As I touched up my makeup and pulled on a shirt that hugged my curves, topping it with a soft draped cardigan, I forced my mind to still. Because if I let it go, all kinds of unwanted thoughts raced through it. I found myself asking questions.

Like how much was it going to hurt when Will told me he was leaving? And would this be the end of my dating life, would it just be one heartbreak too many for me? Would I die old and alone? And how the hell did Will get his hair to stay perfectly styled but still be so damned soft?

If I got answers to none of my other questions, I needed to find out what kind of product the man was using.

Will was waiting for me outside, his big body folded into a casual pose sitting on the curb in front of the resort as I pulled in. I didn't go around to the parking lot—it was late, and no one else was going to be parking out here tonight. As I pulled into the circle, Will stood, a smile pulling the sexy bows of his lips out and highlighting the dimples in his cheeks.

Something inside me thrummed like an engine that had just sprung to life.

I loved and hated the effect this man had on me.

But seeing him now, standing there grinning at me like there was nothing else going on in the world . . . it made me realize there was no easy way out of this. I was already in way too deep. Every cell inside me reacted to him, and just being near him had me thinking about things I'd decided long ago were fairytales for other girls.

"Hey Firecracker." Will met me at the driver's side of the truck and I let him lift me down.

"What do you use in your hair?" I could at least get that question answered, and I needed to do it before I forgot.

"Nice to see you too," he laughed, leaning down to kiss me softly on the cheek.

"I need to know," I whispered, letting one hand sift through the soft perfection at the back of his neck.

He brushed his lips over mine and then stepped back, letting me close up the truck and then taking my hand to lead me inside. "It's a closely guarded secret," he said, a playfulness in his voice that made me want to skip the drink altogether.

But that would not help things.

Will led me into the bar. No one else was around, but soft music played on the speakers overhead and the long space glowed with soft golden light.

"What can I get for you?" He asked me, stepping behind the long counter.

"What's your specialty?"

He leaned over the bar, resting on his forearms and giving me a smile that was clearly engineered to make my clothes fall from my body. "I've already shown you my specialty, but I'm more than happy to demonstrate again." His voice was rough and low, and the timbre of it made every one of my skin cells ache to be touched.

"Later," I breathed.

"Dirty martini?" he asked, straightening up. "Margarita? Manhattan?"

"So you specialize in drinks that begin with M."

He frowned. "Never thought about that. I guess I need to expand my bartending alphabet. How about a Negroni? Or an old fashioned?"

"How about a glass of pinot grigio," I suggested. "So I can drive myself home later."

"Or you could just drive home tomorrow morning," Will said, winking at me as he pulled a bottle of wine from the cooler beneath the bar.

"I need to get home tonight," I said, mostly to remind myself. Falling deeper wouldn't help things.

"So we are agreed. We'll decide later."

I rolled my eyes, but found myself already admitting internally that I'd probably end up staying all night. This playful and light version of Will was the perfect balm for the heavy thoughts that had been weighing me down.

Will pulled a beer for himself and then came to sit at my side. "To the resort," he said, lifting his glass.

I touched mine to the edge of his, and he added. "To us."

I sipped my wine, his simple toast making questions race through my mind again. Was there an us? What was the expiration date on that?

"So your dad left?" I asked him. I wanted him to assure me that nothing was going to change. That for now, at least, I could settle back into the knowledge that he was here for at least a year and that I had work during that time, for me and for the guys who depended on me.

"He did." He sounded like there was something he was going to add, but then was quiet.

"And?"

"And he's still impossible."

"But what about his proposal?"

Will dropped my gaze and traced a circle on the bar top, maybe trying to decide what to say. Then he looked up at me, something inscrutable in the deep blue gaze. "It's a lot of money," he said. "And Ghost thinks it would make it possible to get the resort open sooner."

"It would, I'm sure." I tamped down the fear I felt as I realized he was considering this seriously.

"But he also realizes that he can't just come in here and rock the boat."

"Meaning?"

"You. The guys who work for you. You're all locals. This place needs the support and loyalty of the local community to succeed. Ghost doesn't want to alienate everyone in Kasper Ridge right out of the gate."

Relief washed through me. "So he said no?"

Will took a sip of his drink, put it back down and took a deep breath. "He said no to Dad coming up and taking over."

I wasn't sure what to make of that.

"But yes to a small investment."

Relief lightened the load resting on my shoulders. "That makes sense. So nothing really changes, except maybe we can bring in a few more people and get started on a few things sooner."

Will hesitated just long enough to make me think I'd misunderstood, but then he smiled and said, "Right."

The smile didn't quite light those ocean eyes though, and worry beat a rhythm through my heart. What wasn't he saying?

Chapter 31
Wildlife Encounters

WILL

I didn't want to tell Lucy everything yet. Selfishly, I wanted another night of freedom, a night where neither of us was worried about the future or the job. I wanted it to be just us.

But even as I took her hand and led her up the stairs in the lobby, I could feel the change in her. She was thinking about something, worrying about something, and she wasn't telling me what it was.

Which allowed me to pretend I didn't notice.

We moved side by side down the dark hallway to my room,

and just as we got close, Lucy stilled at my side, pulling me to a stop.

"Don't move," she breathed, sending my nerves spiking with alarm.

"What? Why?" I glanced around the dimly lit space, and my eyes fell on the thing that she was staring at, round eyed.

A bear. Adrenaline surged through me. The thing was standing maybe fifteen feet from us, staring at us unmoving through beady eyes. Its head was enormous, and as it stood there on two feet, glaring at us like we'd rudely interrupted its resort vacation, I realized I needed to act. I pushed Lucy behind me.

"With bears," I whispered. "Is it play dead? Or is it make a ton of noise and get as big as possible?"

"Neither," Lucy whispered. "It's back slowly away and hope they ignore you."

Together, we began backing down the hall.

The bear didn't move.

Like, it didn't move at all. I wasn't sure it was breathing.

"Hang on," I said, the fear slipping from me like a useless coat. "That's not a real bear."

"I was starting to wonder," Lucy said, and I felt the tension leave her too as she laughed.

We both stood still for just a moment, as if daring the bear to charge. But it still hadn't moved a muscle.

"That's gotta be Rufus," Lucy said, and she pulled me back toward the bear.

There was still some internal instinct screaming inside me to stay back, but when Lucy dropped her hand onto the bear's big shaggy head and it didn't react, my brain finally accepted that this bear was not a threat.

"Rufus," I said, taking one of the bear's little round ears between my fingers gently.

"Papa keeps talking about this guy. I guess he was like Marvin's pet."

"When he was alive?"

"No," Lucy laughed. "He just had a particular fondness for this stuffed bear for whatever reason."

"And how the hell did Rufus get outside my room?" I asked. But I knew. This smacked of squadron shenanigans, and there would be retribution. But not right now. Right now, I needed to remind Lucy why she found me so utterly irresistible. Because if she made it clear that there was something here between us, then it would make everything else that was weighing on me a whole lot easier.

I pushed open my door and followed Lucy inside, catching her hand and spinning her around as soon as the door was shut again.

"Hey," she said softly, her eyes liquid sapphire as she looked up at me.

"Hey yourself," I said, leaning down to pull her closer to me, to ghost my lips along the column of her neck.

She sucked in a breath. I let my lips skim along her smooth skin while one of my hands dropped low, molding her hips against me. It sent my blood racing, feeling her respond to me, the way her hands gripped at my back and the little noises escaped her throat.

I lifted my head to capture her mouth, using the tip of my tongue to tease her bottom lip before nipping it softly. When she pressed against me harder, I deepened the kiss and Lucy opened to me instantly. One leg wrapped around mine, and I slid my hands lower, filling them with the soft perfection of her ass and lifting her to my waist.

Like a pre-choreographed dance, we moved together, her legs wrapping my waist as my tongue met hers and her hands went to my hair. Her breasts pressed deliciously against my chest, and I spun her around, pushing her back to the door so my hands were free to explore.

I could feel the heat of her against the iron length in my jeans, and the dual sensations of the wet heat of her mouth and the promising warmth emanating from her sweet center had me forgetting everything else.

I unwrapped her slowly, my hips keeping her trapped between my body and the door as I pulled her sweater and her shirt from her body, pausing to drop kisses onto every inch of exposed skin I could reach. Lucy Dale was utter perfection—fierce determination and intimidating intelligence wrapped up in an impossibly soft and sexy package. I loved everything about her.

I had just realized, actually, that I loved her.

"Bed," she mumbled, her hands pulling at my shirt, trying to free it from my body.

I carried her to the bedroom with reverence, and deposited her gently on the bed before pulling my shirt off over my head and kicking off my shoes all in one movement.

Lucy's hands went to her own waist, but I beat her to it, capturing her hands and pinning them over her head with one of mine while the other hand unfastened her jeans. I kissed her as I wrestled her jeans down with one hand, and she helped by lifting her hips and kicking them off her legs.

I held her like that, trapped beneath me, her arms over her head making her breasts jut deliciously forward in the soft pink cups of her bra. And while my mouth explored hers, taking detours over her jaw and down to her throat, my other hand teased the soft silk covering her center.

Lucy moaned and writhed beneath me, and I slid my hand inside her panties, loving the softness and heat I found there. My fingers grazed her, skimming and sliding over her before I let one delve a bit deeper, slipping between her folds to land on the sensitive pulse that made her gasp.

My mouth and fingers worked together, my other hand keeping her pinned, and Lucy slowly unraveled beneath me, beginning with soft breathy moans and finishing with a thrashing cry that nearly set me off. I let her hands go, and she clung to me, her breath coming in gasps until her body stilled beneath me.

I watched her, holding myself above her and enjoying every-thing about the way she responded, the way she let herself go. She was perfect. The knowledge made something deep in my chest ache.

"You're still wearing pants," she pointed out after a moment.

"I am."

"Let's fix that." She pushed at me until I was on my elbows and knees over her, and then slid down beneath me so I could feel her breath on my navel.

"What are you doing?" I asked, worrying a little about my self control with her breath so close to my cock.

"Helping you out of your pants," she said, her hands unfas-tening the button of my jeans and then pushing them off my hips, along with my boxer briefs.

"Aha. Well, thanks."

"Stay like that," she said after I'd kicked off my pants. She was still beneath me, her mouth just level with my—

"Oh shit," I moaned as the soft heat of Lucy's lips grazed the tip of my cock. Her hands slid down the backs of my thighs and she licked along the bottom of my dick, sending shivers racing through me and making everything inside me tense in antic-ipation.

"You like this?" she asked, taking me into her mouth and then sucking before releasing me.

"Yes," I managed, using every bit of control I had inside not to pin her down and fuck her senseless. "God, yes."

Lucy's mouth found me again, and this time she teased and licked before sucking me deep. Warm wetness enveloped me and the urge to thrust was nearly overwhelming. I heard myself let out a choked moan.

And then she began working up and down, taking me deeper and deeper until every muscle in my body was starting to spasm with the need to release.

"God, Lucy," I managed. "I'm gonna—oh, fuck." It was meant to be a warning, but I felt myself hitting the back of her throat and the sensation was too much.

She didn't stop. And sensation rocketed through me, every bit of tension within coiling and then releasing in a violent explosion that sent stars shooting behind my eyelids.

I tried to pull out, but Lucy held me firm, keeping me ensconced in that hot wet tunnel that was one of the best things I'd ever experienced—second only to actually being with Lucy. I loved holding her in my arms while we were together, feeling her surrounding me, looking into her face, losing myself in her eyes. But this was pretty damned good.

"Shit," I breathed when I had regained myself and Lucy had let me go. I rolled to the side of her and she wiggled back up until we were face to face again. I lifted a hand to her beautiful face, using a thumb to wipe at the tears on her cheek.

"You definitely didn't have to do that." I said, feeling guilty that it had made her eyes water.

"I wanted to. I liked it," she said, molding herself to me and wrapping a leg around my hips. We were aligned, and the heat of her was causing a surprising reaction in the part of me I would have been pretty sure was down for the count.

"You're amazing," I told her, marveling not just at the physical pleasure I felt with her, but at the way my heart felt settled, at the way my mind cleared. "You make me really happy, Lucy."

She smiled and I would have sworn I felt the tension leave her body. "You make me happy too," she said, holding my gaze. "I've been fighting it . . . but I can't anymore."

"Fighting it? Why?"

"Because it's going to be so damned hard when you leave."

"When I—?" Had I told her more than I'd intended to? Had I shouted out what was in my head when I was in the midst of climax?

"I know you'll go eventually. I guess my best plan is just to try to make the most of it while you're still here." She sounded sad, but her arms tightened around me.

"I don't have to leave," I told her, hoping she might say something else, something that made me believe there could be a good reason to stay here forever.

"You do," she said. "And it's okay."

It was like a stone had just been tossed into my gut. That wasn't what I wanted her to say. At all.

"I'm not in a hurry to go," I said, wanting to make her say the words. "I love it up here."

"But it's not where you belong," she said. "I know that."

She might as well have started my car for me. She'd already decided everything. Was it already over then? Before we'd really gotten started? Did she not feel what I felt? She'd just said she was done fighting it. But now she was pushing me away. The urge to step back, to protect what was left of my heart was growing.

"But you're here now," she sighed, her hand slipping between us to grasp me. "Let's not waste time."

Lucy stroked me until I thought I'd explode again, and then I slid into her after quickly rolling on a condom, her gaze on mine the whole time. We moved slowly, in perfect unison, our bodies and breaths coming as one. But our minds and hearts, I realized, were not in the same place.

And as I held her in my arms that night, I realized that leaving sooner would be better than staying too long. I was already too wrapped up in this woman, and if she wasn't looking for anything serious, I needed to go. Before the act of leaving would break me.

* * *

Lucy slipped from bed early the next morning, kissing my cheek before she stepped out to use the bathroom. I got up and dressed quickly. I needed to talk to her.

"Got a sec?" I asked when she was dressed and making moves to leave.

"Yeah, I just need to run home to change so I can get back for work."

I nodded, rubbing the back of my neck. "It's about that, actually. And about my dad's offer."

She sat down at the little table and I took the chair across from her. Words felt lodged in my throat and I felt a little nauseated. I needed to get this out. Now.

"Dad wanted to run things up here, but I told him you're the best he's going to get, and that the people up here are counting on the work. So he agreed to leave you in charge, to keep you as the final say on how things get done."

Lucy was frowning at me, but she didn't speak, so I went on, steeling myself.

"So you'll run both crews, and whoever Dad sends up will answer to you."

"Both crews. Because you'll be . . ." she said slowly.

"Dad offered me a project of my own, back in LA." There. It was out. It was done. A cold sadness washed through me.

Lucy dropped my gaze and stared at the tabletop for a second, a breath whooshing out of her. When she looked back up, her gaze was steely and hard. "So you're leaving now."

God, I didn't want to. I wanted her to tell me not to.

"I haven't promised anyone anything."

Tell me what you want, Lucy. Ask me to stay.

"It's probably a good career move for you. Lot bigger market down there. Plus, your dad clearly has faith in you. It's what you wanted, right?"

"It is, but—" God, I didn't want her to think about that. I wanted her to tell me what we had was more important. That we could make it work. The words were on the tip of my tongue when Lucy spoke again. Her voice flat and loud in the quiet room.

"There's nothing up here for you, Will. Just a lot of trees and small-town people." She shook her head, writing off everything we'd shared.

"And you."

We stared at each other, and it seemed for a second like each was daring the other to say something, to break the tension between us.

"It'll never be enough for you," she said quietly. "I'll never be enough. If we tried to stay together you'd resent me. You'll always wonder what you could have been down in the city. This is a whole different world, a different scale. It's definitely not for everyone."

My stomach dropped. She wasn't right, was she? "You want me to go? You're telling me to leave?"

She took a deep breath and then met my eye. "Running a job like this is kind of my dream come true. And the one down there is yours," she said.

"That doesn't answer the question."

"I think you were going to leave at some point anyway. Easier for everyone if you do it now."

A deep aching heaviness settled into me. I couldn't bring myself to tell her I loved her. Not now. Maybe things would have been different if I'd told her before this, before she'd essentially banished me. But maybe not. Lucy was right—if I left, she had her dream job and I could go take mine. Maybe this was the right thing for us both. She'd never wanted to answer to me at work anyway.

"Okay," I said, wishing my voice sounded stronger. "We'll let the guys know today and I'll tell my dad I'm coming back."

"Yep. Good. Okay." She stood, not meeting my eye again. "I'll be back in an hour."

And then she was gone.

I watched her walk down the hallway, never turning back. And when she disappeared down the stairs, I knew it was really over.

I turned on my heel to find Rufus waiting there, staring at me, looking smug like only a big stuffed Grizzly can.

"Fuck off," I told him, and I punched him in the nose.

Stuffed bears are tougher than they look. My hand hurt like hell. But not as much as my heart.

Chapter 32
Critical Pomade Queries

LUCY

"He left? He's gone?" CeeCee was having trouble processing my new reality.

"Yes." I hadn't told them immediately because it was hard enough for me to accept. Only a week after he'd gone did I feel like there was a chance I could talk to them about it without breaking down. "He left a week ago."

"And you're just mentioning it now," Bennie said thoughtfully. "This is why you've been dodging our calls and telling us you're too busy to get together."

"Part of that is true," I admitted. "But I have been really

busy. Will left me in charge of everything, and with the influx of crew and equipment, there's been a lot to organize. We're trying to complete a project that was supposed to take years in a matter of months."

CeeCee's eyes rounded. "Is that a good thing? I thought this job was going to give you security for the next couple years. Help you take care of Papa."

"It will. The heavy lifting is just happening a lot faster now. There will still be work for a long time." I almost wished it weren't true. Everything about the Kasper Ridge Resort project reminded me of Will. And that he was gone.

Bennie nodded, and poured herself another glass of beer, gazing around the Toothy Moose. "It's a shame though," she said. "He sure prettied this place up."

CeeCee jabbed her in the ribs with her elbow.

"What?" Bennie asked, feigning innocence. "He was nice to look at."

"He was," I agreed, trying not to think about how nice he'd been to touch, to lie next to, to talk to. My heart actually ached in response if I thought about him too much. I'd let myself get way too deep.

"Have you heard from him?" CeeCee asked, tilting her head so that her long curls fell over one shoulder. The sympathy in her eyes and her voice were too much. I hated being the object of pity. I hated all of this.

"He's texted a couple times," I told them.

"Are you going to see him again?" she asked, the hope in her voice skewering me.

"Why are you so invested in this?" I snapped. "It's really none of your business. It was my business, my mistake. It was a stupid fling, and it's over." I picked up my glass and finished my beer, hoping maybe the liquid would fill the gaping hole that my lack of judgment with Will had left within me.

"First of all," Bennie said, straightening. Her cheeks were turning pink, and I realized I might have been a bit short. "Don't yell at us. We're your friends and we care about you. If we're bugging you, it's because we're worried."

"Well, you don't need to be," I said, not meeting her eye. I felt like a petulant first grader being scolded. Maybe because Bennie taught first grade, so she'd pretty much perfected her teacherly scold.

"That's bullshit," CeeCee threw in. She did not teach elementary school. Her mouth would disqualify her from any job that involved children. "That's what friends do, and you're my ride or die. You both are."

Bennie smiled at her, and I gave her a little nod. They were mine too. I just wasn't big on words at the moment. Or ever.

"Okay," I said, sinking into the back of my chair. "The thing that bugs me the most is that before he left, it was like he was waiting for me to tell him not to go."

"Did you?" Bennie asked, leaning forward. She knew the answer. She was doing the teacher thing, leading me down a path to prove a point. Maybe that's what I needed.

"No," I said flatly. "It's not up to me to tell him what to do. He's an adult. He makes his own choices."

"Maybe he didn't know he had a choice," Bennie said.

CeeCee looked at her for a long moment, frowning. "The fuck does that mean? Don't be all mysterious. Lucy needs answers!"

"I'm not being mysterious," Bennie said. "I'm just saying, if you never told him how you really felt or what you wanted or hoped for, then he was operating without all the information."

"Speaking of which," CeeCee said, interrupting the thoughts Bennie's words had caused to spike around in my mind. "Did you get the info we asked for before he left?"

"Tell me you're not asking her about his hair right now," Bennie said.

"Yes. About his hair."

"This is not important."

"It is though," CeeCee said. "Very fucking important. Because it has to be some kind of product and I bet we could order it. Maybe Miss Bea could even get it in at the salon." She paused, looking around the bar at the faces we'd seen here pretty much every day since we were kids. "On second thought, it could be just our secret." She nodded.

I sighed. "I did ask, but he didn't tell me. And I did go into the bathroom in his room a few times, but I did not see any special secret magic hair products."

"You think his hair just does that? Like, it's all ridiculously perfectly mussed and just stays that way all on its own? Maybe he knew you were going to poke around, so he hid it."

"I think they had a little more going on together than some hair product intrigue," Bennie told her.

"Text him and just ask," CeeCee said.

I stared at her. "You've lost your mind." I hadn't responded to Will's texts at all. I was not going to suddenly inquire about his relationship to Vidal Sassoon.

She sighed, but her eyes fell to my phone on the table at my side.

"Do not," I warned.

"What kinds of things has he been texting you?" Bennie asked, proceeding as if CeeCee hadn't just derailed her interrogation with a lengthy detour into the secrets of Will's perfect hair. Which, to be fair, I wondered about too.

The dark hole inside me seemed to be getting wider and wider, the longer we talked about Will. He was gone, that was all there really was to it. "It's not important," I said. "Listen, can we talk about something else? Is there still lice going around at school?"

"Ew." CeeCee scooted her chair away from Bennie.

"No," Bennie said, sounding offended. "We handled that situation."

"That's good," I said, my mind far, far away from the issues cropping up at Kasper Ridge Elementary. "I'll be right back." I excused myself to head to the bathroom, more because I needed a break from the wide concerned eyes and endless questions of my friends than because I needed to pee.

When I returned to the table after taking a few deep breaths and staring at myself in the mirror a little too long, CeeCee had my phone.

"What are you doing?" I asked her, fury making my voice tight.

"It can't hurt to ask," she said, sounding innocent. "He says it's some kind of pomade. He's sending a link."

"I don't think girls with long hair can use pomade like that," Bennie said, twirling a piece of her own hair around her finger and looking at it.

"You're texting Will?" I seethed. "From my phone?"

"I didn't have his number," CeeCee said, putting my phone down again. "And I don't know why you haven't responded. His texts were so sweet."

"Well, I've responded now, haven't I?" Worry over what my friends might have said on my behalf had me vibrating. I snatched up my phone and dug through the texts that had been flinging back and forth since I went to the bathroom.

Me: Hi there. I miss you too. I wish you were still here. I've been a miserable beast since you left, and my friends think I'm an idiot for not telling you how I really feel. But while I have you,

can you tell me what product you're using in your hair?

Oh. My. GOD.

Will: Do you have time to talk? Can I call you?

Me: Focus first. Hair?

Will: It's this pomade my barber recommended. I'll find a link and text it, okay? Talk?

"Oh my god," I hissed. "I can't believe you texted that."

"I really wanted to know," CeeCee said, shrugging.

"Not that part. The part about missing him and not telling him how I feel." My cheeks were hot and a confusing mix of emotions was surging around inside me, making me feel nauseated. "Why would you do that?"

"You told me your passcode, remember?" CeeCee said.

"Sorry, Lucy," Bennie said, putting an arm around me. "I told her not to."

I shoved my phone into my purse, realizing that now Will thought I wanted to talk about things, that CeeCee had just reset the clock on getting over whatever had happened between us.

"I do not want to talk to him," I told them. I wanted to get over whatever misplaced feelings I'd developed and go back to how things were before he showed up.

"But maybe you should," Bennie said. "Get some closure and then you can move on."

CeeCee nodded, but I didn't acknowledge her. I was going to continue being pissed at her for a long, long time.

"What would you have told him if you could have just said how you felt when he mentioned leaving?" Bennie asked.

"Nothing. Which is exactly what I did. I am not having regrets about not spilling my guts for him, and I'm not pining away for him now that he left." My insides churned with every lie I sputtered.

"Beg to differ," CeeCee said, but I was getting good at ignoring her.

"I made a good choice and I'm sticking with it. In fact, there was no choice. He told me he was leaving. That's all there was to it." Except I knew that wasn't quite true.

"Just talk to him," Bennie said.

"You're going to be an insufferable c—"

"Don't say that!" Bennie stopped CeeCee before she could utter one of her favorite words.

"I was going to say cookie. You'll be an insufferable cookie until you get out whatever pent-up feelings you have about this guy." CeeCee smiled sweetly at Bennie.

Finally, the conversation turned to other things, and soon I was back in the truck, heading home.

Papa was already in bed when I arrived, and I sat in the kitchen for a long time, staring at Will's texts on my phone.

I really didn't know what to do, but I didn't think that talking to him and exploring the fact that he was gone would do anything to alleviate the dark ache of loneliness inside me. Decisions had been made. It was time to move on. I deleted the text string so I wouldn't have his words to obsess over anymore.

A clean break.

Chapter 33
Swapping Seats at the Table

WILL

"I get it, man. We just miss you around here." Ghost's voice on the phone made me miss Kasper Ridge even more. But at least he wasn't holding my sudden departure against me.

"Lucy will do a great job though. Especially with all the extra resources." I swallowed hard, staring out my office window at the ocean. I'd traded the shelter and closeness of trees and mountains for the endless expanse of the Pacific, and for the first time in my life, I realized all that open space made me feel uncomfortable. It was too much, too open, too endless. And I was nothing next to it. Small. A speck of dust.

"I know she will," Ghost agreed. "She's determined, I'll give her that. At Monday's meeting she wouldn't let us get off topic for even a second. Not even to acknowledge the fact that my sister and Wiley had dragged Rufus down to the kitchen and positioned him just inside the walk-in cooler."

I laughed, thinking of how terrifying it would be to find a grizzly lurking in the fridge if you weren't expecting it. "Genius."

"Hey, I meant to thank you for the heart attack when you left, by the way."

"You liked that? You looked lonely." I'd paid Ghost back for sticking Rufus outside my door and slipped into Ghost's bedroom with him before I got an early start out of town. We all agreed Ghost needed a bedfellow, so I gave him one. Maybe a little hairier and huger than what he had in mind...

"I'm getting all the door locks modernized this week thanks to you."

"Where's Rufus gonna stay when construction's done? Lucy says he was important to your uncle. Her grandfather remembers him."

"Yeah," Ghost said on an exhale, as if the topic of Marvin was exhausting. "He told me that too. I don't know. I'm starting to think Uncle Marvin was just bananas and that maybe there's nothing to find anyway."

"No luck on the hunt, huh?" Part of me thought he should give up, but another part worried that the disappointment over the treasure hunt being a bust might be devastating for Ghost.

"Not really. We've gotten nowhere on the Mountaintop Studios thing except a poorly written Wikipedia entry that's like two lines long. I've been digging through maps and comparing them to those posters, looking for a word that matches the name of a city or canyon, or some kind of clue to tell us where to go next, but it just feels like a dead end."

"If I have any flashes of brilliance I'll let you know," I said.

"Yeah, thanks." Ghost was quiet a second. "Hey, man, are you doing okay?"

I knew why he was asking—he knew being back with my dad, under his thumb, was a double-edged sword for me. He also knew how I felt about Lucy. "I'm doing okay."

"She call you yet?"

"She texted, actually."

"That's something."

"I guess so. She's gone silent again, though." Lucy had gotten my hopes up the other night, telling me she missed me and then weirdly quizzing me about hair product, which was a little out of character. But I'd talk about pretty much anything as long as we were talking.

"I'm sorry, man. I know you had feelings for her."

"Wasn't meant to be." I let the words carry a casual tone I definitely didn't feel. "She'll get in touch if she wants to."

Except Lucy Dale was one of the most stubborn people I'd ever met. So maybe she wouldn't. Not if she had it in her head that there was a good reason not to. She was too tough for her own good. I knew how much I was hurting, and I guessed she might be hurting too, but I had a feeling Lucy would ignore a femoral bleed if it got in the way of doing her job.

"Yeah," Ghost said. "Suppose so."

I could hear my dad's voice outside my office in the hall, and I turned back from the window and sat at my desk. "Hey Ghost, I gotta go."

"Take care," he said. "Come visit."

"Yeah." I put my phone down, just as Dad appeared in my doorway, his still-impressive form filling the space.

"Got a second, Will?" This was how we did things now. Dad had started coming to my office instead of ordering me to his. He asked if I had time for him instead of assuming I'd shove things aside just because he showed up.

"Yes, of course. Have a seat."

Dad sat across my desk from me and I marveled at the strange twist in our relationship. We were in my office. I was sitting at my desk. I was in the power position, and it was unsettling and insane at once. It was everything I'd ever hoped for. But it wasn't comfortable.

"Looked over your plan for the Newport project," he began. "Looks good. A couple tweaks." He nodded toward my computer and I pulled up the plans.

"Okay, I see." His changes were clear, and they were minor.

"You're cleared to get started on this," he said. "Markie asked to be your second, but I'd have to take her off the Esplanade, and I also think you'll do better with someone you choose yourself. Plus, having that ridiculous dog on site has always been annoying. You don't need to deal with that."

I chuckled. "Sounds good."

Dad sat back in the chair and was uncharacteristically quiet. Then, in a voice I rarely heard him use—the one where he asked people for things instead of telling them what to do, he said, "You coming to dinner this week, Son?"

"Sure," I said. I had nothing else to do. I'd had enough quiet nights back in my condo to know anything was better than wishing my phone would ring and thinking about Lucy.

"Good," he said. "Your mother and I have some things to talk about."

Something about his words lodged a spike of concern inside me. "Everything okay?"

He stood. "We'll talk Sunday." He turned to go, then turned

back around. "You're doing a good job here, Will. I haven't told you this enough, but I'm proud of you."

My father might as well have slapped me in the face. I was stunned, and didn't manage to find any words before he turned and left me alone again.

I had everything I'd ever thought I wanted. Dad's trust and support, a position of power at work... but I knew exactly why none of it felt like enough.

I missed Lucy.

I decided to text her once more before I went to bed that night, not caring anymore if she responded. I just wanted her to know some things.

Me: Hi. You don't have to text back. I just wanted to tell you that I think about you all the time. I worry that I made a mistake leaving, that I might have ruined the one chance at something real I might ever get.

I paused, reading my own words. I had nothing to lose, I figured, and I typed out one more line.

Me: I love you, Lucy.

My fingers hovered over the send key, but then I realized that it was pointless. Sending texts into the void was like tossing pennies down a well. I'd never know where they landed, and I'd never get them back. Lucy and I were done, and I needed to accept it.

Clearly, she already had.

I deleted everything and went to bed, the darkness in my mind claustrophobic and suffocating in a way the empty black of my condo never had been before Kasper Ridge.

* * *

"Hi honey." Mom greeted me at the door of the house where I'd grown up, and wrapped me in a hug. I held her close for a moment, inhaling the familiar comfort of her scent. She was small and wiry, but my mother had always made me think of softness and warmth.

"Hi Mom."

"I missed you. I'm glad you're home." She stepped away, but took my hand and smiled up at me. The little spike of concern that had lodged there at work Friday twisted deeper at the look in her eyes. "Come have a drink," she said, pulling me toward the kitchen.

"I brought this for you guys, actually," I said, handing her the bottle of Half Cat Whiskey I'd brought from Kasper Ridge.

"Half Cat," she said, a giggle lighting her eyes as she put it on the counter and looked at the logo on the front. It pictured a shaggy cat with two front legs and a little wheeled contraption attached to his back end. The little cat's eyes glowed with something like mischief, though how that came through in the line drawing, I wasn't sure. It always made me smile, and it seemed to have the same effect on Mom.

"It's a real cat," I told her. "Wiley—the guy Ghost brought in to run the bar at the resort—he and his brother own a distillery back in Maryland. They make this stuff, and it's really good. But I guess the distillery and the bar are in one space, and there's a cat that lives there, who runs around in this squeaky little wheelchair."

"You're kidding," she said, her eyes widening with mirth.

"His name is Mr. Fluffyknuckles or something. I can't remember, but it's ridiculous."

"I love it!" Mom clapped her hands in front of her and opened the bottle just as Dad came in and took a seat at the counter.

"We having a drink?" he asked.

"Whiskey?" Mom asked him, holding up the bottle. "Will brought this from the resort."

"Sounds good." Dad dropped a hand on my shoulder and left it there for a long beat, and I had a fleeting thought that this must be what it was like to have a regular family. To have parents who were proud of you. I wasn't complaining about it now, but how might my life have gone differently if Dad had always treated me this way? Did I really have to go away to earn his respect? It seemed ridiculous, considering all the years I structured my life specifically to try to impress him. Hell, I might not have even gone into the Navy if I hadn't thought it was the only way to get him to love me.

I struggled to put that thought away as we took our whiskey into the living room and my parents sat close together on the couch. Closer than normal, actually. And Dad's big hand held Mom's shoulder.

There was something wrong. I knew it even before Dad began talking.

"We need to tell you something, Will," he said, and Mom sucked in an audible breath, as if she needed to steel herself for this.

"Okay," I said, putting my glass down on the table next to me.

"I've been to the doctor a lot over the past few weeks, and we've gotten some bad news."

My blood froze inside me, making me shiver as I held my breath, waiting for the rest.

"Lung cancer," Dad said, and the words fell between us like a rock tossed into the center of the room.

I shook my head to clear it as my heart iced over in my chest. This couldn't be right. I'd misheard. "You've never smoked," I pointed out. This couldn't be real, could it?

"Nope. Not a day."

Mom leaned into Dad's side, her eyes shining. "There's a surprisingly high incidence of cancer among military aircrew," she said. "I've been doing a lot of reading. We're going to donate some money to help the research."

"So this . . ." I trailed off, scanning my memory for whatever limited knowledge I had of the topic. "You can treat it, right?"

"They can try," Dad said. "But it's not a game most people win."

Suddenly, things were making sense. Dad must have known, when he came to Kasper Ridge. His sudden desire to be involved in my life, to give me the chances he'd never handed me before. He thought his time was running out.

"God," I said dropping my head to look at the rug between my feet. I wanted to say something smart, to find an answer for this problem, but I knew it wasn't something I could fix. Definitely not with words. "Dad, I'm so sorry."

"You have nothing to be sorry for. You've been everything I could ever want in a son. I just wish I'd made a point of telling you that a little more often."

I raised my head, meeting his eyes then. And for the first time, I really looked at my father. As a man, as a human being who was getting older, maybe failing. I saw the lines around his eyes, the way the strong jaw was beginning to sag. He wasn't the formidable figure who'd dominated my life for so long, and maybe he wasn't the immovable granite stone I'd always figured him to be. He was just a man, and he was telling me he was dying. And in his way, he was apologizing. Making amends.

"We'll be okay," I told them, feeling like I needed to be strong for them. "We'll get through this."

"We will," Mom agreed. "But we wanted you to know. Things are going to . . . change a bit."

Dad nodded. "I'm leaving the firm. Taking time to focus on my health. My family."

That made sense, though I would never have predicted it. "Okay."

"I'd like to leave you in charge."

"Wow." It wasn't the most well-thought out response, but it was all I had. Did I want to be in charge? Did I want to run the company? Could I even do it?

"Obviously, you'll need time to think about it all," Dad said. "I don't need an answer right away."

"Okay," I said. Then I remembered the whiskey at my side and I poured the whole glass down my throat, relishing the way the burn grounded me in the real world even as I felt like I was floating away. "Okay, yeah," I said, doing my best to pull myself together.

We had another drink, the conversation between us quiet and careful. We were a new version of the family I'd known my whole life, and I thought we were all adjusting to it a little bit.

I stayed longer than I usually did after dinner, sitting in the den with my parents, having a cup of coffee and turning on the television.

"Your room is ready for you if you want it, Will," Mom said, leaning toward me. "You're welcome to stay here whenever you want to. You know that. It's your home."

I blinked hard, working to keep the tears from springing to my eyes. Something about the idea of coming home, really coming home, had the emotions I'd been stifling for weeks climbing my throat and threatening to swamp me.

"Okay, yeah," I said. "I might stay tonight."

We watched part of an old movie, one I'd never seen before, and Dad fell asleep in his chair. When Mom saw me staring at my phone instead of watching, she lowered the volume and turned to me.

"We'll be okay, Will."

I looked up, meeting her gaze. "I know."

"I mean you, too."

"Okay." I wasn't sure what to say to her, but the steely strength I'd seen in her my whole life was back. I had no doubt she would be fine, whatever the outcome of Dad's situation.

"This movie," she said, turning toward the screen with a little smile dancing across her face. "I saw it when I was a kid."

"Yeah?" I thought of the movie posters in the bar at the resort. "Ghost's uncle was into old movies." I showed her the photos I'd taken of the posters, told her about the hunt. She smiled as she looked at all the photos, and I sensed she was as happy for a distraction as I was.

"What do they mean, do you think?" she asked, tilting her head.

"No idea. We've been searching all the words for connections, trying to identify the casts and see if they're somehow linked to Colorado. But so far, all we're getting are dead ends. One of the actresses is in a few of them—Annie Lowe. But that didn't get us anywhere either. The only thing we've got is that the scripts all came out of one studio called Mountaintop."

Mom nodded, staring at pictures and scrolling through them. "Maybe there's some kind of connection in the stories," she suggested. "Some theme you're supposed to find?"

"We talked about that, haven't been able to find anything."

"Or something else, something simpler."

"I'm starting to see that nothing about Ghost's uncle was simple."

Mom smiled and shook her head. "Human beings rarely are." She stood, then leaned down to kiss my cheek. "I love you, Will. So much. And so does your dad. We're so proud of you."

"Love you too, Mom."

I stayed on the couch after Mom had woken Dad and

walked slowly with him back to their room. I sat there after the movie ended and the house grew dark and quiet around me. And finally, I climbed the stairs to my childhood bedroom and laid down, closing my eyes and falling into an empty, dreamless sleep.

Chapter 34
Surprise, Surprise, Surprise

LUCY

I t had been three weeks since Will had left.

Papa watched Golden Girls reruns with me until he finally announced that he couldn't take one more minute of it and excused himself to go play poker with his friends or hide in his puzzle books.

Dorothy and Rose made me feel better about my life choices. They were single, after all. Of course, in the show, they'd had husbands and children before deciding to live together in a big house in Florida and commit themselves to a fully polyester-clad, perm-powered lifestyle. Maybe if CeeCee and Bennie ended up alone too, we could all get a house together and eat cheesecake.

Will was gone. And nothing had changed.

At least nothing inside me. On the other hand, it was mid-August here in Colorado, and the outdoor spaces at the Kasper Ridge Resort were nearly complete. The west patio was finished. I could imagine skiers and snowboarders sitting around one day at the many tables and fire pits we'd installed, visiting the built-in service windows for coffee and snacks, or meandering in and out of the ski shop and school. It felt good, to envision all that I'd worked for up and running.

On the east side, things were nearly finished as well. Three enormous hot tubs had been installed on tiered patios, so once the resort was operational, guests could lounge in bathing suits in the steaming water while watching others fly down snowy slopes just beyond the walls of the terrace. It was gated so people couldn't just wander in, and raised enough that swimmers wouldn't be on display exactly, but still felt like a part of the incredible outdoor environment we'd built behind the Kasper Ridge Resort.

There was an enormous fire pit, which the team staying at the resort had already taken to lighting in the evenings—it was propane fueled but put out heat with the flick of a switch and looked like real flames, or could be switched to glow in shades of blue and green. There was the outdoor patio that was part of the restaurant, and the crew had begun sitting there on lunch breaks.

The crew and machines Will's father had supplied were top of the line and efficient, and they'd made all the difference between completing the outdoor spaces in phases and getting them all done at once. It was incredible. And as I stood in the center of it all, watching the final stones being set, the last bricks being laid in the paths, I wished I was standing there with Will.

We had accomplished this together, and it was something I would always be proud of.

But Will had stopped texting me, and I assumed that he'd been reabsorbed into the glitzy world he came from, focused on whatever big project his father had asked him to take on. And I had no doubt he was doing well.

I just wished I hadn't gotten so involved.

But that wasn't quite true. I wished somehow I'd been able to have it all. The discovery of someone who fit me like a puzzle piece I'd been searching to find, and the knowledge that I could keep him.

But that wasn't how my life worked. I'd chosen Kasper Ridge. And Papa. And it took a special kind of guy to choose me when those were my priorities. I knew going in that Will was not that guy. And I should never have let myself believe that he could be.

"This is amazing." Aubrey was standing above me on the top tier where the highest hot tub had just been tested and qualified to run. "I can't wait to sit up here in the winter!"

She grinned down at me and I smiled back up at her. I hadn't spent much time with Aubrey, but I recognized something in her that I knew I had myself. Some kind of spark, or defiance of the standard system women were supposed to adhere to.

"You and Fake Tom really hit this out of the park," she said, looking around at the amazing outdoor spaces.

I absorbed the pain that came unexpectedly with her mention of Will, the reminder that he'd left. "Well, I'm not done yet. There are a lot of interiors that need complete rehabbing."

"Right," she said. "I cannot wait. This is amazing. Fake Tom is going to lose his mind."

"I guess we can send him photos," I mused. "It won't really capture the scope, but he knows what we were doing."

"We don't have to," she said, leaning dangerously over the railing above me. "He'll be here tonight."

I'm sure my mouth dropped wide open. And then I had irrational thoughts about my lack of makeup and the fact I hadn't even brushed my hair today before pulling it into a low knot to fit under the hardhat. I wanted her to explain, but I didn't want to give away the nerves and confusion that had burst into a freaking conga line the second she'd dropped that bomb.

"Will, what? Tonight?"

Great. So articulate.

"Yeah, he had something about the treasure hunt to tell us, or show us, I guess." She watched me process this news and I tried to keep my face neutral.

What had I expected her to say? That he was coming back because he had realized that he couldn't stand to be away from me? Not gonna happen. And I didn't want it to. Did I?

I did.

"Lucy?" Aubrey called, her voice softer. I looked up at her again. "It's bullshit. We all know that."

"What is?"

"He might have something to show us that has to do with my uncle's zany plan. But we all know he's coming back for you."

"No. We . . . but . . ." I couldn't process this. I wanted it to be true, but if he was coming back for me, if he'd changed his mind, wouldn't he have texted me? Or called?

Except I'd never answered before.

"Go change clothes and come back," she suggested. "We can have dinner on the patio to celebrate the completion of the back spaces, and you have to be there anyway. Now you've got one more thing to celebrate." She winked at me.

Did I? Or would he pop in and out, sweep me off my stupid feet again, and then disappear? That would just reset the countdown on my heartbreak timer, and I didn't know if I could survive it.

But I wasn't going to refuse to come celebrate the completion of this phase of work, either.

"Yeah. Okay."

I was going to see Will again. Tonight.

As I drove the truck back home, I let my mind wander through scenarios. I wondered what would happen if I let myself actually feel the things I already knew I felt for him? What if I told him?

Was there any way he might stay?

But if he did, would there be a life here for him besides me? I couldn't ask someone to sacrifice everything else just because I could never leave Kasper Ridge. That was a recipe for resentment, and it was the main reason I'd resigned myself to flings.

But was there ever a fling meaningful enough to erase all the other considerations? Could real love ever be enough?

I sighed and pulled up outside the house, my heart filled with something I worried might be hope.

Chapter 35
Return of the Man

WILL

The drive to Kasper Ridge from the Denver airport felt a lot like coming home. The wide open spaces quickly gave way to deep canyons, emerald green pine trees, and views that gave me a sense of awe as I contemplated their picturesque beauty. I'd never been the guy who pointed out things like the dew on the petal of a flower, or the way the sun dappled the ground as it came through the leaves of a tree—but looking at the mountains looming in the distance draped in shadow and topped with snow, even in the summer—it made me realize how lucky I was to be here. How many things I had to be thankful for.

The resort came into view around the last bend. Aside from the turnaround out front being a bit cleaner and there being a lot more cars in the parking lot, the Kasper Ridge Resort looked about the same as it had the first time I'd driven up here to see the place.

But this time I was different.

I stepped out of rental car looking around me with new eyes, and an unfamiliar feeling inside me.

"Hey, man." Mateo greeted me, stepping back out of the truck he'd been climbing into. "Lucy just told us you were coming back."

So she knew. I guess I shouldn't have expected that my return would be a secret. A little wave of excitement flashed through me at her name. "Yeah," I said. "Couldn't stay away."

Mateo nodded, his shrewd gaze never leaving my face. I didn't know the guy well, but I knew he was serious and reliable, and it was becoming clear that he was also protective of Lucy. "You staying this time?" His voice was a gruff challenge.

It was my turn to give him a narrowed gaze. "I'm staying for now."

He crossed his arms, pulled himself taller. Lucy told me that Mateo had been through a lot, that he was a single father. It had made me feel sorry for the guy, but right now I felt mostly irritated at being quizzed about my intentions by a guy I barely knew.

"You hurt her again, and you're going to have a lot of guys to answer to."

"I didn't mean to hurt her." Did that mean Lucy had been talking with him? Was she really hurt? Did I have a chance still?

He squinted as if he was considering my words. Or like if he squinted hard enough he could activate his X-ray vision and see inside my head. Creepy. "Yeah, probably not."

"Not probably. Certainly. She told me to leave."

"You had good reasons to go."

"I did."

"Do you have good reasons to stay?"

This was becoming a bit like a game of Wordle, which my mother had gotten me addicted to while I'd been home. I didn't have all the information, but was being asked to guess what might come next. "What are you trying to say, Mateo?"

"I've been pretty clear, I think. But I'll spell it out for you. Lucy fell for you. We could all see it. And then you just left, and she hasn't been the same. Lucy is tough and she puts up a front so it's hard to see what's really going on, but it's obvious enough. If you love her, you're gonna have to get her to drop the front. And that means sticking around a while."

"Does Lucy know you put on this protective big brother act when she's not here?"

"If she was my sister, I'd have my fist in your face for the way you hurt her already." I realized Mateo was a pretty scary dude, now that he was leaning in, just inches from my face. We were about the same height, same build. I could probably take him. But he had some kind of axe to grind, and that could give him the psycho advantage in a fight. Besides, I didn't come here to get in a brawl. I'd somehow found myself on the right side of the make-Dad-proud line, and I didn't want to stumble onto the other side of it again.

"Noted." I stepped back, lifting my hands in front of me.

Mateo's fierce frown didn't lessen.

"Look, she's lucky to have you. And I'm glad you're looking out for her. But I'll let you know right now that if she'd given me a reason to stay, I wouldn't have gone anywhere."

Mateo looked disappointed, his lips pressing into a thin line and his eyes shooting left like he hoped a better version of me might be standing over there. "Figure it out, man."

I was going to argue some more, tell him that I had figured it out and that was most of the reason I was back here, but he was already storming off to get into his truck.

"Nice seeing you," I said, waving a hand over my head as I strode around the back of the resort. I wanted to see Lucy's work. Ghost told me it had turned out spectacularly.

He wasn't wrong.

A glow of pride burned brighter with every step I took through the finished outdoor spaces of the Kasper Ridge Resort. It was functional and stunning. Lucy and I had done this together, but she'd put the final shine on it. I couldn't wait to see her to celebrate.

"Fake Tom!" Ghost was coming out of the bar as I strode through the lobby from the back patio.

"Hey Ghost," I said, pulling my old friend in for a hug he clearly hadn't expected.

"Getting a bit handsy in your old age, aren't you?" he stepped away quickly.

"Nah. Just realized a few things about letting the people I care about know I care about them while I have the chance."

He nodded. "Good policy, probably. Very warm and fuzzy."

"I'm gonna grab my stuff out of the car. My room still available?"

"Yep. I'll help you." Ghost walked with me back to the parking lot and shouldered one of the bags I'd packed.

"You know, I'm really sorry to hear about your dad," he said as we climbed the stairs.

"Thanks." There wasn't a lot more to say. "He's a fighter, you know. Maybe he'll beat it." We had agreed as a family to just take it day by day.

"If anyone can, it's Terminator." He chuckled, but it was hollow.

Ghost pushed open the door to my room, and that sense of coming home hit me again. I fought the urge to run through the living room and jump on the big bed. We put my things down inside the door.

"Brought a lot of stuff for a weekend," he pointed out.

"Thought I might stay a while. If you can still use the help."

A wide smile spread across Ghost's face, wrinkling the corners of his eyes that looked haunted far more often that they should for a guy his age. "Yeah. We can use the help."

"Thanks."

"Thank you," he said, turning to face me. "Do you really have a clue on the hunt, or was that just an excuse to get back up here to see a certain feisty construction forewoman?"

"No, I do. Mom figured something out, actually. But it was also an excuse."

Ghost laughed. "You gonna tell me?"

"I'll tell you all together. Dinner?"

"Sure. We're gonna eat on the back patio to celebrate the completion. Monroe's got something planned."

"Sounds good," I paused, wanting to ask about Lucy, but also not wanting to be too painfully needy. "Everyone coming?"

"Lucy's invited, yes."

"Mateo too?"

Ghost gave me a confused look. "Mateo?"

"The big guy on Lucy's crew. Kinda scary dude."

"Probably. I think they're all invited."

Great. I was going to have big brother Mateo watching me while I tried to get my shit together to talk to Lucy. No pressure.

"Okay. What time?"

Ghost looked at his watch. "Nowish. Wanna clean up first and then meet me in the bar?"

"You calling me dirty?"

"No, but I know you've been in the car a while. Thought you might need to take a piss. Or maybe give that perfect hair a spritz or something."

I tried to stop it, but one of my hands went to my hair, as if to check it was all in place. "My hair always looks perfect, you know that."

"Then let's go, asshole." Ghost punched me in the ribs and went back to the door. I followed him down to the bar, where our friends were gathered, music playing and drinks in front of them. This explained some of the distant noise I'd heard when we'd gone upstairs.

"Will!" Aubrey launched herself at me, and I caught her for a hug, and then greeted everyone else.

"We missed you," Monroe said, lifting a martini glass in my direction.

"Thanks." It felt a little like the old days, like I was part of something important. I'd missed these guys too.

"I have to get to the kitchen," Monroe said, turning to go. "Just came in here for some lubrication."

"Wait, Fake Tom is going to tell us what he figured out about the hunt. Right?" Aubrey's eyes were huge and round.

"Yeah. Okay." I looked to Ghost, who nodded eagerly. "So maybe it's nothing," I began.

"Better not be nothing," Brainiac whispered.

"So you figured out that all the movies came out of Mountaintop Studios, right?"

"Yeah," Brainiac said.

"Mom suggested we head over there, so we took a little field trip to Hollywood." I paused, loving the way they were all leaning in, waiting for my discovery. I had become strangely invested in the treasure hunt once Mom got interested.

"And?" Aubrey said. "I thought it didn't exist anymore."

"Doesn't," I said. "The only address we had for the place was actually a residential home."

"Go on," Ghost said, leaning in.

"Mom is very charming, you know," I told them. "She insisted we go to the door and ask some questions, so we did. Mostly she asked the questions."

"Who lives there?" Wiley asked, leaning forward as if my story was enthralling and not just a compilation of random crap my mom and I had done in LA.

"A lady with her family. Bunch of kids."

"FT? Is this going anywhere? You didn't come all the way back here to tell us stories about the housewives of Hollywood, did you?" Ghost looked impatient.

"Funny. No." Just to get him back, I settled back into my stool a bit, sipping my drink.

"And?" Aubrey said again.

"So Mom got her to invite us in. And guess what was on the walls?"

"Movie posters?" Brainiac said, as if this was obvious.

"Yep. Same ones we have here. And the woman we talked to? Her maiden name was Fusterburg."

"Poor woman," Aubrey said under her breath.

"Familiar?" I asked, looking between my friends.

They all stared back at me with blank faces, so I pulled up the Wikipedia entry for Annie Lowe on my phone again and read them the part about her disappearance and the name of her ex-fiancé. "Rudy Fusterburg?"

"Shit," Brainiac breathed.

"This lady's dad," I explained.

"Did you find out who he was? If he was involved in this somehow?" Ghost's face had taken on that optimistic shine again.

"Yeah. He was a screenwriter. He wrote all these movies." I pointed to the wall of posters.

"And?" Ghost was leaning forward now, expectantly.

"That's it. He was Mountaintop Studios basically."

"What?" Aubrey slumped over the bar.

"He's gone, but it was pretty clear he left a shit-ton of money when he left, if the house and the cars out front were anything to judge by. We didn't exactly quiz the woman about her dead dad's finances."

"Did she know about Annie Lowe?" Aubrey asked.

"She didn't. She was actually surprised to hear about it, but she said she'd get in touch if she found anything else out."

"Well, that's more than we had, I guess," Brainiac pointed out.

"I was going to dig a bit more, but things got busy at home."

Brainiac and Wiley donned matching sympathetic expressions. "How's he doing?" Brainiac asked.

"He's Dad. He's doing what he always does, ordering me around and trying to be in charge of everything."

They laughed, and I felt a strange responsibility to stop being glib and be more charitable toward Dad. "Actually, he's changed a little. Become . . . softer, in a way. He wants to give me the company. Make me the CEO."

"Shit, man," Ghost whispered. "What the hell are you doing here then?"

"Figuring a few things out," I said.

He nodded, as if he understood exactly what I meant, and then Monroe appeared back in the doorway of the bar.

"Take this party outside, will you? The crew's arriving."

"On it," Wiley said, grabbing a few bottles on his way around the bar.

"Can I help?" I asked him.

"Got the outdoor bar mostly stocked," he called over his shoulder. "Just grab another bottle of Half Cat, would you?"

I did as he said, and we all went through the lobby and out to the back patio as my heart rose in my throat at the thought of seeing Lucy again. The lights had come on as dusk fell, high-end Edison bulbs strung overhead and built-in footlights within the patio itself that served to give the whole space a warm glow. Candles flickered on the tabletops, the fire pits were lit, and one of the hot tubs had been activated, the water bubbling softly and glowing an inviting turquoise as steam rose into the night air. It was incredible, but something was missing.

Lucy wasn't here.

Chapter 36
Rocky Roads and Nuts of All Kinds

LUCY

I dragged my body through a shower back at the house, at war with myself the whole time.

Most of me felt like a twelve-year old girl, desperate to see the object of my heart's obsession again. But the rest of me was an experienced woman, one who knew how the world worked outside of Hallmark movies and idealized versions of love. One who knew that a guy like Will Cruz would probably never be happy in Kasper Ridge in the long run. One who knew that no matter what we wished for on any of the millions of stars that looked down over the Rockies at night—love was not enough.

I hadn't mentioned the completion of the first phase of construction to Papa yet, and I didn't tell him about the dinner I was supposed to attend, which meant that when I slumped out to the couch in my most comfortable sweats with my hair piled in a wet knot on my head, he didn't think anything was off.

"Want to order a pizza?" I asked him, every cheerful word feeling like a Herculean effort.

He frowned at me. He was sitting in his chair, working a puzzle in a magazine he subscribed to.

"Pizza is fine," he said. "As long as you're talking about ordering it, not cooking it."

"The kind I pick up works out okay," I said. I was tired of everyone insisting I couldn't cook. I could operate an oven, at least. Sometimes.

"Last time you got one of those, you forgot to set the timer and we had to eat pure carbon. I'm sure my doctor wouldn't approve. Not enough vitamins." He gave me a toothy grin.

"Fine. We'll have it delivered. Already cooked. With vegetables on it." I punched at my phone until pizza had been confirmed and then set it on the coffee table with a sigh I didn't mean to unleash.

"Oh no." Papa's gaze found me over the top of his magazine, the blue eyes clear and steady. "What's wrong?"

"Nothing at all," I told him, my heart convulsing at the lie. "Just tired. How are you? Feeling peppier?"

"I'm fine," he said. And he had seemed better. I'd never really thought about how vitamin deficiencies might affect someone over time, but the diagnosis Papa had received had me taking my own multivitamin regularly, and I'd chatted with my doctor about getting some extra vitamin D in the winter. Unfortunately, being up on my vitamins didn't seem to be helping my mood as it had done for Papa.

"That's it," he barked after we'd spent a few moments in silence.

It was my turn to frown at him. "What?"

"You sighed again. Like they've announced that they're not making your favorite face cream anymore or like Rocky Road is going to be discontinued."

"I don't like Rocky Road," I told him. "Nuts."

"Whatever. Something is wrong with you."

"Not everyone likes nuts in their ice cream."

"I don't mean about the ice cream." He put down his magazine and stood. "Tell me."

"Let's just watch *Jeopardy* and eat pizza." If I talked, he'd convince me to go to the party.

Papa crossed the room and sat down next to where I was tucked into the couch.

"Tell me about work today."

"It was all finishing touches outside. We tested power to the lights and the hot tubs, cleaned up some mortar on the patios, and collected our equipment. Patios are done."

"That explains your ebullient mood."

"Ebullient?"

"I have a word of the day emailed to me. Keeps the brain working."

"I see. Good."

"What's going on, Lucy? Something's wrong. Shouldn't you be out with the guys, celebrating?"

"They're all at the resort. Some dinner or something." I shouldn't have told him. I knew he'd throw a fit about me not going, but now it was out. I braced myself.

"Not invited?"

"I was invited."

"But you aren't there because . . ."

"I just didn't want to go. Sometimes I do what I want instead of what everyone else thinks I should do," I snapped.

Papa's eyes widened, but he didn't say anything else. He flicked on the television and we watched Jeopardy until a knock at the door broke the thick tension in the living room. I went to retrieve the pizza and brought it back, setting it on the ottoman in front of us and then going to get drinks.

"Get me a beer," Papa called.

That sounded like a good idea. I brought two in and sat heavily on the couch, working very hard to keep my mind off the resort. I didn't want to imagine Will sitting out there among his friends, laughing and talking. I didn't like knowing he was just a few minutes' drive away. It was easier when I knew he was in California.

But this was best. I was at least sixty-five percent certain of it.

Whatever had grown between us would fade with time, and it wasn't fair for me to keep Will close just because I missed him when he was away. The guy was the definition of worldly—his Navy career had taken him to places I'd only read about in newspaper articles. The idea of a guy like that ever being happy in as small a place as Kasper Ridge was ludicrous.

I could feel Papa's eyes on me as we sat side by side watching television, and I knew what he was thinking. Mostly because a moment later he said, "you need to go over there, Luce. Celebrate your accomplishment."

"There's plenty more work to be done. This is only a mid-point."

"If we don't celebrate the little things, what's the purpose of life?"

I turned my head to stare at him. Papa had never been big on deep thoughts, but that one kind of struck home.

I was about to respond when another knock came at the door. I put aside the plate of pizza I'd been ignoring and went to answer it. We weren't peephole people, and there were no fancy glass panels in Papa's front door. That's why I was utterly unprepared to see the person standing on the other side of the heavy wooden door.

"Will," my voice said, all breathy and surprised. I didn't recall authorizing speech, but my body was clearly going rogue, because in the next second, I was stepping closer to him, and a second after that, I was in his arms.

"God I missed you, Firecracker," he whispered, his strong arms around me and the scent of him filing my senses.

"I missed you too," I said, honesty clearly being a symptom of whatever had taken over my body.

He stepped back, not releasing me, but staring down into my face. "Really? Because other than to ask about my hair, I never heard from you."

I swallowed hard, ashamed at my own cowardice. "Things were really busy, and—"

"She wasn't that busy," Papa called helpfully from the couch.

"Let's, uh . . ." I stepped all the way out of the house onto the porch and pulled the door shut. Will and I moved to the wooden chairs on the front porch and sat overlooking the tree-studded hill at the front of Papa's property.

"I came by because you didn't come to dinner." Will's gaze was open and clear. It didn't feel right to lie at this point.

"I thought it would be better if we didn't see each other."

"Why?" It was almost a whisper.

I shook my head, dropping his gaze. My words were catching in my throat, blocked by an enormous lump of emotion I was struggling to keep down.

"Just easier," I managed, staring at my lap.

"Everyone was asking where you were." He was silent a moment, then he went on. "I thought Mateo was going to punch me when he figured out that the reason you didn't go to celebrate your own accomplishment was because you didn't want to see me. That guy seriously hates me."

I smiled a little at the thought of my old friend Mateo looking out for me. When I didn't say anything, he added, "maybe you hate me too."

Was it better to just let him believe that?

I battled the doubt and confusion in my mind. I couldn't let him believe I hated him. I had to give him that, at least. "I don't hate you," I said, risking a glance into those bottomless blue eyes.

"So why stay away?"

I felt a tear teetering on the verge of falling and my frustration grew. I didn't want to cry, didn't want to sit here like a heartbroken girl, wiping away my tears. This wasn't who I was. But Will deserved the truth and it was going to be hard to tell it without tears.

I took a deep breath and faced him. "Look," I began, trying to put on my serious construction foreman voice. "I just figured it was better to keep it clean. You left, you're leaving again, and I didn't want to confuse matters by potentially falling back into whatever we were doing when you were here before."

"What were we doing, Luce?"

"I think you know as well as I do." I was waging an internal battle. Should I really be honest? Let him see how hard this was for me? What would be the point?

"I thought I did. But now I think maybe I was wrong. Maybe I thought one thing, but you thought something else entirely." He looked so sad, I had to force myself to stay strong, to ignore those shining big eyes that melted my heart.

"You live in California. You're the kind of guy who seeks

adventure, who travels, who thrives on new experiences. You're polished and cosmopolitan, and I knew from the first second I saw you that Kasper Ridge wasn't big enough to hold your attention. You were only ever going to be temporary here. You never made any promises or gave me any reason to expect anything else. And still . . ."

"And still what?" Will was leaning forward, watching me intently as I struggled to keep it together.

The night sky was deepening around us and the sound of a horned owl sounded just beyond the porch.

"And I still let myself fall in love with you," I told him, my voice breaking. "I couldn't help it. I knew it would end like this, and I let myself do it anyway." Relief and a deep sadness washed through me.

"Luce," he said, his voice soft and tender.

I wanted to hear what he might say, but I couldn't bear it. I didn't want him to offer me any words of sympathy, or any false promises. I needed him to go. "Will, just go."

"Listen to me," he said, coming to face me, squatting down and taking my hands. "What if I stay?"

This was exactly what I'd been afraid of. "It'll never be enough. I'll never be enough and you'll end up resenting me. I can't do that to you."

"You wouldn't be doing anything to me except giving us both a chance to be happy. To be together." His face was open, his hands warm. I wanted to say yes. It would be so easy. But I knew I was right.

"Do you know how my parents died?" I asked him, knowing he didn't. Papa had told me a long time ago, and Mimi had been furious at him for it.

"A car accident," he said. "Right?"

"They were arguing," I told him, pulling my hands from his. "They were arguing about this place. About staying here, raising me here. Mom grew up here, but Dad was from North Carolina. He wanted to move back, head to a bigger city with more opportunity, more life. Kasper Ridge was too small for him. It's too small for most people. Papa said they were screaming at each other when they got in the car that day."

"I'm sorry that happened, Lucy, but that doesn't mean it would happen to us."

I stared at him. Didn't it? "I think the odds are against us."

"Give us a chance, Lucy." Will took my hand again. "I came over here tonight to tell you I love you. That I want to stay. For you. With you."

"You can't stay for me. I won't let you." The pain that tore through me at those words was almost unbearable. I stood suddenly, trying to escape the rending torture inside me. "Go home, Will." I stepped away, fighting with myself. But if I turned to look at him, I might never find the strength I needed to set him free.

I steeled myself and opened the door, closing it firmly between us. And then I looked at Papa and fell to thousands of pieces on the floor.

"Oh honey." Papa stood and came to collect me in his arms. They were thin, but they were still warm and comforting.

For a few minutes, I couldn't speak. I stifled sobs as tears gushed down my face and Papa led me to sit with him on the couch. I heard Will's truck start up and pull out of the gravel driveway, and a cold dark emptiness spread within me. What had I done?

"I did the right thing," I said, hoping to convince myself if I said it out loud.

"What did you do?" Papa asked quietly, keeping an arm around my shoulder. His shirt was soaked, but I didn't have the strength to lift my head.

"I sent him away."

"Why?"

"Because he'd leave eventually anyway. Just like Daddy wanted to. He wouldn't be happy here."

Papa sighed, and I felt his chest heave. "Lucy, look at me." He pushed me back a little forcing me to sit up on my own. I took a deep breath and looked up into his clear eyes. "I never should have told you that," he said. "Your grandmother was right. It was too much for a little girl to hear, and now you're building your life around ideas you have that are just plain wrong."

"This place wasn't enough for him, and they fought, and they died."

Papa nodded, his eyes shining. "It was like that, yeah. But they fought a lot about everything, honey. It wasn't just about this place. That was the nature of their relationship. And who's to say whether it would have lasted, had they lived to see. But that's not the point."

My heart was too broken to hurt anymore as I thought about my parents fighting constantly, about whether they would have divorced some day.

"The point is that you're making critical decisions about your life based on fear."

I didn't like to hear this, but he wasn't wrong. I dropped his gaze. I was afraid. I was terrified.

"What is the worst thing that could happen if you let that man stay here for you?"

"He could resent me forever."

"Or maybe he'd talk to you about things. Maybe you would find a solution."

I shook my head. "I can't leave here."

Papa's lips formed a thin line. "You sure as hell better not be staying for me."

I squinted at him. "Of course I am. And for the business."

"Dammit, Lucy, it's your turn to live. If you told me you wanted to move to Timbuktu, I'd be the first one at the goodbye party, sending you off. Or maybe I'd even come with you. But you have to live for you. Not for me. I won't let you do that."

"Who will take care of you?"

"I will, dammit. And I've got friends, you know. I wouldn't be alone. And if you decided to go live somewhere nice and warm like LA, hell, maybe I'd come too."

I stared at him. I couldn't picture him anywhere but here.

"I'm not tied to this place, and neither are you. There's a whole world out there, Lucy. Don't limit yourself. And don't turn your back on someone who loves you."

My mind spun as something I'd believed forever sifted away like sand. More tears gathered inside me and Papa held me again while I cried. This time it was different though. It almost felt like tears of relief were flowing from me, like I was letting go of something I hadn't ever meant to hold, something heavy that was weighing me down.

I looked up at my grandfather. "Oh Papa. What do I do now?"

"We'll think of something." He smiled and patted my back. "And it's gonna have to be good."

Chapter 37

Finish Your Beer

WILL

My head was spinning. I sat heavily in one of the wooden chairs on the back patio at Kasper Ridge, staring out into the darkness.

She'd said she loved me.

But as happy as that information made me, it didn't seem to matter. My heart was still a bloody pulp because she was refusing to even try.

I wasn't sure how long I'd sat there, but the back door opened eventually and Ghost came out. He handed me a beer and then sat in the chair at my side.

"Party still going in the bar?" I asked. I'd come around the side, hoping to avoid the celebration that had been moving inside when I'd left.

"Yeah." Ghost didn't say anything else, but his quiet presence made me want to talk.

"She wants me to leave." I took a long drink of the beer in my hand, mostly because I wasn't sure what else to do.

"Maybe she's just telling herself that."

"She told me that. Pretty clearly."

"Maybe she's scared."

I knew I was. "Yeah, maybe."

"Fear is a powerful motivator," Ghost went on, surprisingly eloquent all of a sudden. "It often wears a disguise and we might be tempted to believe it is common sense. Or wisdom. Maybe Lucy's just confused by the disguise her fear is wearing."

I'd never thought of fear that way, but I realized now that he was right. "I get that," I said, acknowledging that I'd worn a disguise too, when I first arrived. I'd been cocky and arrogant, but realizing it now didn't help the situation at hand.

"What do you want, Fake Tom? What about the CEO gig in LA?"

"I'd stay here if she'd give us a chance. I don't want to run the company. I only ever wanted Dad to believe in me. I thought if he gave me the company it would prove he trusted me."

"He does."

"Yeah. I guess so."

"That's gotta feel good."

It did, but it was a hollow victory given my worry for his health. And it was hard to feel happy about anything when my heart was aching so much over Lucy. What if she was the one I'd been meant to find? I couldn't imagine ever feeling this way about anyone else.

"I think I have to go back."

Ghost turned and looked at me for a long minute. "You have to do what seems right to you. You always have a spot here."

I nodded. "Thanks."

Chapter 38
Thin Mints Are Balm for the Soul

LUCY

I spent the weekend working feverishly on a plan, augmented by wine and Girl Scout cookies Papa had managed to hide from me up until now. But this, he said, was an emergency situation, and that called for heavy ammunition (supplied by little girls in green uniforms.)

He stayed by my side, reminding me there was a chance. I was torn. Part of me believed that I could show Will how much he meant to me and that I was willing to try, but another part worried it was already too late.

Saturday morning I put in a call to Archie Kasper. I was going to need help, and if Will hadn't already gone back to LA, then I needed to make sure he didn't leave.

"He's got a flight Monday night, Lucy," Archie told me, sounding sad about the fact.

"Perfect. Think you can keep him from leaving early for the airport Monday?"

"Hard to say. He's not exactly chatty right now. He's stayed in his room most of the weekend, and has been communicating in grunts for the most part."

"I'm just glad he's still there."

"You change your mind?" Archie asked, sounding like maybe he thought he was prying.

"About everything. Yes. And I'm going to need your help." I told him what I'd need. "And will you mind if I'm a little late Monday morning? I should be there before the meeting ends. Just need a few minutes while everyone is distracted to set things up."

"That's fine. Especially if you being late means Will's going to stop punching Rufus."

"He punched Rufus?"

"At least twice. The bear's face is starting to look a little malformed."

I didn't mention that I thought the bear had looked a little wonky to start with. Had Will been bear punching because of me?

"Try to keep Will from heading out early if you can."

"I will," Archie said.

I didn't have much time to fix the enormous mess I'd made, and at least two hearts were riding on my ability to undo everything I'd done.

Will had told me he loved me. No one had ever uttered

those words to me, not romantically. Papa had said them, for sure, and I had a vague memory of my parents tucking me in, whispering words of love to me. But I'd never let myself really get close enough to anyone else, not romantically.

I pulled into the resort parking lot Monday morning, ready to pretend to be ready to get to work on the next phase of construction. Guest rooms on the third floor had to be completely renovated by October, and the lobby and restaurant needed to be ready to go too. Some of my guys were shifting to other projects I'd contracted for long before Kasper Ridge Resort had hit my radar, but most were getting ready to do everything from drywall to tile to set things up inside the resort.

It was strangely quiet outside. The dumpsters had been moved to one side, where they'd stay even when guests were here—at least for the short term, and most of our heavy equipment had gone to other jobs, back to the depot, or headed back to wherever Will's father had sent it up from.

I headed inside and ran around the resort like a crazed spy, sneaking around corners and dodging through doors in an effort to set things up without accidentally running into Will. Was he even still here? I hoped it wasn't too late. If everything was going according to plan, he should be upstairs in the Monday meeting.

When everything was ready, I headed up to Archie's suite. I could hear masculine laughter from inside, and the distinct timbre of Will's voice made everything inside me jitter with nerves and anticipation. I froze, full of doubt. It would be easier to slump into a puddle of jittery nerves and second-guessing out here than it would be to step in there and pretend I was fine.

But I was nothing if not strong and determined, I reminded myself. I was the kind of woman who could direct an entire crew of huge gruff guys without being questioned, because that's the kind of confidence I projected. I meant business, took no prisoners, and didn't go in for drama. I was Lucy fucking Dale, and I could do this.

When I stepped into the suite, every eye hit me at once, and the laughter around the table died. For a second, the world moved in slow motion as my self-consciousness spiked to new levels.

"Morning everyone. Beautiful day. Can't wait to get started." I took the only seat left at the table, which unfortunately was straight across from Will. As conversation resumed, I let my eyes wander up to him, but he wasn't looking my way. In fact, through the entirety of the meeting, he didn't look at me once.

"Lucy, can you walk us through this next phase of the build?" Archie asked me. "I know things have changed a lot from your original plans and I think I know what's next, but just to make sure we're all on the same page and you've got the resources you'll need. With Will heading back to LA, let's be sure you're all set here to run the show."

"Sure," I said. My voice came out weak and scratchy. I cleared my throat violently and straightened my shoulders.

I was Lucy Fucking Dale.

I was a firecracker.

"Sure," I said again, much more forcefully. And then I explained in detail exactly what would be happening on this project for the next month. I talked about the materials we'd already ordered, the sequence in which finishes would be installed, and described the potential complications that could arise depending on what we encountered as we pulled out old fixtures and walls. But my mind was not on the job.

"Perfect." Archie said, and he turned his attention to Monroe, who began explaining that the Kasper Ridge Resort website was going live this week and that the online booking system was ready to go. Even as my mind reveled at the speed at which we'd accomplished so much, my heart ached inside me, and it was poisoning every single one of my thoughts and reactions. Working here without Will would be torture, I realized.

All the more reason why my plan couldn't fail. As soon as the meeting wrapped up, I glanced over at Archie, who gave me a quick nod. Then, with one more look at Will, who was still pointedly ignoring me, I left.

Chapter 39
Featured Matinee

WILL

I didn't look at Lucy until she was almost out of the suite, and then I let myself have one last look. Her hair was pulled up in a high ponytail, and she wore a fitted tank top and another pair of those denim jeans that were both completely job appropriate and ridiculously sexy at once. I wanted her with a burning desire I'd never felt for anyone else. It wasn't purely sexual, though there was no denying that.

I loved her. And I knew it was going to take a long time—years, maybe—to get past this feeling. But I couldn't do it here.

I turned to Ghost. "I might just head out. No point in me

hanging around here. Might as well get to the airport. Maybe I can get an earlier flight out."

"Actually," Ghost said, looking panicked at the idea. "Actually no. I have something I need help with."

"Oh. Okay, sure." I'd help him with whatever it was and then head out. "What's up?"

"Can you come with me?" he asked, heading toward the doors where Lucy had disappeared a few minutes earlier.

I followed him, my heart twisting painfully as I realized we were heading to the movie theater, where I'd touched Lucy for the first time, where I'd seen a glimmer of a future that would never be. Not for me. Every part of this place echoed with painful whispered memories now. I really needed to get out of here.

"It's just in here," Ghost said, pushing open the door to the screening room.

The room had been transformed—kind of. It was still torn to pieces and falling apart, but tiny glowing lights were strung everywhere, and all the rotting seats had been removed. A little couch sat in the center of the room facing the big screen up front.

"Why don't you sit?" Ghost suggested, pointing to the couch.

I wasn't sure what to think. A tiny flicker of hope was trying to ignite inside me, but Lucy wasn't here. She was nowhere to be seen, and she'd been pretty clear the other night. But if this wasn't about Lucy, then what the fuck was it? "What are we doing, Ghost?" My words came out angry. The rash of violent emotions bouncing inside me were exhausting.

"Just sit, okay? A little trust."

"Fine." I sat, crossing my arms tightly over my chest.

Ghost turned to leave.

"Where are you going?"

"This is a private showing," he said, and slipped out through the door at the back of the theater. And then the whole place went black.

"What the fuck," I whispered into the darkness.

A second later, I heard the projector in the booth over my head whirl to life, and the screen ahead of me lit up. An image of a little girl appeared on the screen, an old home movie. She was tiny, with light blue eyes and dark hair pulled into pigtails, and she wore a pink leotard and ballet slippers, but held a hand saw in her hands as she turned to face a man behind her who was standing next to a piece of wood set between a couple sawhorses.

My heart swelled, seeing Lucy as a kid. A contradiction even at three, she glowed with the same fire she possessed now. But what the hell was I watching?

"This is one of the few videos I have of my dad." Lucy's voice came through the speakers in the theater. I turned to see if I could find her up in the booth, but she was nowhere to be found. "I used to think it was because my parents died when I was so young, but Papa tells me it's because Dad wasn't around a lot. He and my mother weren't happy. So he found other places to be."

My chest ached. I wanted to find Lucy, to hug her. Why was she showing me this, though?

Another video slid onto the screen, replacing a tiny pink Lucy doing her best to saw a thick board as her dad looked on. In this one, Lucy was a little bigger, sitting on the lap of a woman who looked so much like Lucy did today that I would have believed it was her.

"My mother grew up here," she went on, and the movie advanced, showing me lots of images of Lucy with her mom. "She loved this place, just like her dad—Papa. And they made me love it too." Images of Lucy hiking, picnicking, on tiny skis, flashed by.

"But Dad didn't. The thing I never understood—not until Papa told me more about it—was that Dad wouldn't have been happy anywhere. It wasn't about Kasper Ridge or about this place being too tiny or too small-town for him. It wasn't about this place at all. It was about him."

Lucy danced by on the screen, her mother clapping and cheering as the tiny version of the woman I loved leapt and turned.

"I was too little to know any of that. And I think we tend to hang onto ideas we form when we're little, especially if they're built around tragedies that impact our lives in other ways. I lost my parents when I was four, and Papa and Mimi, my grand-mother, were right to keep some of the troubles of their marriage from me then. But now, I understand that something I spent my life believing is tainting the way I'm living it.

"I had plenty of other examples of people leaving Kasper Ridge as I grew up. Boys I liked in high school, whose families moved away. Guys I dated in college who couldn't imagine coming to live in a place so small. Men who visited this place, but had entire lives built elsewhere. In every instance, I drew lines back to my dad, to my parents. I decided that people didn't stay here. That I was going to have to choose between this place, and the man who raised me, and the rest of the world."

I watched photos of Lucy slide by on the screen, lost in watching her grow and mature into the woman I was completely in love with. Her hair and clothes changed, and the backgrounds all morphed from a little girl's world into a teenag-er's life and then to photos of her in college, somewhere with brick buildings and dorms.

"The thing is, Will..." she paused and my heart leapt at hearing my name on her lips. The photos on the screen came to an end, and the theater was completely dark again. I turned toward the doors, wondering where she was, needing to see her, just as her voice came again, closer. Not over the speakers now. The lights flickered back on as she spoke. Lucy stood at the back of the theater.

"The thing is, I never stopped to think about what all those people were returning to. It never occurred to me that they weren't choosing between Kasper Ridge and someplace else. Or between me and something else. They'd never had a choice because this isn't the kind of place you decide to move to—not like New York or Denver. There aren't scads of jobs, or hundreds of great neighborhoods. This place can't absorb people like those cities can. But I'd already decided that every time someone left, it was because I wasn't enough for them to stay."

"Lucy," I said, starting to stand, needing to go to her.

"Let me finish," she said. "I'm getting to the point, I promise." She moved closer, until she was standing just to the side of the couch where I sat.

"It was never really about me," she went on. "And when it might have been, I had already pushed them away and given them more reasons to leave than to stay.

"But I don't want to do that anymore. It never mattered before, because I'd never met anyone who made my entire body feel like some kind of reactor. I've never met anyone who felt like a magnet, who was so impossible for me to resist that it was almost painful to stay away from him."

She moved to sit next to me on the couch. "Until I met you." Her eyes met mine, and they were shining with emotion, her face uncertain. I wanted to hold her, but I forced myself to freeze, to let her finish. I was pretty sure I knew what was happening here, but I didn't think I could take being hurt again. I needed to hear the words.

"Will," she whispered. "I've been so stupid, so stubborn." She shook her head lightly, and a tear dripped down her cheek. She pushed it away with the heel of one hand and let out a nervous laugh that made everything in me want to reach for her.

"I love you," she went on. "I've loved you for a while now. And that realization was terrifying. Because, I told myself, you would inevitably leave. I built entire scenarios that had you leaving, that gave you no choices, because I thought it would be easier if I never considered that you could stay. With me. For me."

"I love you too," I whispered, my heart pounding inside me chest so loudly I was surprised it wasn't echoing off the walls.

"I've been an idiot," she said, dropping my gaze. "And I was trying to show you—with this silly movie—that there was a reason. It wasn't a good one, but it wasn't about you. It was just this story I'd built up in my mind, this defense system—"

"I get it," I said, reaching for her hand. She let me take it, and the contact with her soft skin smoothed over so many of the rough hurt patches inside me, the wounds that had erupted at her refusal to give us a chance. "I've had time to think too," I told her. "My life has been about one thing, Lucy. And it wasn't about me. Or what I really wanted, or who I really was."

"It wasn't until I came here, to Kasper Ridge, that I started to understand what I wanted from life. It wasn't until I met you that I saw what could be possible, that I considered what life would be like if I didn't live it for someone else—to try to please my father. You made me see what it might be like if I were to live for me."

Lucy's eyes gleamed, and she slid closer, her lips parting slightly.

"People have always said things like 'follow your heart,' and I've never understood what they meant," I told her. "Because through all those years, my heart was quiet. It wasn't an organ I led with because I needed to be smart. I needed to figure out how to finally achieve something that would get my father's attention, earn his love."

"God, Will," Lucy whispered, "I'm so sorry."

I shook my head, pulled her closer. I needed her to know that I was past all that, that she'd helped me figure out a few things about life. "If I'd listened to my heart a lot earlier, I might have realized that I didn't want the things he wanted. I didn't want to be him. I just wanted him to tell me I was good enough. And I didn't see another path.

"But you helped me find it, whether you meant to or not. Lucy, my life isn't going to be about exotic travel and cosmopolitan locations. And it's not going to be about making my dad proud of me. I want it to be about the future, and I want to build the future with you."

"I want that too," she whispered, and a cool soothing feeling flooded me, giving me the confidence to go on.

"You make me feel seen and understood in a way I've never been before. You challenge me and infuriate me, and I love every single second of it. When I close my eyes at night after I've been with you, your voice fills my head, and when I dream, it's of your laughter, your smile.

"I have been searching for something, Lucy. And a year ago I would have told you I was searching for success or money, maybe. That I was trying to accomplish something.

"But now I realize that I was searching for you. And that happiness and success in this life are not about a location or some kind of accomplishment that some guy hands you a medal for. Those things are about other people and connection. And it took coming up here and meeting you to make me realize it."

"Will," she whispered, leaning into my body as I put my arms around her.

I held her close, my mind finally still as the thing that had been missing slipped back into place.

"I'd like it if you would stay," she said quietly. "If you want to. And maybe we could go on a date or two."

"Lucy Dale," I whispered, "you're everything I never knew I was looking for, and now that I've found you, you're going to have to chase me out of here with a herd of buffalo to get me to leave."

"Buffalo?" she asked, a light chuckle escaping her.

I hesitated. "That's a Colorado thing, right? Should I have said mountain lions or bears?"

"Mountain lions and bears don't run in herds."

"Do you suppose we could hold off on the Colorado wildlife lesson for a second?"

"Yes," she agreed.

"Firecracker," I whispered, pulling her close. My fingers were in her soft hair, but they'd run into a surprising little bit of something. I pulled it out. "Is this a cookie?"

Lucy moved back to see what I had pulled out of her hair, and her face morphed into a frown as she identified it. "A Samoa," she confirmed. "It was a hard weekend."

I didn't ask, just put the cookie piece next to us and pulled her back into my arms. I could feel her heart beating in her chest, firm against my own, and it was all I needed.

"I love you," I told the woman in my arms.

"I love you too," she said.

And then she kissed me, and it was the kind of kiss you can only truly appreciate if you've lived your life believing you'd never find a kiss like that. The kind that sears your insides with heat, but also makes your heart swell with comfort, the kind of kiss that is as reassuring as it is arousing. The kind of kiss that doesn't promise forever—the kind that says, "whatever I have, whatever might come my way... I'll share it with you."

It was all the promise I needed.

Epilogue
Not Everyone Can be Right

WILL

For the next six weeks, everything in my life including the resort, became more certain, more complete. The guest rooms on the third floor were ready for guests, the elevator was finally in working order, the kitchen in the restaurant was complete and the restaurant interiors were close behind. The lobby was the last thing we finished, right after the overhang on the circular drive up front, and when it was done, it was the crowning touch on a place that was already promising to be a sought-out destination.

"You were right," Lucy said, bumping my shoulder with

hers as we both looked up at the new fixtures hanging from the lobby ceiling and lighting the finished space with a glamorous shine.

"I usually am, don't you know that by now?"

"Weird," she laughed, "because I'm usually right too."

"So as long as we agree, we'll be good." I put an arm around her shoulders. I wouldn't have cared if she'd been insistent on the other chandeliers, a more modern dark iron fixture that she thought went with some of the newer touches we'd added. They would have worked just as well as the ones I'd found that were pretty close to the originals and gave the place a Hollywood flare. I just liked that we'd done it together. In fact, looking around the shiny finished spaces at the Kasper Ridge Resort, it was pretty damned hard not to be proud—of both of us. We'd done it all together.

"We're not always going to agree on everything," she said, a hint of warning in her voice.

"I don't expect that we will."

"Sometimes I'll fight you just on principle," she warned. "To keep you on your toes."

Her bright eyes were shining with laughter, and I pulled her even closer to my side, the warm glow that burned hot when she was near getting bigger and stronger every day.

"No sex in the lobby," Monroe quipped as she strolled past, carrying a tray of plates into the bar.

"Funny," I shot back.

Lucy turned to face me and pushed up onto her toes to give me a quick kiss. "I need to go home and get ready for tonight."

"Okay," I said, and I watched her turn and head out the front doors of the lobby, her perfect ass doing the same thing to me that it had been doing since the first time I saw her. I took a deep breath and looked around me, feeling like the luckiest guy in the world.

"Don't you have work to do?" Ghost's voice came from the stairs as he descended, heading toward me.

"Look around. Done. And ahead of schedule."

Ghost nodded with satisfaction. "This place is incredible," he said, his voice low and reverent. "I'm not sure I ever expected we'd really get it done."

"Oh ye of little faith," I quipped.

Ghost gave me a serious look. "Faith is one thing I'm not sure I have much of anymore." Then his face cleared. "But this place is amazing. Thanks for all the hard work. I know it wasn't all easy."

"None of it was easy," I told him. "That's why it feels so good to see it finished."

He nodded. "Your folks on the way?"

I checked my watch. Mom had called from the airport a few hours earlier. "Another hour or so probably."

He nodded. "Monroe's mom is coming, and Wiley's brother and his girlfriend got here this morning."

We'd invited friends and family for a private happy hour to celebrate the soft opening of the Kasper Ridge Resort. A bunch of our old squadron mates were coming up to put eyes on the place, and assorted family members had been invited too.

"I'm gonna go get dressed," I told him.

As I moved toward the stairs, Ghost called back. "Hey, your dad . . . how's he doing?"

"He's good. Mom says the first round of chemo was hard on him, but that he's doing better." It had been a rough time for my parents, but when I'd offered to come home to stay, they'd refused. I'd flown home a couple times, only for a few days at stretch when Lucy insisted she had things under control at the resort. Dad and I had made some arrangements for the company when he was feeling up to it, and Mom had reassured me constantly that they were doing fine.

I'd struggled with some guilt, still did. But Dad had made a point of telling me he wanted to see me live my life, that no matter what happened, he didn't want me to spend one more day doing things because I thought they were what he wanted.

"I want you to be happy, Son. To make choices based on what you want. That's what will make me most proud. To see you happy."

It was a strange realization for me—that I could feel simultaneously the happiest and saddest I'd been all at once. But life was funny like that.

"I'm looking forward to seeing him," Ghost said, snapping me back to the present.

"Yeah, me too."

My parents would be some of the first guests to stay in the newly completed guest rooms upstairs, and in a way this weekend was a dry run for the real opening, which was still a month out. Everything was ready, and for the first time in my life, I was looking forward to seeing my father, eager to show him something I didn't have to wonder if he would be proud of me for.

* * *

An hour later, I was back in the lobby, taking my mother's bags and listening to my father's ongoing narrative about the renovation.

"You should have seen the place last time I was here," he was telling Mom. "It was a disaster. Will, you've done amazing things here in a really short amount of time."

A warm glow of pride washed through me at his words.

"It looks gorgeous," Mom said, looking around the space with a smile. "Very old Hollywood meets the mountains."

"I think that's probably close to the original feel," I said. "Marvin was very into Hollywood for whatever reason."

"Sir," Ghost said, striding into the lobby from the bar. "Mrs. Cruz. We're so happy you could come. It's really good to see you." He directed this last part at Dad, and my father acknowledged the subtle reference to his health. I knew that would be all the conversation about the situation that he would allow. Though he'd become a somewhat mellower version of the demanding and determined man I'd always known, he was still concerned with appearances, and he didn't want to appear weak to the officers he once commanded. That was who he was, and I would respect it.

"I'll show you the rooms," I told them, turning toward the newly functional elevator.

"I'll see you tonight at the party," Ghost said, waving as the elevator doors closed.

I got Mom and Dad settled, and then went back to my room to finish the surprise I'd been working on for Lucy. I wasn't going to give it to her at the party—there'd be too much going on already. But I hoped we would end up in my room when it was over, and I'd surprise her with it then.

By the time I went back downstairs, the lobby was filling with guests. Monroe and the others had erected cocktail tables and seating areas in the big space, and big band music flowed through the overhead speakers. It felt a bit like stepping back in time, with the dark paneled walls polished to a high shine, the chandeliers dripping with glimmering light, and the sleek marble floors underfoot.

People were circulating through the bar and back to the lobby, and we'd set up a buffet and lit the enormous fire pit out back, so the entire space felt alive and vibrant. It was almost as if it had been waiting for this moment to come back to life, waiting to be returned to its original purpose.

"There you are," Lucy found me out back, where I was sitting with Mom and Dad near the fire.

"You look beautiful," I told her. Lucy had done her hair in an ornate arrangement at the back of her head that reminded me of the pinup girls I'd seen painted on the bombers from the forties. "Let me introduce you to my mother. You've met Dad before. Dad, you remember Lucy Dale?"

My father stood and took Lucy's hand, kissing her cheek. "It's wonderful to see you again, Lucy."

"I'm pleased to meet you," Mom said, and then her face broke into a huge smile and she pulled Lucy into a hug that nearly sent them both tipping sideways.

"Don't knock her over, Mom," I said, reaching out to steady them both. Lucy was recovering, but clearly hadn't expected to be attacked by my tiny mother.

"This is my grandfather," Lucy told them, introducing Papa, who stood behind her, looking around with glowing eyes and a tiny smile playing beneath the grizzled short beard he wore. I was happy to see him looking so pleased, and it felt good to know Lucy and I could restore some part of his childhood for him to enjoy again.

"Ernie Dale," he said, shaking hands.

We all sat, and it was strange how comfortable the situation was. I got up at one point to get drinks for everyone, and my mother came with me.

"What are your plans, Will?"

I looked down at her as we waited in line for the bar, trying to figure out what she meant. "My plans for what, Mom?"

"For Lucy."

Mom had been dropping hints about weddings and grand-children ever since I'd told her about Lucy, and this was her less subtle way of pushing the idea.

"We haven't been dating long," I reminded her.

"But you love her. And she loves you. And you're not getting any younger."

"Thanks for that," I said handing her the gin and tonic I'd ordered for her.

"You know what I mean. I just love seeing you so happy."

I picked up the rest of our drinks, handing Dad's to my mother. As we walked back across the patio, I told her a tiny part of my secret. "I do have a plan. I was going to show it to Lucy later."

Mom looked disappointed, and I decided that maybe I could share it now instead. I'd already talked part of it over with Dad, so it wouldn't be a shock for him.

I handed drinks to Lucy and Papa, and set my own down. "Will you excuse me for a moment? I'll be right back."

I went upstairs and gathered the plans, heading back down to the patio where it was relatively quiet compared to the bustle of the lobby and bar.

"What's that?" Lucy asked immediately, noting the rolled. up papers I carried.

I took a deep breath and sat, rolling the plans out over the low table in front of us. "I was going to show you this later, but Ernie, it makes sense for you to see it too." My breath caught in my throat. I was surprisingly nervous.

"Is this the resort?" Mom asked, pointing to the building plans. "It looks small."

"Not the resort," I confirmed. "That's a house."

I explained that the resort property included a small subdivision that had never been built, a private drive that had been set up with power and sewer lines, but never developed. Archie had granted me the deed to that land for my investment in the resort, and given me license to develop it. We agreed that some kind of permanent staff housing would make sense—we couldn't live in the hotel forever.

I took a deep breath, looking between Lucy and Papa. "It's the house I'd like to build for you and Lucy," I told him. "And for me."

They exchanged a look and then turned matching expressions of amused confusion on me.

"Will, are you suggesting we're ready to move in together?" Papa asked me, chuckling.

"I thought we might be," I told him, glancing at Lucy.

Mom was sitting with her hands clasped tightly under her chin, and I thought she might have been holding her breath.

"Lucy," I said, turning to face her. "Will you move in with me?"

"I mean . . ." she didn't say no, but she looked hesitant. "Wait, this house isn't built yet, is it?"

I shook my head, grinning. "No. You'd have to continue to date me for the next twelve months while it gets built. Could take eighteen. So I'm asking for the future."

"You're building yourself a house here," she said, almost whispering. I'd told Lucy many times that I intended to stay, but I thought this concrete symbol of my intent might have finally made her believe it.

"No," I told her. "I'm building *us* a house here. By the time it's done, I'd like to ask you to marry me."

No one spoke as I let that terrifying suggestion fly, and I took a deep breath to cover my nerves.

A tear rolled down Lucy's cheek as she stared at me.

"Hey," I said, wiping it away. "It's okay. We don't have to do anything fast here. We have lots of time."

She shook her head, a wide smile overtaking her face. "That's why I'm crying," she explained. "I think I'm finally realizing that it's true. We have time. We have the future. You're not leaving."

I smiled.

Lucy laughed, more tears running down her face.

"Oh honey," Mom said, and I wasn't sure if she was taking to me or to Lucy, but there were tears standing in her eyes too.

"Walk us through this plan," Papa said, pointing at the house. "Is this a Kasper Ridge Construction job?"

"That's the other part of the plan," I told them, grinning at Dad. "Cruz Construction is opening a satellite office here in Kasper Ridge. We have some connections and assets that could be helpful up here."

Lucy looked uncertain, as if realizing this might mean competition for Kasper Ridge Construction.

"But all the jobs will be subcontracted," I explained. "We'll source business, but we're not going to crew the sites, unless we're subcontracted by a local company. And anything we bring in gets subcontracted out."

Lucy frowned at me. It wasn't the savviest of business moves, but it allowed me to establish an office here, from which I'd manage Dad's company. Markie was going to be the on-site management at the Orange County office.

"So yes," I told Papa. "This will be a Kasper Ridge Construction job. If they can fit it in the schedule . . . which Cruz can help make happen."

"And where did you say my room was?" Papa asked, squinting down at the plans.

I shuffled the blueprints and showed him what he was looking for. "Not your room. Your wing." I'd set the house up with a separate apartment on the first floor that allowed Papa his privacy, but also flowed into the common areas of the main house if he chose to leave the connecting doors open.

Papa let out a little laugh that I was pretty sure meant he was okay with this idea. I hadn't been sure if he'd be willing to move or not. I knew he had a lot of memories in the house he and Lucy shared now.

My parents were quiet through all this, but when I turned to glance at them, I saw that they were holding hands, my dad silently squeezing my mother's fingers as their eyes shone with what I thought was happiness. Maybe even something like pride.

"What do you think?" I asked Lucy.

She stood and moved to where I sat, placing herself on my lap. And then she wrapped her arms around my neck and kissed me quickly. "I think we'd better prioritize this build," she said. "I'll get to work on it Monday morning."

"So you like it?"

"I love it. And you."

In that moment, I was pretty sure I felt my heart actually swell like the Grinch at the end of the Dr. Seuss story. Happiness was a tangible thing that filled the space inside me and floated in the cooling night air around us. It lit the faces of the people I loved, and I knew it was written on my own. For the first time in my life, I felt complete.

I squeezed the woman in my arms and settled back into my chair, careful to remember everything about this moment. I knew the future was uncertain, that the plans we were making might not come to pass exactly as we hoped. But we had now. We had this moment, and it was perfect.

Bonus Epilogue
Just a Crush: Sneak Peek!

LUCY

As summer rolled into fall, I tried not to second guess things. I was happy, and that was enough. Papa was healthy, Will was every bit as charming and sexy and incredible as ever, and the refurbishment of the resort and this new job—building custom homes on resort property—had work going well too.

The third-floor guest rooms were complete, but those on the second-floor were being carpeted and painted and were on track to receive their first guests in mid-November. Monroe—whose real name I still didn't know—had talked us into wallpapering the bathrooms, which was taking a little longer than I'd hoped since it wasn't something the guys had a lot of experience with. But I had to admit, the finished product did look pretty chic. I made a note to wallpaper the downstairs powder room in the house I was building with Will.

"Hey Lucy!" Mateo's voice called down the wide second-floor corridor, sounding more flustered than usual.

I stepped away from the door I was hanging with Andrew, and headed in his direction.

"What's up? You sound panicky," I told him, stepping into the room where he was working. He and Herman were standing in the small sink area of the suite's bathroom, wearing matching frustrated expressions and covered in wallpaper paste. One long vertical strip of wallpaper was stuck to the wall at an angle, the corner drooping and a huge bubble in the center.

"This is impossible," Herman told me.

It did seem like applying wallpaper was kind of an art form, and while my guys were pretty good with paint and caulk, this was one thing that seemed to have them stymied.

"Well, that's not gonna work," I said, pointing at the sheet beginning to peel off the wall.

"We kind of figured that out. We might need to bring someone in to do this, boss," Mateo said. It was clear it pained him to admit it. Like me, Mateo tended to bulldoze through things, willing to try just about anything before asking for help.

"Let me see," I said, climbing the ladder to the top so I could grab the corners of the strip. "If I pull this off, can we reattach it straight? Maybe you can kind of smooth as I stick it up here." I pulled the wallpaper from the wall, and lifted the whole strip, sticking the corners up snugly against the ceiling. The top, at least, looked perfect for one second before it began to slide down and go wonky again.

"Why is this so hard?" I heard myself shriek.

"That's what she said," came a feminine voice, followed by a peal of light laughter.

Monroe.

I was still a little suspicious of the woman who seemed to be everywhere, know everyone, and always look fantastic. She was a bit handsy with Will, but I'd been around her long enough now to know she was like that with everyone. I wondered what she hid beneath all that bluster and charm.

She strode into the room with Will, and despite my unease around the blond bombshell, my heart rate always calmed just a bit when Will's ocean blue eyes met mine.

"Well, that's not gonna work," Monroe declared, sticking her hands on her generously curved hips and tilting her pretty head back to take in our work.

"How many contractors does it take to hang a piece of wallpaper?" Will asked, chuckling until his eyes found my face again and the chuckle died in his throat.

"This isn't funny," I told them. "If we don't get this devil paper stuck nicely to these walls, we'll fall behind schedule. And while I'm sure guests will appreciate this lovely French countryside toile you've picked out, Monroe, they might want sinks and toilets even more."

Monroe was unfazed by my quip, and she waved a hand at me. "Come on down, I'll show you. It just takes a little coaxing."

I climbed down the ladder and backed purposely into Will, who immediately wrapped his arms around me and dropped a soft kiss onto my neck before stepping away. Everyone knew we were together, but we still did our best to be professional at work.

Monroe climbed the ladder, and I tried not to admire the perfect roundness of her denim-clad backside or the curve of her legs in the tight-fitting jeans, but they were pretty much in my face. And a woman can acknowledge another woman looking good without it being a thing.

Mateo, however, seemed to be struggling with the view, maybe because he was squeezed into the corner and the ladder's position had him pretty much pinned at eye level with Monroe's booty. She seemed to realize this too, and I thought she was wiggling a bit more than was strictly necessary as she explained exactly how to hang the paper.

"Give me a hand here, will you Mateo?"

He squeezed out from behind her and took the bottom section of the paper in his hands.

"You've gotta have a little extra up here," she said, tugging the whole sheet higher so there were a couple inches of over-hang at the top. "And you make sure the dominant part of the pattern is on the dominant wall so it's where the eye lands. Hand me that sponge?" She pointed to a sponge next to a bucket of water on the plastic laid out over the floor.

I handed her the sponge, and watched as she expertly pressed and smoothed the paper down until she was standing face to face with Mateo, who still looked a little flustered by her sudden appearance in his personal space. A tiny defensive urge reared up within me, but Mateo was a grown man. He could step back if he wanted to.

Monroe showed the guys how to press out bubbles with the long plastic squeegee and how to align the next sheet so the pattern matched.

"Equal parts arts and crafts and engineering," she said, step-ping back from the first two pieces hung perfectly on the wall.

"That's going to look incredible," Will said. "Luce, we should—"

"Already ordered some for the downstairs powder room."

"Monroe will have to hang it for us."

"These guys can do it," Monroe assured us, looking between

the two men. "Can't you?"

"Yeah," Mateo said, finally breaking out of his buxom-blond-induced stupor. "Maybe you can hang out and help us finish this first room? We should be good from there."

Monroe gave Mateo a smile that I thought was engineered to send his brain swirling, and agreed to stay and help. As we were leaving the room, Will leaned in close. "She's flirting with Mateo, you got that, right?"

"I got that," I told him. "I'm just not sure how I feel about it."

"She's harmless."

"He's got a kid. He just ended a relationship. If she hurts him, I'll stomp on her myself."

Will turned his head to look at me, eyebrows high. "Remind me not to get on your bad side."

I smiled up at him, love and gratitude and a sense of calm contentment filling me as we headed down to the lobby in the elevator. I snuggled into his side and let his mountain tropical scent wash through me. "I love you," I whispered as the doors opened.

"I love . . . where is this fucking bear going to go, Ghost?" Rufus was positioned just outside the elevator doors, essentially impeding our ability to exit. We pushed him out of the way to find Ghost and Aubrey laughing hysterically.

"Aren't we a little too busy for jokes at this point?" Will asked them.

"Asks the king of Navy shenanigans," Ghost said, making some kind of point neither Aubrey or I understood.

"What's—" Aubrey began.

"Another time," Will said.

"You know, my grandfather said he belongs in the bar on that high ledge."

Ghost nodded. "Yeah. We should put him where he

313

belongs, I guess. C'mon Rufus. Give me a hand?" He nodded at Will.

They tipped the bear over and Ghost picked up his head as Will lifted his back, putting the bear's feet in the air. Aubrey and I stood back, but a second later, I was stopping them.

"Wait!"

"What?" They asked in unison.

"Oh shit, yeah . . ." Aubrey stepped in closer to the stuffed bear. "Did we know this was here?"

"What?" Ghost asked, putting down the bear's head and stepping around to where Aubrey stood, pointing at the bear's foot. A tiny metal plaque was bolted to the underside of one of his big paws, the print on it almost too tiny to read.

"Light?" Ghost said, and Will turned on the flashlight on his phone.

"What's it say?"

Ghost read aloud: "Rufus was named for Rudy 'the traitor' Fusterburg. May he rot in hell."

"Well, that's cheery," Aubrey said.

"Rudy Fusterburg," Ghost said. "That name keeps coming up. He was the screenwriter, right?"

"Right," Will said. "The one whose house we went to in Hollywood."

"It's a clue!" Aubrey shrieked. "We finally have another clue!"

"We kind of had that one already," I pointed out.

"True," Will said. "But now we know Marvin wasn't too fond of this guy. We need to figure out why."

We hoisted Rufus up to his spot in the bar, where he did seem to look at home. That night we all went up to put eyes on the wallpaper work in the first two bathrooms. Evidently, Herman had been dismissed from wallpaper duty and Mateo and Monroe told us they'd developed some kind of system.

"She's a genius with this stuff," Mateo said, and Monroe grinned at his praise and then shot him a wink I could only call lascivious.

"Hey," I whispered to him, feeling protective of my old friend. "Be careful there, okay?"

His smile faded and he gave me a serious look. "It's okay, Lucy. We just hung some paper."

"I'm looking out for you. She's a player. You should hear the stories they tell."

"I'm not proposing marriage. We're just getting these rooms put together. You should be happy—your precious schedule is intact." He elbowed me in the shoulder.

That night, Will and I relaxed on the balcony of his room overlooking the hills and trees behind us.

"Hard to believe there's going to be snow up here soon," he said.

"I know," I sighed, leaning in to rest my head on his shoulder. "It's weird though, I'm looking forward to this winter in a way I never have before."

"How come?"

"You, mostly." I turned my head to meet his eyes in the fading light.

"Oh yeah?"

I nodded. "Work slows down, and I like the idea of being here with you, the fireplace going, just relaxing for a while instead of going all the time on this ridiculous schedule."

"That you set."

"That I set."

"Speaking of which . . ." Will said, trailing off as a wide smile crept across his face.

"What?"

"Well, I was talking to Ghost, and we had an idea."

Any hopes I had for this being some kind of romantic surprise fizzled at the mention of Ghost. "Okay."

"We don't like the thought of you driving back and forth from here to your place down that highway."

"Hold on," I interrupted. "I grew up driving these roads. If anything, I should be worried about you city types up here with your SUVs telling everyone that you'll be fine because you've got four wheel drive."

Will stuck his tongue out at me.

"Cute."

"Just listen for a second, woman, will you?" He chuckled and then continued. "I wondered if you might just move in here with me. Until the house is done next summer."

I began to protest immediately. I wasn't leaving Papa alone.

"There's a room for Ernie," he said, cutting off my argument. "You might as well both live here."

There was something appealing about the idea of having Papa so close, and definitely of being with Will.

"I don't know if Papa will want to move," I said, though I already knew that he would like the idea of living at the resort, being part of the mystery surrounding the place, being involved in his old friend's final plan.

"Maybe he wouldn't complain if we were married," Will said lightly.

My head snapped around to stare at him. "What did you say?"

Will stood and went inside, returning with a soft smile on his perfect lips. He pushed his chair out of the way and dropped to his knee in front of me, a little box in his hands.

"I know it's fast, Lucy," he said. "But I've already got Papa's blessing. Now I just need to know if I have yours."

I knew what was coming, but my head was spinning and I

felt like I might float right off the chair. I wrapped a hand around the armrest to anchor myself as my heart pushed its way into my throat.

"I came up here looking for something," Will went on. "A new beginning, a different version of myself. And what I found was a home. A place where I was the person I was meant to be, and a place that was already home to the person I was meant to spend my life with. You've already taught me so much—about knowing myself, understanding my strengths, admitting when I need help—"

"And about high altitude construction," I added.

"I don't think you're supposed to say anything yet. I'm going to ask you a question and then you get to talk."

"Sorry," I said quickly, heat climbing my cheeks.

"But yes, about high altitude construction too. Mostly, Lucy Dale, you taught me that it was okay to be vulnerable. That it was okay to not be perfect. And that the only person I needed to make proud was myself.

"I came to Kasper Ridge to find myself, and I was lucky enough to find so much more than that. And I would love it if you would marry me, if you would stand by my side, and if you'd be willing to navigate this world as my partner. I love you, Lucy. Marry me?"

I wanted to scream my response, to leap from the chair and dance, but my voice was lost in the elated chaos inside my body. I tried to say yes, but a squeak was all that came out. Lucy Fucking Dale was speechless, and that was a first.

Since words were failing me, I nodded my head vigorously, and then threw my arms around Will, pulling him up and kissing him like he'd told me he was shipping out tomorrow.

"Don't you want to see the ring?" he asked, his words muffled by my attention.

"Yes," I managed finally. "Yes, I'll marry you. And yes, I want to see the ring."

He found enough space between us to pop open the box, and the ring inside was familiar, but I couldn't say exactly why. It was an emerald, ringed by tiny diamonds and set in an antique ornate setting. Still slim and delicate, but slightly more substantial than a solitaire. I loved it.

"It's perfect," I said.

"It was your mother's," he said softly, his tone suggesting that maybe I knew this. "Papa gave it to me and insisted that you have it. But I'll happily buy you your own if you'd prefer it."

My heart did something odd inside my chest, and words slipped out of my grasp again. I felt tears threatening.

I put out my left hand, and Will slipped the ring on. I'd tried this ring on once before, when I'd been snooping through Papa's things. I'd found it and put it on, and Mimi had found me in their room looking at it.

"That," she had told me. "Is your mother's ring. And for now, I'm going to keep it safe for you. One day it will be yours, Lucy." I never saw the ring again until now.

"I love it," I whispered. "It's perfect. You're perfect."

We stood there, the mountain, trees and clear Colorado sky bearing witness to the happiest moment of my life. And as Will Cruz put his arms around me, I felt myself finally settle into the life I was meant to have. Here, with this man.

* * *

Ready for Monroe and Mateo's story? Don't miss this grumpy single dad meets sunshine party girl romance, and get more clues to solve the Kasper Ridge Treasure Hunt!

Pre-order Only a Crush here!

Also by Delancey Stewart

Want more? Get early releases, sneak peeks and freebies! Join my mailing list here or scan the QR code and get a free story!

The Kasper Ridge Series:

Only a Summer (prequel)

Only a Fling

Only a Crush

The Singletree Series:

Happily Ever His

Happily Ever Hers

Shaking the Sleigh

Second Chance Spring

Falling Into Forever

The Digital Dating Series (with Marika Ray):

Texting with the Enemy

While You Were Texting

Save the Last Text

How to Lose a Girl in 10 Texts

The MR. MATCH Series:

Scoring a Soulmate

Scoring the Keeper's Sister

Scoring a Fake Fiancée

Scoring a Prince

Scoring with the Boss

Scoring a Holiday Match

The KINGS GROVE Series:

When We Let Go

Open Your Eyes

When We Fall

Open Your Heart

Christmas in Kings Grove

The STARR RANCH WINERY Series:

Chasing a Starr

THE GIRLFRIENDS OF GOTHAM Series:

Men and Martinis

Highballs in the Hamptons

Cosmos and Commitment

STANDALONES:

Let it Snow

Without Words

Without Promises

Mr. Big

Adagio

The PROHIBITED! Duet:

Prohibited!

The Glittering Life of Evie Mckenzie

9 781956 195026